Impasse

An Arthur & Irma Blake Mystery

by

Richard Davidson

Imp Mysteries Volume 5

Books by Richard Davidson:
Self-help:
DECISION TIME! Better Decisions for a Better Life

Mysteries:

The Lord's Prayer Mystery Series:
Lead Us Not into Temptation
Give Us this Day Our Daily Bread
Forgive Us Our Trespasses
Thy Will Be Done
Deliver Us from Evil

Imp Mysteries:
Implications
Impulses
Impostor
Impending
Impasse

Anthology: (Editor)
Overcoming: An Anthology by the Writers of OCWW

"Impasse," by Richard Davidson
ISBN 978-0-9976381-3-4
An Arthur & Irma Blake Mystery

Published 2018 by RADMAR Publishing Group, P.O. Box 425, Northbrook, IL 60065, U.S.A. Copyright 2018, Richard Davidson.
Manufactured in the United States of America

This book is dedicated to those who discover the unexpected.

CHAPTER 1 – CAT'S CLAW

The big yellow Cat clawed into the earth and scratched up major trouble.

Jerry Krizda nudged the lever on his massive Caterpillar backhoe to force the toothed bucket downward through the stubborn clay and building rubble. The hard obstacle resisted intrusion and then collapsed under the relentless pressure. He rotated the bucket to capture its contents. Then he raised and swiveled the arm to deposit the retrieved conglomeration onto the growing pile alongside the trench. He reached for the lever to rotate the arm back to its digging position, but stopped as his gaze scanned the large pile of debris. His training had prepared him for this eventuality, but he never considered it to be a likely outcome. He sounded the big machine's horn long and loud. Then he waited three seconds and sounded it again. Everyone else on the job stopped what they were doing and came running toward him.

The boss, Ron Barabee, was the first to reach him. "What's the emergency?"

"Look at the top of my pile. We have to stop the job."

Protruding from the hill of debris were three long bones and a human skull. Ron Barabee knew that Krizda was right. The contract documents included American Institute of Architects A201-

2007 – General Conditions of the Contract for Construction. Among many other provisions, that document required the contractor to *immediately suspend the operation upon the discovery of human remains or other archaeological findings*. He would have to stop work, contact the police department, and examine the insurance policy covering this job to see whether they honored claims for forced work stoppages. Excavating the site of a strip mall of stores torn down years before should be simple, not bizarre.

Ron Barabee hoped that the bones would turn out to be relatively few and of recent demise. A simple murder or murders would involve only the police. If the forensic pathologist decided the bones were old, the construction delay would be much longer. Archaeologists would have to evaluate the significance of the remains and their appropriate relocation. Those academics could even turn his worksite into an archaeological dig, inaccessible for months or years. Per Ron's instructions, Chuck had already called the police. The piercing throbs of sirens in the distance, changed tone as they got closer. This had turned into Barabee's worst work morning in a very long time.

CHAPTER 2 – CONTACT

Irma Blake responded to the unexpected ring of the doorbell by walking rapidly toward the front door while brushing off her jeans and pushing her tangled hair back into some version of normalcy. Why did such interruptions always come when you were in the middle of a dirty task, in this case emptying the vacuum cleaner and extracting hair from its rollers? Sometimes she wished their dog, Rex, didn't shed so much. Hopefully, the visitor would be a salesperson who would be easily dispatched.

Irma opened the front door to find United Methodist Bishop Howard Chandler standing on her porch holding his snap-brimmed cap and absentmindedly torturing it with tight twists as he waited.

"Hello, Howard, we haven't seen you for quite a while. Please come in and forgive my appearance. Today is a work day in our house. Time to catch up with a few of the chores we left for *someday*. Let me take your hat. I don't remember seeing you wearing one before."

"Thanks, Irma; please forgive me for arriving unannounced, but I have a somewhat urgent request for you and Arthur. The hat is actually a defensive device. Thanks to my newly expanding bald spot, I have to protect my head from the sun. I

normally wear a baseball cap. I select either a Cubs
or a White Sox version depending on what church
in the Northern Illinois Conference I'm visiting. I
don't know your baseball preferences, so I wore my
flat cap instead."

"For future reference, Arthur and I are Cubs
fans. Let's go into the kitchen, and I'll set you up
with coffee at our big table while I get Arthur. He's
fixing the fence around Rex's dog run out back. Rex
managed to break through it for the third time this
year."

"The coffee sounds great. I should have realized
that you'd have some handy, knowing the way
Arthur goes through it. Go ahead and get Arthur;
I'll be quite comfortable in the kitchen."

Irma paused in the back yard while she waited
for Arthur to finish securing a new fence board to
replace the broken one. As she approached
afterward, he looked up.

"I think this new board should do the job. It's
oak instead of pine, and I mounted it with screws
instead of nails. Rex knows how to pound and push
on nailed boards until they either break or come
loose. I'll paint it to match this afternoon."

"You may have to defer the painting. We have a
visitor. Bishop Chandler is here, and he's upset
about something. I think he's about to ask you to
rescue him from some difficult situation again."

"We're back to Howard not being able to live
with me and not being able to live without me. He
said my sideline investigations were detracting from
my pastoral assignments, so he put me on an
indefinite and unpaid leave of absence. Today, he'll

ask me to investigate something for him, because he knows the normal church administrators can't handle it. I feel like a yo-yo."

"I'm glad that you've finally admitted you're not normal. Let's go in to hear what he has to say."

"I'll speculate that an older pastor shot a younger one who was trying to push her out."

Irma laughed. "Why, Pastor Blake, what an unchristian thing to say. My guess is that he wants to retire and is nominating you to replace him."

That exchange put them both in a better mood as they went inside to the kitchen. There, they found their golden retriever, Rex, resting his head on Bishop Chandler's lap while receiving the blessing of being scratched behind his ears.

CHAPTER 3 – ASSIGNMENT

As they entered the kitchen, Arthur observed that Howard Chandler had visibly aged since their last meeting. The bald spot, sagging left eyelid, and facial wrinkles were all recent additions. Arthur extended his hand toward Howard and felt relieved that the bishop's handshake was as firm as ever.

"Welcome, Howard; what brings you to Amboy and our old house today?"

"It's more than an old house, Arthur. I appreciate a more-than-a-century-old Queen Anne structure like this, and it's comforting to feel young in comparison to its age."

Irma picked up on the tone of Howard's words. "I hope you're not feeling sorry for yourself. You're just as energetic as ever. The first signs of age mellowing are just starting to appear."

"Thank you, Irma. I don't know whether 'age mellowing' is a medical term, but surely I'm in better shape than your forensic pathology patients. Anyway, you've cheered me up. I apologize for appearing gloomy, but the church has a problem that requires assistance from both of you, if you're willing."

Arthur said, "We're always willing to listen, Howard, but I'll be approaching this matter as a detective rather than a clergyman. You pushed me into a leave of absence to make me get off the fence and choose my primary career. I decided investigations were my long-term calling."

"That's fine and proper, Arthur, but let me assure you that even when you treat your ministry as a sideline, you're much better at it than most of our pastors. ... You do understand that I made that comment confidentially, and I'll deny I ever said it."

"Thank you, Howard. Let's hear about your problem and what you would like us to do."

"As you know, the United Methodist Church, along with many other Christian denominations, has been fighting decreasing membership in recent years. Our society has been riding a secular trend. People aren't going to church regularly like they used to. Because of this, we have a program to build new churches in areas where we're underrepresented. The first of these new churches started construction two weeks ago in a Hispanic neighborhood just inside the northwest border of Chicago."

"That sounds like a good program start."

"It would be, Arthur, except for the discovery of human remains on the property. Once those bones were found, the construction company had to stop all work while the police and pathologists studied them and looked for other evidence. We don't know how long their analysis will take."

"Are you here to ask me to get involved and to determine whether the body parts resulted from a crime, or are you looking to have Irma join the pathology team examining the remains?"

"My answer is yes on both counts. I'm hoping that both of you will get involved and help us find a way to get construction going again. We publicized this new emphasis on Hispanic United Methodist congregations, and we don't want our momentum in that direction to fizzle because of construction technicalities."

Arthur raised his right eyebrow. "It's not appropriate for me to preach to you, Howard, but surely, the significance of one or more lost lives is higher than a construction delay."

"You have me there, up to a point. A minor delay to honor the sanctity of life is fitting, but I chafe at the possibility that archaeologists will get involved if the bones turn out to be old. They'd like nothing better than to study them for months or years under a government grant. Tell me that you'll do everything you can to expedite the required investigation of the remains."

Irma patted Howard on his shoulder. "As spokesperson for this family, I assure you that we'll take on your challenge. We won't be able to predict where our investigations will lead us, but I will predict that you'll receive a sizable bill for our efforts."

Howard looked relieved. "I'd expect nothing less. The days are long gone when the church could cajole its consultants into supplying their services as a charitable contribution."

CHAPTER 4 – ARTHUR AND IRMA

Pastor Arthur Blake's pre-ministry years had been spent as an engineer for NASA in the spaceflight program. During the course of that early portion of his career, he had learned how to dissect an apparently unsolvable problem into manageable segments and then tackle each smaller problem using a creative approach unlimited by preconceived notions. He believed that all problems could be solved if you were willing to think differently as you analyzed them. This background led to preaching creative sermons and applying novel counseling techniques during his ministry at Parkville United Methodist Church in a far northwestern exurb of Chicago. It also made it natural for him to get involved in the investigation of skeletal remains found in the attic of the older portion of his church.

During that investigation, Arthur befriended Parkville, Illinois Police Chief Bobby Andrews and Irma Custis, the forensic pathologist on the case. His friendship with Irma developed over the course of several years into a playful partnership and their eventual marriage. Throughout their relationship, Irma prodded Arthur toward deciding whether he considered his primary career to be that of a pastor or an investigator.

Individually, Arthur and Irma Blake were very talented problem solvers within their respective fields of expertise. Together, they were an extremely well-matched couple and awesome investigators.

CHAPTER 5 – WORKSITE

The parcel of land for the new church had previously been occupied by a strip mall of stores, five in all, including a shoe store, a fish market, an auto parts store, a Subway sandwich restaurant, and a bookstore. The building had been torn down and the debris only casually cleared away three years before. Since that time a simple chicken wire fence had surrounded the property as a nod to the owner's obligation to keep the public away from the unsafe rubble of the building.

When Arthur and Irma arrived at the worksite, they found police yellow tape surrounding the property, two police cars with accompanying officers on diagonally opposite corners of the site, several civilians digging cautiously within a fenced off smaller area, and a man standing next to the construction office trailer. After parking, Arthur and Irma approached one of the police officers and identified themselves as representatives of the bishop. She lifted the yellow tape for them to go inside the perimeter of the property. At that point Irma turned toward the fenced off excavation area while Arthur walked to the office, circling some large chunks of concrete and other obstacles along the way.

He approached the man standing outside the office trailer. "Good morning. Are you in charge of this construction project? I'm Arthur Blake, and I'm here at the request of Bishop Chandler, representing the United Methodist Church, your client on this job."

The other man shook hands with Arthur. "I'm Ron Barabee. I'm supposed to have my crew building a church for you, but my hands are tied until they resolve the origin and disposition of the human remains our men found. I have coffee inside; would you like some?"

"You said the magic word. I work much better over coffee."

They went into the trailer, poured their coffees, and sat across the desk from each other. After a few satisfying sips, Arthur was the first to speak.

"Ron, can you describe what your backhoe operator was doing when he found the bones?"

"He was working in that fenced off area where the archeologists are playing now. We dig with backhoes while they use tools the size of teaspoons. Anyway Jerry's job that morning was to tear out old reinforced concrete sewer pipes that led nowhere and weren't in use. They must have been left over from some earlier use of the property. The bones came up along with some chunks of the sewer pipes, so they must have been buried near them. My personal theory is that these were people who worked to install the pipes, and they got buried alive when the ditch walls collapsed. That's a big danger in digging. Nowadays, trenching is done within steel shields and boxes to prevent accidents, but I frequently hear about workers who didn't take proper precautions and got buried in mud from collapsing trench walls. Quite a few underground workers die every year."

"Do you think a crew would abandon buried workers?"

"Not intentionally, but workers could get buried without anyone realizing they were down there, especially if they had only a few people on the job. Don't forget, the push for safety in construction work of this type occurred relatively recently. Construction firms do their best to downplay the dangers, both to their employees and to the public. We aim to give our workers proper training, but within a competitive bid environment there are more than a few construction firms that cut their costs by minimizing the training of new workers. In the old days, it was much worse. They'd hire anyone with a strong back, even if the worker had little or no training."

"Have you had any fatalities on a job, Ron?"

"Just once, Arthur; eight years ago, we lost a steelworker who fell from a high beam because he wasn't wearing a safety harness. He was an independent subcontractor, and he thought he was too skilled to require the modern inconvenience of a harness."

"That's the gruesome side of the construction business. If your theory is correct, Ron, and these people died in a construction accident, we should be able to document that fact and get you back into operation fairly soon. The authorities will require a much more detailed investigation if those remains turn out to be historically significant or from a sacred site. I'll check with those people working at the excavation to see if they've determined anything specific about the bones. The bishop wants me to do whatever it takes to get you back to work as soon as possible."

"Thanks for your help, Arthur. I'll appreciate anything you can do to expedite things."

Arthur navigated his way through the debris field to the fenced off area and peered over the surrounding slats-and-wire snow fence to assess the process and the participants down in the hole before breaking their concentration with his words. He saw that Irma had been accepted as a member of the archaeological group. She was examining a portion of a body that had shreds of clothing and what appeared to be dried-up decayed flesh attached to it. Another individual was identifying bone fragments and other unearthed items and calling them out to a third person who photographed them and wrote their descriptions on a large pad of paper. Two others were digging carefully with small spades and spatulas and occasionally brushing the surfaces of found items to remove earth and other coatings.

Irma saw Arthur looking over the fence. She set her latest specimen aside and climbed up the ladder to greet him.

"We had two bodies in this area. It's possible that additional digging will unearth others."

"Do you think they were construction workers? The supervisor on this job suspects that they were accidently buried when the trench they were digging for the sewer pipes collapsed."

"It's possible but unlikely that they were construction workers, because the trench collapse theory is a non-starter. The intriguing thing about these people is that they died inside the sewer pipe."

"Now, that piques my interest, Irma. What do you suppose they were doing in there? Due to the water in the sewer pipe, the bodies must be pretty badly decomposed."

"That would be a very astute assumption if there had been water in that pipe. The remains are in surprisingly good condition because the pipe appears to have been dry and tightly sealed. I examined all the concrete pipe remnants I could find, and I saw no evidence that there had ever been water in the pipe. It looks like a sewer pipe, but I think it had another purpose."

"That sounds as though the police should be interested in your findings."

"They probably would, Arthur, if they weren't so busy with street violence and current crimes. The discovery of these remains will be a low priority event for the Chicago Police unless television news reporters or these archaeologists make a big fuss over it. That's why I'm not bringing the circumstances of the victims' deaths to the attention of my temporary colleagues. We should handle this mystery ourselves."

CHAPTER 6 – BOBBY ANDREWS

Irma and Arthur had just finished their meal and were clearing away the dishes when the telephone rang. Arthur answered it while Irma continued to clear the table.

"Pastor Arthur Blake here. May I help you?"

"Arthur, it's Bobby Andrews, and you definitely may help me if you're willing. By the way, I thought you stopped using your pastor title when you decided to concentrate on investigations."

"I didn't look at the caller ID before I picked up the phone. Some folks know me only as a pastor. Don't you identify yourself as a police chief when you receive a call from an unknown person?"

"I only do that at work. I prefer to hide my identity on my home phone to keep things personal. Being just plain Bobby also helps me record and catch scamming telemarketers. I've put a few out of business by relaying my recordings to the appropriate authorities."

"Anyway, Bobby, it's good to hear from you. I hope things are quiet on the criminal front in Parkville. Tell me about the favor you want from me."

"I didn't use the word 'favor', but you're absolutely right that I'm calling looking for assistance. It's an emotional matter. My wife Renee has family on the south side of Chicago, right in the middle of one of the most dangerous neighborhoods. Lawson Redshaw, her sixteen year old second cousin, was shot and killed last week while sitting on his front steps talking with a neighbor. Lawson's mother is frantic about the possibility of losing her older son Jayson who's twenty years old. She wants to send Jay to live with us in Parkville so that he'll be safe. We agreed, of course. We told the mother she could come too, but she's not ready to leave the friends she's had for many years."

"That's very generous of you, Bobby, but how do I or we fit into the picture?"

"If Jay comes to live with us, we won't have anything challenging for him to do beyond baby-sitting our six year old daughter, Thelma Lou. The best I could do for a police job is something part time and clerical. That won't cut it for him. He'd probably get into trouble because he'd have too much time on his hands. I was wondering whether you could use an assistant on whatever case you're currently investigating, at least on a part time basis. Would you have anything worthwhile for him to do?"

"I assume that you wouldn't ask me to use him on a case if he weren't a straight shooter and a clear thinker. Am I correct?"

"To be honest, I don't know him that well, but Renee told me that he did well in high school and would be halfway through college now if his family had the money for it. Since high school graduation he's been doing odd jobs for relatives and their friends to keep him away from the bad elements in the neighborhood."

"Bobby, I want to help you and Jay out, but there are two hurdles to clear before I can take him on. First, I'll have to get Irma's agreement. That will probably be the easier obstacle to overcome. The second problem is that our current case is in Chicago. If Jay assisted us, he might be working where those bad guys could find him, if they're looking for him."

"Thanks for that tentative nod to my request, Arthur. If you'll check with Irma, I'll do my homework to find out whether anyone is out to get Jay or if it will simply be a matter of his having to stay away from the old neighborhood. I wouldn't want to send him back into Chicago either if someone would be hunting him there."

CHAPTER 7 – DNA ANALYSIS

When Arthur asked Irma for her views on hiring Jay Redshaw as an apprentice or assistant, he received an enthusiastic response.

"I think that's a great idea, Arthur, and a timely one too. If we share Jay's time with some duties he has at the Parkville Police Department, he'd be in a perfect position to use the police computers and coordinate with the Illinois State Police Forensic Science Laboratory for me. I have DNA samples from the bodies found at that construction site, and I was wondering whether we would have to ask Penny and Joe Gonzalez's federal agency to search databases for us. Jay may have access to the Illinois State Police databases while working in Bobby's department. That would also keep him out of Chicago, at least for a while. Set up a meeting with him to evaluate his outlook and skills."

"Before he could do any searching, you'd have to teach him the basics of DNA testing and analysis. That's a complex subject."

"I can't think of a better way to evaluate his aptitude for investigative work and give him some college level coursework at the same time."

"You're the doctor, Irma; do you expect Jay to be ready for serious work so soon after losing his younger brother?"

"Doctors don't like to give medical opinions without an in-person examination. Ask Bobby to

Richard Davidson

bring him over for a visit. It will be a social meeting, interview, and examination all-in-one."

CHAPTER 8 – JAYSON REDSHAW

The following evening, Bobby and Renee Andrews arrived at the Blakes' Amboy, Illinois home along with their new houseguest, Jay Redshaw. Bobby and Jay offered a sports-style contrast. While Bobby had the muscular bulk of a pro football lineman, Jay displayed the tall grace of a basketball player.

Following the initial greetings, Renee described her animated discussion with her young daughter when she told Thelma Lou that she'd have to stay home with Momma, her grandmother, rather than visit her Aunt Irma and Uncle Arthur.

Irma reacted first. "Wow, Arthur, we've been elevated to aunt and uncle status. I think that's wonderful that Thelma Lou feels that way about us."

Arthur said, "Without having put a label on our relationship, I think it's always been an extended family thing with her and the rest of the Andrews clan. How do you feel about that, Renee?"

"My checklist says that we're absolutely an extended family. You and Bobby have been best friends for longer than I've known him. You performed our wedding ceremony. I worked with you and Irma in ABC Consultants on government investigations until I got pregnant. Irma and I are close friends. Momma practically wanted to adopt you during your first few evenings spent together. It's official; we're an extended biracial family."

Arthur turned to Jay. "We may joke about family relationships, but we want you to know that the loss of your brother, Lawson, weighs heavily on all of us. He and the other victims of street violence will never know what they could have achieved in life. Tell us about him so that we'll be able to appreciate him as a person too."

"Pastor Blake, Lawson and I were always close. He looked up to me as his older brother, and I looked up to him as the smartest one in our family. He hadn't even gone for his driver's license test, but he was already helping guys in the neighborhood fix their cars. He read books about engines, and could get a car going again when most of us couldn't do much more than change the spark plugs and fluids. Lawson taught himself first aid too. He stopped the bleeding and dressed wounds for a bunch of people, and continued to redress those wounds until they healed. Some of the folks in our neighborhood called him the little doctor."

Irma said, "He would have had a promising future in either healthcare or engineering. I'm so sorry for your loss, Jay."

"It hurts to be without Lawson, but I know so many others who have lost family members too. We're all hurting. Just a few weeks ago, some celebrity visited an elementary school in my neighborhood and asked the kids what they wanted to be when they grew up. They all answered, 'alive'. That's not right. This isn't random crime. It's our society falling apart. Nobody will have dreams and hopes for the future anymore."

Arthur rested his hand on Jay's shoulder. "People keep hoping for a simple solution to street violence, but there isn't one. We have to make the bad elements want to be parts of society instead of destroyers of it. That will take continuous efforts over a long period of time. It could take a whole generation or more before things get significantly better."

Bobby said, "We cops can only react as shootings and crimes take place. As long as people want their freedom, we can't round up groups of people we consider bad and lock them up. They have to do something unlawful first."

Renee disagreed. "Bobby and I have these discussions all the time. Even though I once was a cop and had the same rules he follows, I think that every gang member should be arrested as an accomplice when a gang-ordered crime is carried out. What do you think, Arthur?"

"I see nothing wrong with that approach so long as the legislature passes laws that outlaw gang actions like that and the courts support those laws. The problem comes when you have to arrest otherwise law-abiding individuals who were forced to join the gangs."

Jay nodded. "There are plenty of kids who are forced to join if they want to survive. Then the gangs make those kids do initiation crimes like shootings, beatings, and robberies in order to control them and keep them from trying to leave.... Enough talk about our life and death struggle in the neighborhoods; we're stuck with it. I left the city to give Mom some peace of mind. How would I be working with you Blakes on investigations while I'm living with cousins Renee and Bobby in Parkville?"

CHAPTER 9 - WORKING ARRANGEMENT

Irma faced Jay. "I have some thoughts on how you might assist us, but you'll have to sit down before I discuss them. You're so tall that I have a pain in my neck from looking up at you."

That comment brought lightness back into the mood of the group. Everyone sat except for Irma.

"Jay, you appear to be a bright and active person. I assume you're capable of working on your own without continuous supervision. Am I correct?"

"Give me the tools to carry out an assignment, and I'll take it on. What would you like me to do?"

"One more step in the qualifications discussion. Can I assume that given your age and the fact that you have a high school diploma, you're used to working online with a computer?"

"Lawson may have had the edge on working with cars and first aid situations, but I always took the lead on computer work."

"Good. I'm sure Bobby told you that I'm a forensic pathologist. I do autopsies and try to interpret crime scene evidence. Our latest case involves human remains found at a church construction site in northwest Chicago. Although the bodies were old, they were in relatively good condition because they were sealed in a dry sewer pipe underground. I collected DNA samples from them."

Jay said, "DNA is the code in our body tissues and fluids that uniquely identifies each one of us."

"That's right. Relatives have similar DNA profiles, but only identical twins have matching DNA profiles. I'll give you an introductory course on DNA sampling and analysis. Then I'll ask you to work with the Illinois State Police Forensic Science Laboratory in Rockford to search online state and FBI databases for matches to the samples I took from the two individuals at the construction site. With a little luck we may be able to identify them. If we can find matches, we'll get a clue as to how they came to die there. This assignment requires Bobby to give you a part time clerical job at the Parkville Police Department, so that you would have law enforcement credentials for working with the forensic laboratory. The online DNA databases are available to law enforcement agencies and to forensic laboratories, but not to the general public. How about that, Bobby? Will you have a job for Jay?"

"I'll have a job for you, Jay, but on my portion of your work, you'd be doing boring things like searching for the number of tickets a driving offender has received and tracing ownership of cars from license plate numbers."

"That stuff's interesting too. I know some folks who drive cars they shouldn't be able to afford. If I got their plate numbers through friends, would you let me check to see whether their plates match the models of cars they're attached to?"

"Sure; I exchange info with the Chicago Police all the time. That does raise the question of jurisdiction. How will Jay get away with asking for State Police help from Parkville on a Chicago case?"

Irma said, "It will take a little discussion and negotiation, but I informally joined a forensics team that was appointed by the Chicago Police Department. Jay would be working for me when he interfaces with the State Police laboratory, so by extension, he would be working for the Chicago Police as a subcontractor. Besides, I worked with Jane Ferguson, the Lab Director in Rockford on an earlier case. I'm sure she would give us a little leeway."

Jay stood and faced Bobby and Irma. "I accept both of your jobs. I think I'm going to have fun with these assignments, but for now I have to get up and move around. I get nervous sitting down."

Bobby said, "You'll be spending a lot of hours sitting in front of a computer at the station. You'll have to learn to live with that nervousness."

"That reminds me, Chief; will I get a uniform on this job?"

"No uniforms for clerical staff. You'll have to settle for a bar-coded clip-on identification card. Wait and see what other jobs you work into in the future."

CHAPTER 10 – STRIP MALL

The next day, while Irma outlined her DNA course that she would teach to Jay and other possible future associates, Arthur visited the Chicago Building Department and then returned to the church construction worksite armed with an old architect's drawing of the strip mall stores. He wanted to get a feeling for the location of each store relative to the unearthed sewer line. Did that sewer lead into one of the stores?

When he arrived at the site, he found that the police presence had been reduced to one car parked close to the street corner. He also noted that there wasn't anyone working in the fenced-off area where Irma had assisted the archaeologists. After checking in with the police officer and identifying himself, Arthur headed for the construction office trailer, where Ron Barabee welcomed him.

"Good to see you again, Arthur. I get lonely, staying here guarding the site and watching for an opportunity to get back to work. I notice that you brought a drawing. Is it something I can help you with?"

"If you still have a coffee supply, we could share it and do some analysis of how your excavation results compare with my drawing. Do you have some time for me?"

"Until they let us restart the job, I have nothing but time."

"Good. Here's my matter for discussion. My drawing indicates the locations of the stores on the lot when they were still here. From left to right, the five stores were Walkathon Shoes, Great Lakes Fish Market, Garcia's Auto Parts, a Subway sandwich restaurant, and Paige's Books."

"This is the first time I've seen the layout of the old stores, but it looks efficient. What's your question to discuss?"

"Ron, I know you had to stop work before you made much progress, but can you suggest which of these stores was connected to that sewer pipe tunnel?"

"Thanks for the new information, Arthur. I wondered about the purpose of that large eighty-four inch concrete sewer pipe. It served as a tunnel. You're also probably telling me that the bodies were in the pipe, rather than underneath it. You're pretty good at this investigation stuff for a pastor."

"Let's just say that at this point in my lifelong education, I'm majoring in investigations and minoring in pastor's duties."

"That's good. You're continuing to look for new challenges. Maybe I should do the same, given my current frustrations with the construction business. Anyway, in answer to your question, we didn't do enough digging to trace the path of that sewer pipe, but from the orientation of the few sections that we did find, I'd say that the pipe wouldn't have connected with any of those stores, unless there was a side connection to it. The sections we found lined up with the long dimension

29

of the parking lot, parallel to the strip of stores, rather than aimed at any one of them."

"Ron, isn't it possible that the pipe turns beyond the area of your initial digging?"

"Sure, it's possible, Arthur, and future digging may show just that, but side connections cost a lot more. I would have minimized the tunnel's length and complexity by aiming it directly at its intended destination."

"So, we're missing a destination."

"True, but we have a clue to it. You're the investigator, Arthur. Do you see the clue?"

"You're enjoying putting me in this position, Ron, but thanks to your needling, I do see it. The drawing of the stores is dated 1999. Something else was on this lot prior to that. It's time for me to search the Building Department archive again."

CHAPTER 11 – IRMA

Arthur heard Irma whistling an upbeat song as he entered the front door. He listened for a minute or so and then went to join her in the kitchen.

"Someone feels she has accomplished something important."

"Right you are my friend. I've accomplished two things. All by myself I outlined the *Elements of DNA Testing and Analysis* course for use in introducing Jay Redshaw to the world of forensics. I also had a conference call with the archaeologists I joined at the construction site dig, and we have agreed on an approximate date for the deaths of those poor souls in the sewer pipe."

"May I guess that date before you reveal it?"

"Arthur, are you going to do one of your magic tricks again? You keep coming up with off-the-cuff answers that match the results of hard work by others. Go ahead and give your estimate. I don't mind telling you that I hope you're wrong."

"The remains are twenty to twenty-five years old."

"You're either terribly smart or just terrible. We had four estimates of the age of the bodies, and they all put their deaths within that five-year range. Are you going to tell me how you arrived at your answer, or are you going to be silent and smug all day?"

"To put it in terms I'm sure you'll understand, I reached my conclusion by thinking like a coroner."

"That's a jab at my background, but I think I understand what you did. Instead of working from the physical characteristics of the human remains, you tied the dating of their deaths to historical events. That's very clever and completely admissible as evidence."

"Thank you, Irma. I'll take my imaginary bow and then congratulate you and your colleagues for reaching the same conclusion through the hocus pocus ceremonies you perform over dead bodies."

"So, we're both magicians. Give me the details of your logical analysis."

"I'll do that, but first I have to give credit to my own analysis partner, Ron Barabee, the construction boss. He steered my thinking in the correct direction, literally."

"That sounds mystical. Fill me in so that I'll understand that 'literally' comment."

"Here's the scoop. I managed to find architect's drawings of the group of five stores that had once occupied the worksite property. Then I asked Ron if he had enough evidence from the excavation to suggest which store would have been the destination for the tunnel pipe."

"Agreed; because it carried no water, it served as a tunnel."

"The surprising result from our conversation was that the tunnel did not go to any of the stores if it was installed based on logical construction procedures. It went to a location under the parking lot. Ron prodded me toward realizing that it went to a structure that was on the property before the stores were built."

Impasse

"And the drawing said the stores were built about twenty years ago. I see how you worked it out. Good thinking by both you and Ron. We owe your new friend a dinner or a few beers for that one."

"Yes, indeed. My drawing of the stores was eighteen years old. They were only there for about fifteen years before they were torn down. Modern business buildings have a limited lifetime, much shorter than residences."

"So, Arthur, your next step in this adventure is to work on discovering what building was on that lot before the stores."

"It is, but once we learn that, we'll have to debate whether we should get the powers that be to allow the construction to proceed and please the bishop, or whether we should do some archaeological excavating of the phantom building's foundation first."

CHAPTER 12 – LABORATORY

Irma Blake contacted Jane Ferguson, Director of the Illinois State Police Rockford Forensic Science Laboratory and discovered that she had done so on a good day. Timeliness and luck were on her side.

Jane's response to Irma's telephone request for assistance was, "If you had called with this request a few weeks ago, I would have had to turn you down. The politicians in Springfield finally came up with a budget for the state of Illinois. It's hard to believe that we had to get along without a budget for so long because of the political stalemate between Democrats and Republicans. I was on the verge of having to lay off a quarter of my staff. If that had happened, we would have been restricted to performing tests for only the highest priority cases. The finding of long-dead human remains at a construction site would not have qualified for our assistance. However, given the glorious prospect of an actual state budget, I'll be happy to work with you."

"That's great news, Jane. I'll bring the samples in tomorrow, and I'll also bring my forensics assistant, Jay Redshaw. He's new to our team, and would appreciate a tour of your lab while we discuss the case. Could that be arranged? We have our own budget problems in the private investigations world, because there are gaps between cases. Because of those pressures, we're sharing Jay's time with Chief Bobby Andrews of the

Parkville Police Department. Bobby was in on the last case we tackled together."

"I'll look forward to your visit, Irma. I do have one question. How senior is your assistant? Should Jay get the technically complex tour or the introductory one?"

"He'll have to work up to the technical version in the future. He's taking an Elements of DNA Testing and Analysis course now. He'll appreciate seeing your people applying the technology he's studying."

"If you don't mind my asking, where did you find Jay?"

"He's working his way out of a bad situation on Chicago's South Side, after his brother was killed."

"With that background, we'll be sure to give him our best quality tour. Improving prospects for victims of street violence and their families is high priority for our department. Too many people in harm's way look at the police as being belligerent and dangerous. We'll do everything we can to change that image of the State Police."

"Amen to that approach. Jay has the potential to move beyond the limited opportunities he would have had in his old neighborhood. Given a little encouragement, he should do well."

The day after her meeting with Irma Blake and Jay Redshaw's tour of the laboratory, Jane Ferguson met with Sarah Jackson, the DNA technician who had conducted Jay Redshaw's tour.

"Sarah, how did the tour go? Did Jay appreciate what we do here?"

"He did, and he asked plenty of questions about the reasons underlying our laboratory procedures. He didn't just want to know what we do; he wanted to understand why we do it. I'd rate him as someone to watch in the future as he learns more about lab work."

"Did he ask you any questions you couldn't answer?"

"Just one; he asked whether there was any significance to your having selected a black technician to give him the tour."

"Ouch. I guess I flunked diplomacy on that one. How did you handle his question?"

"I took the only approach that made sense to me at the time. I have a date with him next week."

CHAPTER 13 – OLD BUILDINGS

Arthur started his search for the mysterious building that had once been on the worksite property using an online computer search. He discovered that the online database of Chicago building permits only covered documents issued since 2006. He also unsuccessfully explored old maps of Chicago neighborhoods and random architectural photograph files.

Arthur was beginning to despair of finding information on the building that predated the stores, when he had an inspiration.

If I can't get my answer the high tech way, I'll revert to the low tech option.

He put on a suit and the clerical collar that he infrequently had worn when he was pastor of his own church. Then he drove to the worksite, parked, and started a door-to-door canvass of the neighborhood, looking for residents who had lived there for more than twenty years. It didn't take him long to find a woman in her seventies, Loretta Langford, who had lived in her present house for fifty-two years. She turned out to be talkative and an Episcopalian.

"It's a shame the way the neighborhood's changed, Father – I mean Pastor. At one time almost all the folks here were of English descent, but now most of them are Hispanic. I don't have any problem with that, but you feel more at home when everyone around you has a similar background. My husband, Phil, passed away twelve years ago, and I'm doing very well on my own, but I have to admit I stopped going to church. At my age it got to be too big a bother. The Episcopal Church is too far away for walking, and I didn't renew my driver's license when it expired last year. I suppose I should reinstate it, but I get along with buses. Once they build that new church you talked about, I might try it. It would be close enough for me to walk, and Methodists are similar to Episcopalians but poorer, at least that's the way I learned about different churches when I was a girl."

Arthur jumped into the conversation when she took a breath. "It's a pleasure to meet you, Mrs. Langford. Nowadays, people tend to move every few years. It's so nice that you've put down roots in this neighborhood and made this house a true home. From your comments, I'll bet you have many memories of the way the neighborhood used to be. You've been here longer than many of the buildings."

"That I have, Pastor. Ask me about anything during the good old days, as we call them, and I'll fill you in. Mary Johnson down the street and I are the only ones still here who remember it all."

"What I'm particularly interested in, is the history of that lot where we're building the new church. I know that there were five stores on it until three years ago, but I'd like to find out what was there before the stores."

"That's no problem. I can remember all the way back to the time when it was a vacant lot with nothing but a couple of scruffy small trees on it. My son Tommy used to climb one of them because its branches stuck out in many different directions, making it easy to climb. He'd get to the top of it and pretend to be a pirate in the crow's nest of his sailing ship. That boy always did have a great imagination. He runs an animal shelter now."

"You do indeed have a fine memory, Mrs. Langford, but I don't need you to remember all the way back to the time of the unimproved vacant land. I'd just like to know what building was on that property before they built those stores."

"That's fine, Pastor. I was just showing off a bit, thinking back to the vacant lot. Everything was spread out then. We even had lots of colorful birds singing during the summer months. I loved to listen to them. The neighborhood didn't have nearly so many people as today. I enjoyed the area then, not that I don't appreciate my home now. It's amazing what they charge for a new house like this one."

"Pardon me, but can we get back to the question about the building on that lot?"

Loretta Langford appreciated a chance to unload her many stored thoughts, so she felt a bit miffed, but she complied with the pastor's request. "Oh, that was an ugly bank building. It was black, and it didn't have any architectural class at all. It was box-like and covered with black marble sheets. They felt cold if you put your hand on them, although I bet they weren't made of real marble. Banks like to convince you they're solid and prestigious, even if they aren't."

"Do you remember the name of the bank?"

"It didn't have a very interesting name. I think it was called Corner Bank, but it might have had another couple of words in its name. That's about as bland as you can get. They didn't realize that their name had nothing in it to attract the established neighbors away from other banks. I could have told them they were losing out on local business, but nobody ever asked me. Oh, Pastor, I'm such a poor host. Please come inside and have some tea and a slice of apple pie. I baked it myself yesterday."

"Thank you for the information, Mrs. Langford, but I really should be going."

"Nonsense, Pastor; I insist. I've been known for my hospitality around here for over fifty years, and I'm not going to lose my reputation now."

"Do you have coffee?"

"Tea in the daytime; coffee in the evening."

CHAPTER 14 – SNAKES

Armed with his property history information, Arthur returned that afternoon to the worksite for another meeting with construction boss Ron Barabee. Before he did so, he stopped at a Duncan Donuts store for a "Box O' Joe" ten-cup container of coffee. When he got to the site, Arthur didn't see Ron, so he knocked on the office trailer door.

"Are you in there, Ron?"

When Ron opened the door, Arthur saw him holding his phone to his ear and holding up his index finger to signal that he would be a minute longer. After two more minutes of animated telephone conversation, Ron put the instrument down and shook hands with Arthur.

"Sorry about not being available, but my insurance company is stalling about paying off on our work delay claim. If I can't get some cash soon, my workers are going to take other jobs, and I'll be stuck with recruiting a whole new workforce when they finally let us return to the job we're here for."

"I can't help with that, but at least I brought fresh coffee for us. I figured that I've mooched off your supply long enough. I was going to give some to the police officers watching the property, but there's no car on duty anymore. They must have left when the bodies were removed to the morgue."

"Your bringing coffee is a friendly gesture, Arthur. You appear to be in a good mood."

"I am, and I have news for you."

"You've arranged for us to be allowed to dig again."

"My news isn't quite that good, but I did find out what the missing building was, and it adds intrigue to the existence of that sewer pipe tunnel."

"Was it located where the tunnel leads?"

"It was, if I can trust the memory of the neighbor who told me about it. People like to talk with clergy. I may have even found a member for the new church when it's finished."

"I hope that's sooner rather than later. What kind of building was it?"

"It was a bank, and the building was a simple boxy affair sheathed in black marble."

"That would probably have been done as three eighths inch thick tiles. Larger black marble sheets are too heavy to be practical for a local building like this was. What else did you learn about this bank?"

"I didn't get its entire name, but the neighbor said part of it was Corner Bank. She couldn't remember the rest of it."

Ron finished his coffee and poured a refill. "You did a great job of finding the property's history, but where do we go from here?"

"You had just started to dig. The bulk of the tunnel might still be intact. Do you think you could clean up the rubble at the end of the sewer pipe and send someone in to inspect the rest of it?"

"No way, Arthur; that would be far too dangerous. OSHA would cite us for taking unnecessary risks. It wouldn't even be part of the contracted work."

Impasse

"I understand your position, Ron, but I suggest that we're going to have to find out about that tunnel and what those men were doing in it before you get permission to continue excavating. How can we do that?"

"There is a way. If you'll authorize the extra expense as the bishop's representative, I'll hire a video sewer inspection outfit as a subcontractor. They'll explore the tunnel with a motorized remote-controlled video camera pulling a long cable behind it. Those things can explore lengthy sewer systems and even turn corners. This tunnel isn't that long; it would be an easy job."

"Can the remote-controlled probe grab something it finds and bring it back out?"

"Some can, if the object isn't heavy. I'll pick an outfit that has that capability. Am I authorized to proceed? We'll have to dig a new tunnel entrance away from the location where they found the bodies so that we don't disturb evidence there, and we'll have to clean up an approach for the truck before they start. It won't cost much more. No offense intended, but any kind of action is better than sitting around here drinking coffee all day."

CHAPTER 15 – PROBING

Rather than recall one of his men for the brief task, Ron Barabee fired up the Caterpillar backhoe himself. He avoided the fenced-in area where Irma and the archaeologists had worked on the unearthed remains, and opened a new hole in the sewer pipe farther along its length. Then he smoothed out the approach area near the hole for access by the video sewer monitoring truck. By prearrangement, that vehicle arrived one hour after he finished the digging and site preparations.

Arthur had called Irma and told her about the old bank building and the video inspection project. She arrived on the scene slightly in advance of the sewer inspection truck to take charge in case they found additional human remains. The inspection company would record their video progress so that other interested parties, such as the police and forensics laboratory personnel could review it later.

Upon the truck's arrival Ron, Arthur, and Irma met with the operator to establish ground rules for the effort. The technician was to take video images of any additional human bodies or body parts without disturbing them, but inanimate evidence would be first recorded and then retrieved, if practical to do so. Because the new pipe tunnel opening was between the point where bodies had been found earlier and the old bank building location, the operator would first inspect the short section of pipe between the new opening and the original excavation, and then turn the device around to examine the longer pipe section between the new opening and the old bank building's foundation.

The remote-controlled camera pulled out cable from the supply reel as it moved through the concrete pipe toward the original excavation opening. On the video screen the pipe appeared to be clear except for minor debris, scattered into the pipe during the digging process.

Irma concentrated on the image. "I expect that if there are any more bodies or body parts to be found, they will be in this shorter section of the inspection run. People in trouble in the tunnel would have tried to get out through the manhole cover where they entered."

Arthur said, "That would depend on whether they expected to find an easy exit at the other end of the tunnel even though it was farther away."

Ron Barabee disagreed. "Arthur, most deaths in a confined passageway like the sewer pipe are due to asphyxia. OSHA standards specify that the oxygen level in such places must be at least 19.5%, and carbon dioxide must not exceed 4%. If the percentage of oxygen is too low or that of carbon dioxide is too high, the worker starts to suffocate. In that condition, they wouldn't be able to go anywhere rapidly. They would be lucky to get back to their entrance point."

"Speaking of that entrance point, did any of your workers find a manhole cover?"

"I wouldn't expect them to find one, Arthur. This property has been covered with rubble for years. During that period, scavengers would have searched it many times for pieces of metal and wiring that they could sell to scrap metal dealers. There's even a substantial business in reclaiming bricks from demolished buildings. It's a secondary economy, making something out of nothing. Some might call it recycling instead of petty theft."

Irma raised her hand in a traffic stop signal. "Concentrate on the screen instead of talking. The camera is almost to the point where you excavated the two bodies. I see a piece of bent steel conduit that your scavengers missed. Let's watch the screen."

As the camera probe continued forward, the bottom of the pipe became bumpy, and the probe had to use its track drive to climb over small objects.

Irma pointed at the screen. "Look; it just climbed over two finger bones. I think there are more coming up, and a few pieces of paper."

Two minutes later, Arthur asked the camera operator to stop the probe. "Take a close look at those pieces of paper. Now that the probe stopped moving, you can see them better. They're filthy, but they're money. I can make out a twenty dollar bill and a hundred. These guys died while they were robbing the bank. We're going to have to call in the FBI."

Ron said, "Damn! That will delay construction even more."

CHAPTER 16 – FLIP SIDE

Irma put her hand on Ron's shoulder. "Calm down, Ron. Arthur jumped to a quick conclusion. He usually holds off until he gets at least most of the facts."

Arthur said, "Sorry, Ron; I'm guilty as charged. We should at least run the camera down the other end of the tunnel pipe before we speculate on what happened here. Irma is a forensic scientist, and she wants as much data as possible before giving her opinion. That's not the first time she called me out for a premature judgment."

They instructed the camera probe operator to reel in the camera and then start it down the pipe in the opposite direction, toward the foundation of the old bank.

The technician put the cable reel into the rewind mode and cleaned the camera once it was fully retracted. Then he repositioned the camera probe to aim it toward the building end of the tunnel pipe.

The first half of the bank-side tunnel was clear of debris, except for minor amounts of soil and concrete dust that had sifted through the joints between the pipe sections over the years. They observed electrical conduit attached to the sidewall of the tunnel. Then, two bulky objects appeared on the monitor screen.

Ron said, "Oh hell! Those are two big bags of money. Arthur was right about the bank robbery."

Irma turned to the camera probe operator. "Just maneuver your camera past those bags. We need to look all the way to the end of the tunnel."

The operator nodded and continued moving the camera forward. The tunnel continued for an additional hundred and twenty-five feet. Halfway along that length the pipe had been crushed by surface demolition operations, leaving only a gap eleven inches across for the camera probe to pass through. The operator threaded his probe through the needle eye of that gap and maneuvered past some additional chunks of broken pipe and other debris to the bank end of the tunnel. At that point the probe ran into a concrete wall.

Irma wrote several sentences and drew a sketch into her pocket notebook. Then she said to the operator, "I think I saw something as we approached the end of the tunnel. Back off the probe about ten feet, and aim the camera upward at a thirty degree angle."

As the operator aimed the camera upward, the monitor screen revealed a large rusty steel plate set into the end wall of the tunnel with a lockable hatch door similar to one that would be mounted on a ship bulkhead to allow watertight access to the next compartment. Above the hatch was a louvered ventilation grill, probably masking a fan behind it.

Irma smiled at Arthur. "I told you not to jump to early conclusions with incomplete data. That hatch means that the men who died in this tunnel were not robbing the bank. They were making a secret deposit."

Impasse

"I'll agree on that one, but either way, Ron is going to be delayed by an FBI investigation."

Ron Barabee stared at the image of the hatch and said nothing.

CHAPTER 17 – FBI AND OTHERS

Doing his best to follow proper procedures, Arthur called the Chicago Police and alerted them to the new developments that would likely require their assigning a detective to the case and the participation of the FBI because it involved a bank and large quantities of cash being transferred. Arthur asked whether he should contact the FBI and, as expected, he received the response that the Chicago Police Department would make those arrangements. Following that call, Irma, Arthur, and Ron returned to the construction office trailer to await the new arrivals. The sewer inspector cleaned his camera probe and cabling and then left for his next job.

Less than an hour later, a knock on the trailer door announced new arrivals. Ron opened it to find two men and a woman standing outside. Ron, Irma, and Arthur went outside to meet the newcomers, due to the limited space in the trailer. The woman, a dark-haired sturdy individual with a square chin, presented her credentials first.

"Good afternoon. I'm Special Agent Ruth Daltry of the FBI, and these gentlemen are Detective Justin Marks of the Chicago Police and Agent Paul Garcia of the Drug Enforcement Administration, I'll be leading our efforts, but we're here as a team to cover all probable aspects of your discovery."

Irma asked, "Did you all come in one car?"

Ruth laughed. "No, we came separately, but our different agencies are getting better at coordinating arrival times. It's necessary when we're carrying out surprise raids on suspects."

Following the remainder of the introductions, the group gathered around the sewer inspection monitor to review the recorded video footage of the tunnel. Ron and Irma initially summed up the worksite background of excavated remains and DNA sampling. Then Arthur provided commentary to go with the video playback.

"You folks are the experts, but the existence of an access tunnel leading to a hatch in the foundation of a financial institution plus two bodies and sacks of cash in the tunnel led us to suspect that the dead men were making a deposit to a money laundering operation, possibly connected to drug smuggling."

DEA Agent Paul Garcia, a quiet man with a bland expression, nodded. "I've seen similar things elsewhere, although not this sophisticated. We do know that the drug cartels have expertise in digging tunnels, although I haven't seen them use concrete sewer pipe in them."

Ron said, "They wouldn't use sewer pipe for a secret tunnel, because it takes heavy duty equipment to do the excavation and installation. You couldn't construct it secretly. My guess is that the tunnel was installed when the bank was built, working quite openly, because no one would have suspected anything improper."

Ruth Daltry agreed. "Mr. Barabee's suggestion is reasonable, and it indicates that the tunnel was part of the initial planning for this bank. We'll have to check our records for the bank name and the people involved in it. I think we can all conclude that the two people in the tunnel were not construction or maintenance workers."

Detective Justin Marks had fidgeted during the entire video playback session, obviously less than intent on studying it. After noting a few details in a pocket notebook he said, "I've seen enough to let you federal folks run this case. Unless this turns out to be something local like a fencing operation, I'll assume that the proper jurisdiction is federal. Because of that, I'll be leaving you and returning to one of our many Chicago cases. We're more than overloaded without this one."

As Marks drove away, Ruth Daltry said, "That's one level of inter-agency cooperation the FBI can avoid. These multi-agency investigations are a paperwork nightmare."

CHAPTER 18 – SARAH AND JAY

Sarah Jackson responded to the doorbell through her apartment's security intercom. "Hello. Who is it?"

"Hi, Sarah. Jay Redshaw at your service. OK to come up?"

"Hi, Jay. You're a little early. I'm in apartment 3A, third floor. Come on up, but you'll have to wait outside the door for a few minutes, if you don't mind."

"That's fine. Buzz me in, and I'll see you when you're ready." The buzz was longer and louder than he expected.

When Sarah opened her door ten minutes later, she saw Jay smiling up at her from his seat on the floor and extending a bottle of red wine in her direction.

"Hi, Sarah; sorry I was early, but I had a borrowed car and an old gas station map. I could only guess how long it would take to get here. My mother told me to always be on time or early, rather than late."

"Come on in, Jay, if you can hoist that long body of yours up from the floor. Didn't your mother also tell you that you have to be twenty-one to buy wine in this state?"

"This wine is as legal as it gets. Chief Bobby Andrews of the Parkville Police bought it for me to give to you as someone who is older than twenty-one. It's up to you whether you share it with me. I'll be legal next birthday anyway."

"I guess I'm robbing the cradle today. Have a seat in the front room while I finish getting ready."

"Don't rush. This will be a casual *getting to know you* afternoon."

A few minutes later, Sarah returned. She had added a floral-figured silk scarf to her blue jeans and denim shirt. "Where would you like to go to get acquainted, Jay?"

"I went online and researched places in the Rockford area. The Anderson Japanese Gardens sounded like a picturesque place to start a friendship. Is that OK with you?"

"Cool; I've wanted to go there for years, and never quite made it. I'll drive if you don't mind because I know my way around Rockford and nearby places."

A half hour later, they stood on a black wooden bridge overlooking a pond with formally natural tree and shrub plantings and a stone Japanese lantern perched on a shoreline slab of dark rock.

Jay took a deep breath. "This place is serene. It's so different from my old neighborhood in the city."

Sarah rested her hand on his as he held the bridge railing. "I heard through the grapevine that you lost your brother in that neighborhood. I'm so sorry."

"You would have liked Lawson. He was only sixteen, but he had already learned how to do many things that thirty-year-olds can't handle. He could turn scrap into a work of art and fix almost anything using bits of junk as parts. I miss him so much."

She squeezed his hand. "His older brother has talent and understanding too. You were the first visitor I ever took through our lab who took such an interest in why we do things the way we do. Most folks never get beyond asking how we do things."

"Thanks, Sarah. How long have you worked there, and where did you grow up?"

"Believe it or not, I grew up right here in Rockford. My dad worked in a plant where they made parts for airplanes. As to my time at the State Police Laboratory, I took some courses in Criminal Justice at Rock Valley College, and that led into Special Topics studies in forensics. I actually learned most of what I know about forensics after they hired me at the lab two years ago. I guess that was a long-winded way of answering your question. Please forgive me if I talk too much."

"I like to listen to you talk, Sarah. You talk about things that interest me. Most of the girls in the old neighborhood spent all their time talking about local personal things and what they did or were going to do that day."

"I was one of those girls once. Everything was about creating an image and then living up to it. Then I realized I didn't care, and that allowed me to spend my time thinking about more important things."

"Well, thanks for spending a little bit of your valuable time with a young guy like me."

"A few years difference in age means less and less as you grow older."

"Is that a hint that we might have a second date?"

"It may be, Jay, but only if you do something to make this afternoon a memory."

"What would you like?"

"I've never been kissed on a romantic bridge in a Japanese garden."

"*Hai, yorokonde.*"

"You speak Japanese?"

"Only a few phrases I picked up along the way."

"What does that one mean?"

"Yes; with pleasure." He gave Sarah a long gentle kiss.

CHAPTER 19 – DNA RESULTS

Jay Redshaw started to connect with the rhythm of police work as he settled into his clerical routine at the Parkville Police Department. He actually experienced a feeling of power as he traced plate numbers of drivers that had refused to pull over when the speed trap officer gestured. Those folks thought they were getting away with something because the Parkville department had a *do not pursue* rule for safety and efficiency. Every car that passed by the speed trap was recorded on a split screen video, displaying the radar-detected speed readout alongside the image of the car and its clearly readable license plate. All he had to do was punch the plate number into his computer, and the system took over. Two minutes later, he had a printout of the registration information for the vehicle and a printed ticket, ready to mail to the speeder. The speed trap officer deliberately set up his equipment on the near side of a traffic monitoring overhead camera. If an offender claimed that the car had been stolen, they could check the overhead camera recording for an image of the driver. For a small-town setup, it was efficient and lucrative as well.

The telephone rang, and he responded in his deeper-than-normal official voice. "Records and Data, Jay Redshaw speaking."

"Hi, Jay; it's Sarah. You sounded very professional. I have good news. We managed to tie both of those DNA samples to names in our databases. Neither one of them was in the Illinois records, but we got lucky when we worked through the FBI's CODIS national database. The first individual was Albert Rivers. He did some time in Massachusetts for fraud. The second person was Theodore Higgins. We have no information on why he was in the CODIS database. My guess is that he's not a convicted felon, but that's only my personal opinion."

"Wow. You are the bearer of good news. I didn't think we had much of a chance of naming those two old corpses. That didn't sound right. They were people, whatever they did, and we should refer to them with some degree of reverence. Ever since my brother was shot, I've had misgivings about treating dead people like statistics."

"We get that same question raised at the lab, but we don't have your personal connection with it. A whole life can be terminated in an instant, and our records dwell on that moment of death, rather than the life that preceded it. I always get the feeling that it isn't right."

"Thanks, Sarah, both for the identification info and for your comments on the importance of life. You're a good person."

"Jay, it feels good to hear that, coming from you. Now, say your next important line."

"What line? I don't have scripted lines?"

"I phrased that poorly. This is the point at which you ask me for a second date. Then I accept and say that this time, I'll come down to see you in Parkville."

Impasse

"Got it, Sarah; how about Saturday afternoon at one o'clock? Meet me at House of Ming Chinese Restaurant for lunch, and wear good shoes for spending an afternoon hiking and being outdoors. After all my years behind city walls, I need the great outdoors."

"I'll be there, and you should practice using chopsticks, because I'll have them take the silverware away."

Five minutes later, Jay sent an email to Irma, being careful to have his words sound like official police jargon. *Regarding deceased subjects in sewer-pipe tunnel, one identified as Albert Rivers and the other as Theodore Higgins. Rivers served time in a Massachusetts prison for fraud. No information yet on Higgins. Do you need a formal report? That's all I have so far.*

Ten minutes later, Irma sent her reply. *Good work. Pass my thanks to the State Police Lab. I'll send you feedback after I learn more about them. Arthur or I will contact you when we have your next assignment.*

Jayson Redshaw leaned back in his chair and relaxed. He felt that he had achieved a few things. He was making useful contributions to investigations, both routine and unusual. He had a romance threatening to bloom, too. Everything was good, perhaps too good. Would his next assignment go as well?

CHAPTER 20 – FLASHBACK

The two men crouched in the back of the specialized truck. Rivers, a clean-shaven forty-eight-year-old was the leader. His companion, an apprentice named Marco, little more than half his age, listened attentively. When Rivers gave Marco instructions he had to speak loudly because of the heavy rain on the truck's roof.

"Here's the way this is going to work. This truck has a trapdoor in the floor of its cargo box. Willie, the driver, will park in the outlined loading zone. The outline of that zone matches this truck, so that our trapdoor will be directly above a square manhole cover in the pavement. When I press the green button on the wall of the truck, a motor will open the hinged manhole cover. Don't worry about the rain. We'll take our bags down into the tunnel through the trapdoor and manhole cover without getting wet and without anyone nearby seeing us in the darkness. Once we're down below, we press a red button on a matching switch that closes the manhole until we're ready to come up again. We have lights and a fan down there, so it'll be dry and bright. I'll go down first, and then you hand the bags down to me. That's a lot easier than trying to squeeze through the manhole while carrying a bag."

Marco agreed. "That sounds as though you've thought of everything. This is a much fancier setup than I expected. It must have cost a bundle to set it up."

"Don't worry about anything except doing your job. Tonight, you're a fetch and carry man. Later on, I'll start teaching you my end of the business. Once you get to that point I guarantee you'll enjoy both the risks and the rewards."

They heard three knocks on the rear wall of the truck cab.

Rivers said, "That's our signal. Willie has parked the truck directly over the tunnel entrance. You open the truck's trapdoor, while I push the button to activate the manhole's motor drive. The beauty of this system is that the manhole only opens when my switch triggers the motor. A man trying to force it open with tools would be unsuccessful."

Marco opened the trapdoor and watched the manhole cover swing upward on its hinge. "Everything's open, but I can't see anything. It's dark down there."

"I forgot to mention that part. We have to drop down into the tunnel without lights so that no one in the area sees us. There's rubber padding beneath the opening to cushion your landing. After the manhole closes, the lights go on. Here I go. Drop the bags down after you hear me clap my hands."

Marco watched Rivers maneuver into the hole below. He hardly heard him hit the bottom of the tunnel, due to the background noise from the rain and the cushioning material below. As soon as Marco heard Rivers' handclap, he eased the two heavy bags into the tunnel entrance and released them one at a time. Upon hearing a second handclap, he sat on the edge of the manhole and let

61

himself drop downward into the darkness. He was off-balance when he hit the floor, but he didn't fall because Rivers grabbed his arm. As he became more dark-adapted, Marco was able to see Rivers reach for the switch button mounted on the wall of the round tunnel. He pressed it and the manhole shut with a muffled thud. Then the motor stopped, and the tunnel lights went on, one at this end and one or two along the way to the other end. It was dry; Marco could feel air circulating; and he no longer heard the rain.

"Hey, Rivers, this is pretty neat. This place is solid enough to be used as a bomb shelter."

"It probably could in an emergency."

They picked up the heavy bags and started walking toward the other end of the tunnel.

Marco asked, "Do you mind if I ask you a personal question?"

"Go ahead, if it's not too personal."

"You call yourself Albert Rivers. That name almost begs the question of whether it was once Alberto Rivera. Was it?"

"Let's put it this way; my dad was Alberto Rivera. I'm Albert Rivers. It sounds more American, and it's better for use in my business."

"Would I be rushing things too much if I asked about your business?"

"Yes, you would be rushing things, but if your training works out as well as I expect, it will soon be our business in partnership, so please be patient."

A loud booming noise penetrated the tunnel.

Marco said, "That sounds as though the rain is changing into a thunderstorm."

They heard two more claps of thunder.

Rivers said, "Drop the bags, and head back to the entrance."

"But these bags are full of cash. That's a lot of money."

"Drop them and run. If the power fails, we're trapped in here. The weakness of this system is that there's no battery backup."

They abandoned the sacks of cash and ran back to the entrance. As Rivers reached for the green button, everything went black.

"We're screwed, unless the power comes back on before we run out of air."

Marco said, "Maybe not. I can still hear a fan in the distance. That must be on a different circuit."

They continued to hear muffled thunder. Then the fan noise stopped, and Marco realized that they were in big trouble. "What about the other end of the tunnel? There must be a door where we were taking the money."

"That won't work, Marco. It's an airlock setup. We open a hatch and put the sacks into a chamber beyond it. Then we lock the hatch again. Our partner on the other side has a locking door at the other side of that storage chamber. We can't unlock the door to the bank, and they can't unlock the door to the tunnel. It's a security design so that the tunnel can't be used to rob the bank."

"Can we go into the space between the tunnel and the bank? The air might be better than in the tunnel."

"The hatch is too small for us to fit through."

"Can Willie open the manhole from the truck?"

"Not without electricity to drive the motor, assuming the circuit didn't arc and fry when the power went off."

"Would he call 911 to get the police and paramedics over here?"

"He might try that from a phone booth, anonymously, but my guess is that he'll drive away and hide somewhere. He has a long police record, and he's not very resourceful."

"In other words, we've had it."

"Don't waste your time on words. Save your breath for as long as possible, and pray that Commonwealth Edison gets the power fixed real soon. That's our only chance. The fan will restart when the power comes back on, even if the hatch motor drive is dead."

CHAPTER 21 – FBI MEETING

FBI Special Agent Ruth Daltry stood facing the conference table at which Arthur Blake, Irma Blake, and DEA Agent Paul Garcia sat with yellow pads of paper in front of them.

"Welcome to our status meeting. I thought we should all meet to exchange ideas and information."

Arthur said, "I notice that our group keeps getting smaller. Earlier, the Chicago Police detective was all too happy to leave, and now we no longer have Ron Barabee, our construction and excavation expert."

Special Agent Daltry nodded. "As we progress into the investigation I'll be varying the involved parties to suit our immediate needs. My colleagues and I decided that we have all the information we need about the tunnel, so I omitted Mr. Barabee from this meeting. I also plan to discuss confidential information that is beyond his need-to-know limit. I may involve him again, depending on the results of today's discussion."

Paul Garcia said, "My supervisors will want me to justify my participation by convincing them that this tunnel discovery has some connection to drug trafficking and that it is relevant to current investigation work, since the tunnel deaths occurred so long ago."

"We'll cover those questions, but first, let's get informal. I've found that social barriers get in the way of investigations. From now on, we'll be on a first name basis. Call me Ruth, and I'll address you as Irma, Arthur, and Paul. Now I'll turn to your concerns, Paul. It's too early in the investigation to state whether drug trafficking was connected to the bodies and money found in that tunnel. However, my superiors and I are convinced that this was a scheme for laundering money through a bank. Regardless of the source of the money, we need someone with knowledge of money laundering techniques on the team. Accordingly, Paul, my superiors have contacted their counterparts at DEA, and I can announce that you no longer have to justify your working on this case. You have been officially assigned to it."

"Thanks, Ruth. That avoids red tape and ongoing questions about my time allocation."

"Irma and Arthur, you're civilians. I can't draft you for the team."

Irma gestured that she would respond for the two of them. "We're on the team because Arthur has a responsibility to the bishop to eliminate obstacles to building a new church on that tunnel worksite and because we bring useful skills and experiences to the investigation. However, as private contractors, we will expect to be compensated for our efforts."

Arthur leaned back and folded his arms across his chest. "She's our business manager."

Ruth opened a folder and handed Irma a stapled set of papers. "Just sign and date these in the indicated places, and you have a contract. Let me know if the indicated compensation amount is not sufficient."

Irma glanced at the sheets and smiled. "That's quite reasonable. We accept."

Ruth closed her folder. "Now that we've handled the preliminaries, what are the next questions in this case that need to be answered?"

Arthur broke the pause while the others considered Ruth's question. "I'm bothered by the fact that the bodies and money were undisturbed in that tunnel for so long. The accomplices in the bank would have wanted to retrieve the money, even if they didn't care about the people."

Ruth wrote his comment on her pad. "My first response to that one is that our FBI technicians don't think the bankers would have been able to get into the tunnel. We don't have the manhole assembly, but the existence of conduit along the length of the tunnel suggests that the entrance was electrically operated. If it was motor-operated and the command circuitry failed, it would have been very difficult to overcome the motor gearing and force the manhole open."

"That's technically reasonable. Congratulations to your people for suggesting that answer. The bankers could have hired a contractor to open that entrance, but they wouldn't have wanted to attract attention to the contents of the tunnel. I still wonder why the scavengers who eventually dug out the entire manhole assembly didn't go down below."

Irma said, "I'll answer that one, Arthur. My guess is they thought it was a sewer, and therefore not interesting, or they thought going down there would be too dangerous. The whole property was covered with rubble at that point. The scavengers had the fancy manhole assembly as a prize. They wouldn't have been interested in going beyond that success. What do you think, Ruth?"

"I think your answer shows good reasoning. Whatever the obstacles, either immediately after these men died or at a much later date, we can conclude that no one entered the tunnel, because the bags of money were still there and undisturbed. Our specialists managed to retrieve the bags of money and other evidence from the tunnel, but they couldn't get past that cave-in with the small gap in it. Now, Irma, tell us about your DNA sampling and results."

"During our first visit to the property, I attached myself to the efforts of archaeologists hired by the Chicago Police Department to determine the age of the unearthed human remains. The City of Chicago is always sensitive to the possibility of accidentally excavating a burial ground with ethnic or religious significance. They take this approach despite, or perhaps because of, their failure to find and relocate all the bodies buried in old cemeteries on the shore of Lake Michigan before Chicago converted and extended that land into lakeside parks. Once we determined that the deaths occurred only twenty to twenty-five years ago, the archaeologists lost interest. Because the tunnel was dry and sealed by either a manhole or a plug of collapsed rubble during all those years, the remains were in good enough condition for me to retrieve DNA samples from them. I convinced the director of the Illinois State Police Forensic Science Laboratory in Rockford to process my samples and search for database matches to them."

Ruth said, "And I believe they found matches."

Arthur noticed that Ruth took a deep breath after making that comment. He awaited Irma's response before saying anything.

Irma said, "Yes, Ruth, The Illinois lab found matches in the FBI CODIS databases. One individual was Albert Rivers, who had a felony record in Massachusetts for fraud, and the other was Theodore Higgins, who had no background information."

Ruth's posture sagged slightly. "Theodore Higgins was an FBI agent working undercover as Marco Locante. Ted and I entered the FBI Academy in Quantico, Virginia together and were close friends. He disappeared while on an undercover assignment, and we had no idea what happened to him until now."

Arthur understood Ruth's earlier deep breath. "Can you tell us the nature of his undercover mission when he went missing?"

"That's the problem. It was a special assignment with only verbal instructions from his supervisor, and that manager died in a suspicious traffic accident four months after sending Ted as Marco into the field in 1992. There are no records."

CHAPTER 22 – DIRECTIONS

For a few minutes the investigative team remained silent, digesting the news that one of the tunnel bodies was an FBI agent, and perhaps saying a prayer for him.

Arthur asked, "Did Ted have a family?"

"His mother lives in Manchester, New Hampshire in a retirement home. She isn't well. I'll have the responsibility of giving her the news of her son's death so long ago."

"I take it that you and Ted were close."

"For a short period we lived together, but his undercover work made that impractical. Even before he disappeared, he had several assignments that each lasted several months, during which he could not be contacted. We agreed that a long-term relationship would not be in our future."

"Why did he take the name of Marco Locante, and was that name a continuing alias, or did he have different identities on his various assignments?"

"Arthur, he became Marco Locante in every aspect of his being. That was one of the reasons for our drifting apart. His Irish ancestry gave Ted an informal and humble approach to life, but as Marco, he became a suave but ambitious man with an Italian family background. He was trained to do undercover work, and he enjoyed it. He said he didn't have to pretend to be Marco very long. He simply became him."

"That's interesting, Ruth. His statement reminds me of another person we encountered in a previous case who was able to change identities at will. You're in charge of this team, but I suggest that we're ready to go off in several directions to explore different aspects of the case."

"What directions do you suggest, Arthur?"

"If we allocate tasks by expertise and interests, it might make sense for you and Paul to find out more about the bank at the far end of the tunnel and the way they handled the mysterious and unofficial cash deposits. I think that I should get Ron Barabee involved again and work with him and his crew to clear and explore the basement of that bank building. That would require a contract from the FBI for the additional excavation work he would be doing. Irma and her assistant, Jay, might look into the activities of our deceased fraud felon, Albert Rivers, and perhaps interview some of the people who had contact with him. How does that sound to everyone?"

Ruth said, "It makes sense, because we would be looking at several aspects of the case at the same time. Irma, if you're satisfied with the assignment of checking on Albert Rivers, I'll get you temporary credentials and passwords for searching our FBI files. You would have to go through security training and clearance to be sure you jump through all of their information control hoops properly."

"No problem, Ruth. We have clearances and background checks from working with another government agency on a regular basis. I can arrange for recommendations if you wish."

"I don't think that will be necessary, but what agency is it?"

"One that doesn't officially exist."

"Understood. I don't have a need to know about them. How about you, Paul? Are you interested in exploring that bank's money laundering techniques?"

"I'm more than interested. While the rest of you have been talking, I've been writing down a list of possible schemes they might have used."

Ruth made a few notes on her pad of paper. "That's the way we'll move forward. I have the initial unwelcome assignment of meeting with Ted Higgins' mother. After that, I'll work with Paul on bank-related matters. Arthur, please keep Ron in the dark about the identities of the two men in the tunnel. He is only involved in construction activities and won't join us in our meetings. Tell him I'll have a contract for him in a few days and that he is authorized to begin work immediately. Irma, access to FBI files will be for your eyes only. You should confine your assistant's research activities to publicly available information sources. We'll meet again when any one of us feels he or she has enough results to justify a gathering. Good investigating luck to all of us."

CHAPTER 23 – WORKSITE

When Arthur knocked on Ron Barabee's office trailer door, it opened promptly.

"Thanks for coming by, Arthur. I'm going out of my skull with boredom."

"That boredom was caused by a skull, so you might want to rephrase that comment. Anyway, I have some relief for you."

"Are you here to give me the green light on the rest of this job?"

"I'm giving you authorization to start a separate smaller job here. It's not the full release you want, but it will relieve your boredom, and you'll get paid extra for it."

"Tell me more. So far it sounds like good news."

"The news is that you're about to get a contract from the FBI to carefully excavate and open access to the basement of that old bank building under the parking lot. When they tore it down, they didn't dig out the foundations, as you saw from that sewer inspection video. The basement walls are still down there. The earlier contractors simply bulldozed the bank building and paved over it when they built the stores."

"That's not best practice, but lots of contractors cut corners."

"Their cutting corners created an add-on contract for you. I'm authorized to tell you to start right away. The paperwork from the FBI will arrive in a few days."

"I'll call a few of my guys in today. We'll have to hand-clear the rubble in the area where we believe the bank building stood. Then we'll probe through the remaining rubble and ground in a grid pattern to determine the building's outline. The actual excavation will be labor intensive using hand work and small machines. I'm assuming the FBI wants us to find and clear the stairs so that they can go down there."

"That's the ideal goal, but I'm sure they'll settle for ladder access if necessary. They'll want you to save interior walls whenever possible. They want to know where all the basement rooms were."

"I don't want to cut my own throat as far as additional contracts, but shouldn't there be a drawing on file somewhere showing the layout of the rooms?"

"FBI people will be looking for that, Ron, but we suspect that the actual building didn't match the original drawings. This bank was a front for a criminal operation. It may have had more than a few secrets in the way it was built."

CHAPTER 24 – NEW ASSIGNMENT

Jay Redshaw looked up from his computer screen when Chief Bobby Andrews and Irma Blake walked into the Police Department data-processing room. He stood, looking from one to the other.

"I must be in trouble if both of my supervisors are coming to see me at the same time."

Bobby tried to look stern, but couldn't keep a hint of a smile from his expression. "We're not here to chastise you, but we are ganging up on you. Irma has a new assignment for you that will also take you into an additional area of police work, so I'm going to let her use my portion of your schedule, even though the Police Department will pay you for that time."

Irma said, "Thanks, Bobby; when we discussed this assignment, I didn't expect you to pick up the tab for the time Jay spends on my case."

"It's only fair, Irma. Jay's learning on the job, and it will make him a better police officer eventually if he chooses to make this his profession."

Jay tried to guess his new task. "Are you guys teasing me, or am I going to get away from the computer and do something active like following someone?"

Bobby laughed and walked out of the room. As he left he said, "Jay, you're so tall, you'd have trouble trying to follow anyone without being noticed. He's all yours, Irma."

Irma motioned for Jay to sit. She moved a swivel chair from an empty desk closer and sat down. "Sorry, Jay, you won't be going out to do field work yet, but you may in the future. For now, you'll be doing computer work of a different type."

"I'm ready for anything, Dr. Blake. Give me the details."

"The first detail is that we work informally. You may call me either Dr. Blake or Irma when we're with Chief Andrews, but we'll stick to first names when officials or strangers aren't present."

"Got that, Irma."

"Good. The DNA match for one of the men who died in that worksite tunnel was Albert Rivers. We're both going to find out everything we can about him. I'll be examining confidential FBI files, and I want you to check police records, perform online searches, and interview administrators at the Massachusetts prison where he served time."

"Do I get to go to Massachusetts and visit that prison?"

"I'm afraid that trip is beyond our budget. You'll have to do your interviewing by telephone or email."

"That's fine, but put me on record as being serious about wanting to do something in the field. I'm too young to be riding a computer all day. Line me up for some physical things too."

"Your request is noted, Jay. I'll try to find some field work for you, after we find everything we can about Albert Rivers."

After Irma left, Jay went online to learn more about the Massachusetts prison system and what he would have to do to retrieve information about Albert Rivers' conviction and behavior while he served his sentence. He learned that Massachusetts had developed a computerized system, Criminal Offender Record Information (CORI) and that he would have to apply to have the Parkville Police Department accepted for use of their system by means of a letter signed by Chief Andrews. He drafted a letter that included the requested background information and took it to Bobby's office.

Bobby was on the telephone when he arrived, so he stood in the hallway until he heard the chief end his conversation. Then Jay knocked on the doorpost.

"Come on in, Jay. You could have taken a seat while I finished up that call. It was nothing confidential. In the future, just come in and take a seat if I'm on the phone with my door open. It would be closed if I were discussing sensitive information. Have you already finished your research on Albert Rivers?"

"Hardly, Chief, I'm still getting qualified to begin that study. That's why I'm here. The state of Massachusetts has all of its criminal records in a database for online retrieval. There's a two-step process required before I can access that data."

"In the old days we could just call someone and ask him or her to pull a file folder."

"You're not that old, Bobby. You could still be playing football if you had chosen that for a career."

"I did have that dream once. I was big enough, but not talented enough. Getting back to your assignment, what do you need from me?"

"I drafted a letter for you to sign. They need the police chief's signature for every department requesting admission to the system. Then there's another step before I can actually retrieve some information on Albert Rivers."

"What's that?"

"I have to contact their technical team and tell them about our computer setup and equipment to determine whether they're compatible with the Massachusetts system."

Bobby signed the letter and mad a note on his scratch paper pad. "That sounds like a ton of work."

"It's extra work for departments like ours that want to access their system, but they avoid the need to have individual interviews with people from other departments, so it's easier for them. I'll follow all of the procedures, but I have a nagging feeling that we won't get all the information we want."

"What's bothering you?"

"The problem is that we can't ask their system a question. It will spit out all the standard format data for our former prisoner, but we won't have access to someone who can answer an unusual question."

"Like what?"

"Like, who were Rivers' cellmates or friends while he was in prison? What were those people's crimes? How friendly or cooperative was he with the prison staff? What were the details of the fraud for which he was imprisoned?"

"I get it. Whatever you learn about someone triggers more questions, and standard format data summaries don't go far enough to let us really understand a convicted criminal."

"That's it, Chief. I'll get the data this system will give me, but it would be useful to come up with someone we could actually question."

"I like your thinking, Jay, but you do realize that Rivers completed his sentence in that prison at least twenty-five years ago. I could call and try the personal approach, but they aren't even likely to have staff members who have been there that long, let alone staffers who remember the specific prisoner we're studying. I'll try to think up a way to get more than the system's standard data, but Rivers' records are practically ancient history."

CHAPTER 25 – BASEMENT

There was a touch of excitement in Ron Barabee's voice as it emerged from Arthur's telephone. "I think you and your associates should visit me at the worksite. We're ready to explore that old bank's basement."

"Your tone suggests that you already have explored it."

"No, Arthur, I wanted to see it when you did. A couple of my workers have hinted at unexpected things down there. That's why I'm looking forward to our inspection visit. I'll be in my office trailer when you get here. Take your time. We have the bank site fenced off to avoid anyone else going down there by accident."

Arthur called Ruth Daltry at the FBI and told her that he and Irma would be inspecting the bank basement along with Ron Barabee. He invited her to join them, but Ruth said she'd have to wait for their report because she was about to go into an all-day meeting. Arthur promised prompt documentation of anything they found. Then he called Irma at the local library and told her that he would pick her up in twenty minutes to join him in the inspection.

After Irma climbed into the car, Arthur asked, "What did you expect to find in our little library that would be useful information for our case? They certainly wouldn't have anything on Albert Rivers there."

"They didn't have anything on him, but they did have quite a bit about a man named Alberto Rivera who claimed to have been a Jesuit priest who left the Catholic Church. He accused the Vatican of untruths and misdeeds. He was older than the apparent age of our Albert Rivers and died within a year of him. I've been wondering if these two men were related, perhaps father and son."

"Why would you suspect that? Outside of the similarity of names, they probably had nothing in common."

"There was one thing. The Catholic Church accused Alberto Rivera of fraud in his claim to have been a priest and in his claims against the Vatican. The other man, Albert Rivers was convicted of fraud in Massachusetts. Perhaps he learned the family business at the dinner table."

Arthur glanced sideways at Irma as he drove. "You frequently accuse me of suggesting a conclusion before I've gathered all of the necessary evidence. Despite that tendency, I've never suggested a connection between two people on such flimsy data as your speculation based on the similarity of their names."

"*Mea culpa.* I'm guilty as charged, Arthur. I simply discovered the possibly fraudulent priest story and let my imagination run with it. At least we'll have hard evidence to study when we go down into the basement of that demolished bank. If you're not in a complete rush to get there, let's swing by the Parkville Police Department and invite Jay to join us. I promised him that I would get him involved in a field task when I found a suitable one."

By the time Arthur, Irma, and Jay arrived at the worksite, Ron's workers had already quit for the day. True to his word, Ron was in his office trailer, completing the FBI contract forms while he waited for Arthur and company to arrive. Arthur knocked on the door with the traditional *shave and a haircut* rhythm, and opened the door after Ron yelled out his welcome greeting. Once inside, Arthur introduced Ron to Jay, who had to bend over to fit beneath the low trailer ceiling.

Jay asked, "If you folks don't mind, could we possibly talk outside? My back is starting to complain already. I can't stand bent over like this."

Everyone agreed to leave the cramped quarters. Once outside, Ron supplied each of them with a flashlight.

"You'll need these when we go down into that basement. We were able to save its ceiling except for a couple of spots where the daylight will shine through. Depending on what we find, we may want to stay down there after dark anyway. I'll be taking photos of anything that relates to the way the bank building was constructed and best demolition techniques. I see that Jay has a camera for your documentation."

Jay said, "Irma wants me to photograph anything we think is significant from an evidence point of view. I'll also take a few people shots as we search the basement for use in our report to the

FBI. Both Irma and Chief Andrews keep reminding me to document everything I do or see."

Irma nodded slightly in agreement. "You're being very deliberate about following our procedures now, but after a while they'll become automatic, like driving a car."

As they approached the bank basement site, Ron took down a section of the surrounding fence. "The guys managed to save most of the concrete stairs going down there, but a few steps have missing sections. They added temporary pipe railings for balance when you have to jump over a gap. Be very careful, and I hope your insurance is paid up, because ours doesn't cover non-workers."

Arthur laughed. "We're building inspectors, working for your clients, so that should get us some measure of coverage. In any case, we'll do our best to be careful."

As they descended the obstacle course masquerading as basement stairs, they scanned the space in front of them with flashlights that moved too quickly for their beams to reveal more than continuously bouncing patterns of light and shadow. All four of the visitors appreciated the temporary pipe railings.

When they reached the floor below the stairs, Ron apologized. "My guys told me there were only a couple of gaps in the stairs. They understated the difficulty of getting down here. Try to remember each place where the concrete is loose or missing for the return trip up those stairs."

As they started to look around, Irma asked, "Ron, our flashlights aren't going to give us enough steady light to completely evaluate this place. Is there any chance you could run an extension cord from the office trailer so that we can hang a light from something? I have two trouble lights in our car. Do you have long enough extension cords?"

"I might have to temporarily steal a couple from their regular uses, but I think I could do it. I'll have to draft Jay to help me put them all together."

Irma gave Jay her car keys to get the trouble lights from the trunk. "Arthur and I will continue to scan this place with our flashlights while you work on getting us some steady lighting."

After Ron and Jay left, Arthur motioned for Irma to join him and walked toward the right–hand corner from the bottom of the stairs. "While you talked about improved lighting, I did a little exploring. Look what I found."

Irma looked into an extremely large room with a wide open entrance. "This must have been their vault area. It has extra-thick walls."

"Notice anything unusual about it?"

"It's hard to see details by flashlight."

"My first observation doesn't involve details."

"Are you looking at the size of the room?"

"Yup. This was a relatively small bank with a vault room the size that a larger bank would have."

"It would have looked smaller when the safe deposit boxes were in place. They removed them before they abandoned the building."

"Now look at the back wall of the vault room."

"That's the other end of the tunnel. The wall is steel, and it has a safe door centered on it and a fan grill near the ceiling above that door."

Arthur banged on the steel wall with the back end of his flashlight. "They couldn't remove that safe door when they left because it's welded to the steel wall, and the steel wall is load-bearing. Part of the building might have collapsed if they had tried to tear out the steel wall. Besides, it would have been an expensive procedure."

Arthur and Irma heard noises behind them. They walked back to the stairs, where they saw Jay daisy-chaining the two trouble lights together and connecting them to the end of an extension cord. Jay spoke into his cell phone. "They're connected, Ron. Turn on the power."

A moment later, the lights came on, separated by the length of a long trouble light cord plugged into the second light's power outlet. The two individual lamps emitted enough light to fill a large room, even the vault. As Ron climbed down the stairs to join them, he dragged an additional extension cord behind him. "This will give us enough slack in the setup to illuminate the entire basement, one section at a time."

Arthur and Jay carried the extension cords and lights into the vault room while Irma explained to Ron and Jay that the steel wall with its built-in safe door was the other side of the airlock compartment where the bags of cash were once deposited.

Jay listened to Irma's summary and then turned to Ron. "Is there a ladder on the worksite somewhere?"

"Sure; there's one under my trailer. Why?"

"I'd like to climb up and look through that air vent grill near the ceiling. I wonder if I could see into the compartment behind that safe door or through the double-walled compartment into the tunnel."

"That's worth trying. I'll help you get it." Ron and Jay climbed up the stairs, and a short while later Arthur heard and saw a ladder sliding down the concrete stairs. He pulled it away from the stairs and carried it into the vault room as Ron and Jay navigated the damaged stairs into the basement.

As Jay positioned the ladder in front of the high ventilation fan grill, Irma said, "We've found the perfect job requiring your height. Looking at that ladder, I don't think any of the rest of us would be able to see into that fan grill."

He started climbing. "We'll soon find out whether I can see anything either."

When Jay reached the top, he stretched, but couldn't get a good viewing angle. He called for assistance. "Ron, Arthur, brace the ladder really well. I'm going to have to go up one more rung to see anything useful."

Jay moved up the ladder tentatively, because he was beyond the safe climbing level. Thanks to the bracing by Ron and Arthur below, he was able to examine everything on the other side of the grill. After a few minutes he descended the ladder.

Arthur asked, "What were you able to see?"

"Three things: The compartment between the airlock walls is covered with steel plate, so we won't learn anything without opening that safe door. When the fan is off, louvers drop over the vent opening to the tunnel, sealing it off and keeping me from looking beyond the vent grill. The third thing I saw was the most interesting."

Irma asked, "What was it?"

"I wasn't the first person to climb up to that grill. A long time ago, judging from all the dust, someone climbed up there and used a long-handled tool to cut the wires to the fan and the wires that lead into that conduit that runs the length of the tunnel. Those men in the tunnel didn't die accidentally. They were murdered."

CHAPTER 26 – SAFECRACKER

When Arthur visited the FBI office to report their basement exploration findings to Ruth Daltry, she was more than interested.

After receiving Arthur's input, Ruth summarized her own preliminary findings. "That bank was definitely a front for something illegal. You had mentioned its name being a Plain Jane sort of thing. The full name was North Corner Savings Bank. It had an Illinois state charter to keep the more rigorous federal bank examiners away and to let it engage in cash-intensive sidelines like a travel agency business. It went out of business during the period when Illinois first allowed branch banking and then affiliating with interstate banks. Some banks changed hands so frequently during this process that accurate audits were virtually impossible. The interstate banks accepted losses due to all the changes and moved forward. North Corner Savings Bank was of such small size compared to its interstate buyer that the new management took over the charter and the active accounts and then sold or wrote off everything else, including the building. That new owner was just looking to get a toehold in Illinois. Then, six months after the razing of the bank building, the interstate owner merged with a larger banking group. That was the wild west era of banking in Illinois."

Impasse

"The interstate bank probably didn't build a bigger facility at that location because their planners didn't think they would do enough business there."

"Most of those big banking outfits built small branches in wealthy suburbs or took over existing stores with a limited-time lease. The age of the imposing bank building is over, Arthur."

"Were you able to get a list of the key people running that bank? Your comment about multiple ownership changes suggests confusion and poor record keeping."

"We have the names of three stockholders, but we suspect that they were invented identities to disguise people with criminal records. As soon as the North Corner Savings Bank went out of business as a separate entity, the public records of the officers and stockholders terminated. They didn't renew their driver's licenses, register to vote, or file tax returns."

"Perhaps they all died."

"That's possible, but I doubt it, Arthur. No death certificates were filed, and we found no life insurance paid out in the officers' names. The operating people may have been listed as officers under different names to hide their identities. I wouldn't be surprised if one of those officers was our tunnel corpse, Albert Rivers, using a different name. He certainly knew how the bank worked its money laundering magic."

"If that was the case, they had a falling out, because someone who had access to the bank vault, probably at night, trapped the two men who died in the tunnel by cutting the electrical wires that powered the ventilator and their exit manhole mechanism."

"Arthur, my question on that one is whether the killer's target was his associate, Albert Rivers, or an FBI agent whose alias as Marco Locante had been discovered."

"We may learn more when we get that safe door in the back wall of the vault room open. Have you arranged for an expert to open it?"

"I have. She'll meet us at the bank basement site at ten o'clock tomorrow morning."

The following morning, Arthur and Irma arrived at the bank basement site to find Ruth and another woman waiting for them. Ruth introduced the newcomer as Donna Spelsby. Her posture suggested athletic capabilities, casually hidden by the loose blue jeans and flannel shirt she wore.

Arthur asked, "Donna, I understand you're an expert at opening safes. Did the FBI train you in that skill?"

"No, I trained myself with some input from my uncle. The FBI interfered with my entrepreneurial use of my skills."

When he raised an eyebrow at this response, Ruth said, "That's right, Arthur; Donna is a reformed safecracker. She served a number of years in prison and, upon her release she volunteered to assist the FBI when safe doors needed to be opened."

"Ruth, don't distort the details. I never volunteered to do anything. I get paid big bucks for every safe I open for the FBI. They also pay me an ongoing retainer fee in between assignments so that I won't feel the urge to return to my independent business again. It's not as glamorous as the old days, but I have a guaranteed income and no risk."

Ruth said, "Anyway, Donna is very good at what she does. Let's get down into that old bank basement so that she can demonstrate her skill."

Arthur led the way down the broken concrete stairs, plugged the temporary trouble lights into the extension cord, and guided the newcomers to the old vault room. Irma decided to take her flashlight and explore other areas of the basement while Donna tackled the wall-mounted safe door.

When Donna saw the safe combination lock dial, she identified it as a standard combination lock mechanism, known to safecrackers as Old Faithful. She reasoned that the bank people would feel that offered them adequate protection, because it was installed in a room secured by a more modern vault door. Donna asked Ruth and Arthur to leave the room while she worked so that she would be able to concentrate and not reveal her techniques. She promised to call them back as soon as the safe door was open.

When Ruth and Arthur left Donna alone in the vault room, they saw a beam of light at the other end of the bank basement and realized that Irma was exploring areas they had not previously searched. They walked to the illuminated area, dodging minor piles of broken plaster and concrete along the way. When they reached the beam of light, they saw Irma kneeling next to an old carton full of papers.

She looked up as they approached. "I found this carton on a shelf underneath that built-in counter over there. The people who emptied this basement prior to demolition of the bank building must have overlooked it."

Arthur looked into the carton. "I see travel brochures on the top. Is there anything underneath them that reveals details about their business?"

"There may be. I have both typed and written loose sheets of paper plus some printed forms. I'll have to take these away from here to clean and study them."

Ruth said, "Photograph the carton here and on the shelf where you found it for evidence purposes. After you remove the carton to a better location, list the contents in detail and sign that inventory list, indicating that it is complete and correct. We don't know yet exactly where our investigation will go, but we have to follow good practices for handling evidence that we find along the way."

A shout from Donna echoed through the basement. "Where did everyone go? I have some secrets to show you."

When they returned to the vault room and saw the open safe door, Arthur said, "That didn't take you long, Donna."

"If you hire a professional, you get top-quality results. Actually, this was such a standard lock mechanism that I felt as though I had opened it before."

Impasse

Ruth shook Donna's hand. "Congratulations. You came through for us again. Did you find anything interesting in there?"

"My job is to open doors and locked compartments. Your task is to analyze the contents, which in this case are quite disgusting."

Ruth climbed two rungs up the ladder and aimed her flashlight into the hidden wall compartment. She stared downward into the space between the safe door and the hatch from the sewer pipe tunnel. Then she climbed down the ladder to the floor. "Irma, get over here please. Take a few pictures looking down into there, and then do a preliminary analysis. This case just got weirder."

Irma climbed the lower rungs of the ladder and looked into the compartment with her flashlight. Below her she saw two skeletons and an open leather and canvas bag full of money, with many loose bills on the floor. "My preliminary comments are that I see the remains of two people, one male and one female. They appear to have been dead as long as the two we previously found in the tunnel. At least one of them died from a gunshot wound to the head, because I can see a bullet hole in the right side of one of the skulls. I suggest that the open bag of money has been here at least as long as the two victims because the loose currency decayed along with the bodies. From the positions of the bodies, I would say that they were killed elsewhere and then their bodies were pushed through the safe door opening into that compartment. The positions of the skeletons are not natural. Their bodies were wedged in there by the killer due to the limited space. The ladder we're using came from the construction crew, so I would say that the perpetrator had a ladder or stepstool that he or she took away from here, or that the perpetrator was quite tall. That's about all I can say for now. I'll take some pictures, and then we should move the remains to a laboratory for more thorough analysis."

Ruth said, "That's a pretty detailed preliminary summary you've given us already. What do you think, Arthur?"

"Irma always has a good eye for examining the scene of a crime. We may find additional artifacts and belongings when your technicians remove the bodies. I'm intrigued by the suggestion that the killer was quite tall. That would suggest that the perpetrator of these murders was the same individual who cut the ventilator and actuator wires to trap Albert Rivers and FBI Agent Ted Higgins in that tunnel."

Ruth said, "It's much too early to reach a conclusion, but perhaps that tall person killed the two individuals in the wall compartment to eliminate anyone who might interfere with his or her cutting of the wires. What do you think, Arthur?"

"It's an interesting question as to which pair of murders occurred first, the tunnel or the safe compartment. It's the old chicken or egg puzzle. Whoever killed these two must have had some reason for abandoning the cash that's in there with what's left of the bodies. Perhaps he or she planned

Impasse

to come back for the money later, but never had the opportunity."

CHAPTER 27 – HOUSE OF MING

Sarah Jackson sat across the table from Jay Redshaw at House of Ming, wondering whether this would be the first of many meals they would share together. She decided that they needed to get beyond polite surface-topic conversation.

"Jay, are we good enough together to express our feelings on different matters?"

"We are, Sarah, but I'm not quite ready for you to tell me you're madly in love with me."

"No danger of that at this point. For starters, I wonder why everything we've done so far has an ethnic ingredient in it. We had our first date because you wondered why my boss at the lab picked out an African American guide for you as an African American visiting client. Then we went to a Japanese garden, where you romantically said something to me in Japanese. Now we're at a Chinese restaurant. I don't emphasize ethnicity as you do. I work with folks having many nationalities and backgrounds, and before you, I hadn't dated an African American guy in close to two years. I won't want emphasis on one ethnic group or another if we continue dating. Will it bother you to select your friends and entertainment without an ethnic ingredient?"

"Not in the slightest. I'm working for Irma Blake and Bobby Andrews, supervisors from two different ethnic groups. We're here because I like Chinese food, and I hope you do too. Arthur and Irma brought me here several times, and they're close friends with the very ethnic proprietor. Excuse me for one minute. I'd like you to meet him, and then we can continue this conversation."

Jay got up from the table, went down the hallway by the kitchen, and knocked on the half-open office door. He waved to the man sitting at the desk. That individual stood to shake his hand.

"Hi, Jay. Welcome back. What may I do for you?"

"I'm here with a date tonight, and I'd like to introduce you to her."

"Let's do that. I'm not busy right now."

The two men walked out to the table, where Sarah was sitting with her back toward them. They circled the table so that they stood in front of her.

Jay said, "Sarah, this is our host, Tony Fleming. Tony, I'd like to introduce my friend, Sarah Jackson."

The two shook hands, and then Tony said, "I'll bet you're wondering why I don't look Chinese, Sarah. The fact is that I have a serious business that I love, but it's based on a joke. House of Ming is named after the last syllable of my name, Fleming. I learned to cook Chinese food in Chicago, and it has always been a labor of love for me. I hope you enjoy your meals tonight. Try not to get completely filled by the main courses you order, because I'll have your waitress bring you a unique dessert that I save for special occasions like this. Enjoy yourselves, and I hope we'll be seeing the two of you in here again soon." Tony gave a slight bow to each of them and returned to his office.

As Jay sat down he said, "So much for my supposed emphasis on ethnic purity. Tony's Chinese food is as good as any you've eaten at other restaurants. Order anything on the menu, and I'm sure you'll enjoy it. He's a good guy, whether he's Chinese or not."

Sarah said, "Now I'm embarrassed. I thought I saw a side of you that wasn't there. I hope you'll forgive me."

"There's nothing to forgive. We're all just people. It's more a question of your neighborhood that determines who your friends are. You do your best to get along with the people who are near you, regardless of their race. In your case, you don't live very close to me, but I'll go out of my way to remain friends with you."

"After that speech, Jay, I hope we get to be very close friends. Let's order our food, before our conversation gets weird."

Jay covered Sarah's hand with his and nodded.

By the end of the meal, Sarah had become as big a fan of Tony Fleming's Chinese food as Jay was. They decided to complete the afternoon by walking the path around Mallard Lake, which was located across the street from Parkville United Methodist Church, where Arthur Blake had once served as pastor.

When they reached the lake's parking lot, Jay asked, "Sarah, did you follow my instructions from when we set up this date? Did you wear comfortable walking shoes?"

"I remembered, and I did wear them. Even so, I'd like to sit on those rocks over there and talk a bit before we start hiking. Would that be OK with you?" They talked as they walked to the rocks and then sat facing each other.

"Sure, Sarah, is anything bothering you?"

"That's exactly what I wanted to talk about. Is anything bothering you, Jay? How are you coping with your brother's death? That must be a terrible burden for you to carry."

"Of course it is, but I have to keep going without Lawson. As my younger brother, he was my one person fan club. He's in my thoughts and my dreams, but at least they caught the kid who did it. The shooting was another one of those gang initiation challenges. They make a new kid shoot someone at random, so that the gang has a permanent hold on him to keep him from quitting. Now that bastard will spend most of his life in prison in exchange for the life he took from Lawson. It's all crazy, but what can I do except keep moving forward? That's what Lawson would have wanted for me. If I do go on to becoming a police detective, maybe I'll be able to get some gang members convicted and sent away for a long time. I don't know how else to fight what happens on the streets."

She reached out and held his right hand with her left. "Your parents must have looked at you and Lawson as a matched pair, even though you were older by several years."

"Why do you say that?"

"They named you Jayson, and when he came along, they named him Lawson. They're matching names, almost as though you were twins."

"I never would have considered that important, but it gives me an idea."

"What's that?"

"From now on, I'm going to ask everyone to call me Jayson instead of Jay, but I'll think of the *son* part of my name as transplanted from Lawson's name. I'll learn more about fixing cars, junk art, and first aid medical treatments. I'm going to do my best to keep him in my thoughts and live the rest of my life for both of us. Maybe that would make my mother feel better too. I could try to act like him sometimes when I'm with her."

Sarah looked at him without saying anything for what seemed like a long time. "I have no problem with calling you Jayson instead of Jay, but there's no way I'm going to get attached romantically to a guy who thinks he's two different people at the same time. I think you need to reconsider your new outlook, and just be yourself. I also think that Lawson would agree with me and would tell you to push on without him."

CHAPTER 28 – CRYPT AND CARTON

After discovering skeletons behind the safe door in the back wall of the vault room and finding the carton of documents under the bank's travel agency counter, Ruth, Arthur, and Irma discussed their next steps in the investigation. The safecracker and another FBI agent had already departed. Ruth said that she would have FBI forensics specialists study the compartment behind the safe door, which Arthur had christened a crypt because of its skeletal contents. They would collect DNA samples from the two victims who had been killed elsewhere and crammed into that crypt. Ruth proposed that Irma should study the contents of the carton of papers she had found, while Arthur would research the travel agency business that once operated out of the North Corner Savings Bank, drawing upon brochures contained among Irma's papers.

Before they left the old bank's basement, Arthur asked, "Ruth, how much time will the FBI need for additional studies of this basement and the rest of this property after your technicians complete their study of the crypt? We need some scheduling so that I can tell Ron Barabee when he can have his construction crew restart on the new church."

Ruth made a few mental calculations. "I don't see that we'll need much more time after the crypt study, but I need to allow for something unexpected. Let's tell him that he can get back to work ten days from today. He'll probably want to get an earlier release, but at least that will give him a known schedule."

Arthur said that he would pass the timing information to Ron. Then they all climbed the damaged concrete stairs, Arthur struggling a bit for balance as he carried the heavy carton of papers while dodging gaps in the stairs.

When they arrived home, Irma announced that the papers in the carton would not be available for study until she cleaned and photographed or scanned them. After many years in the partially filled-in bank basement, the documents were damp, deteriorated, and covered with concrete dust. She suggested that in most cases they would be better off magnifying the digital photographs of the papers and examining them on a computer screen rather than working with the faded originals.

Arthur decided to try a computer search on the old bank's travel agency while Irma did her photography and scanning. From a brochure on the top of the stack of papers, he learned that the North Corner Savings Bank had chosen the obvious name for their travel agency, North Corner Travel. He googled this name and learned that the search engine had no information on this business, but had many entries for other businesses with north or corner in their names. Given the fact that the bank had ceased operations about twenty years earlier, Arthur was not surprised by the lack of online information. He would have to wait for Irma to make photographic copies of the brochures and other documents available before going further with his search. The information about the travel agency contained in that old carton would be better than anything he could expect to find online.

The telephone rang and Arthur answered it without even thinking of his usual formal response. "Hello."

"Hello, Arthur. It's a voice from your past. This is Cindy."

Arthur's mind was still focused on the travel agency, so he asked, "Cindy who?"

The tone of the telephone voice changed. "Cindy, your first wife. That's who. I assume you have a second wife by now. Maybe we should increase those numbers by one to include that NASA engineer you lived with for years before I entered the picture."

That speech focused Arthur's thoughts in a hurry. "Hello, Cindy. This is a surprise. How did you get my phone number?"

"From a clergy directory. I remembered that you became a man of the cloth, as they say."

"That was very resourceful. How may I help you, Cindy?"

"Arthur, I'm going to ask you for a favor that would affect several lives. ..."

CHAPTER 29 – SURPRISE AND PRESSURE

When Arthur walked into the room that Irma used as her office and laboratory, she said, "I've done all of the photography. We can work at two computers, with you studying the travel related documents while I study the bank's business papers and anything else that's in the carton batch."

After receiving no response from Arthur, Irma studied his facial expression. "You look like you've had a shock. What's wrong?"

"That telephone call was from my first wife, Cindy. She told me some things that are hard to believe, but apparently true."

Irma put her arm around her husband's shoulders and led him to the couch. She could feel his heartbeat racing. "Do you want to sit for a few minutes to calm down before talking about this?"

"No, I'll be alright. Cindy told me that when she got angry about my NASA engineering schedule and left me for that stay-at-home weatherman, she was pregnant. She didn't think anything of it at the time because they were already in the midst of an affair before she left me. They had a daughter, Nancy Tillingham, who is now fifteen years old, with health problems. She needs a kidney transplant, which can be done from a living donor. The hospital tested Cindy and her husband Tom to see who matches her requirements better, and it turned out that Tom was a complete mismatch. Follow-up DNA testing proved that he is not Nancy's father, and when Tom learned that, he left Cindy and filed for divorce. Now, Cindy is telling me that I have a fifteen year old daughter I never met and that I have to donate a kidney to her."

"How do you feel about that?"

"How would anyone feel? It's a shock, and it will take a while to feel comfortable about it. The unknown daughter is a big surprise, and I'm also a bit unhappy to learn that Cindy had an active affair with Tom Tillingham for months before she left me."

Irma leaned over and kissed Arthur.

"What was that for?"

"That kiss was to show you that I appreciate how naïve you are in some ways. When Cindy broke off your marriage, didn't you at least suspect that she already had intimate knowledge of her new guy?"

"I guess I got completely wrapped around her story that she hated my long NASA hours and needed someone with a stay-at-home schedule."

Irma held Arthur's hand while sneaking a finger onto his wrist to take his pulse. It had settled down to its normal rate. "While you were gone on those extended assignments, she got involved with her new man. I'll have to confess that I wondered about that stay-at-home husband story when you first told it to me."

Arthur looked out the window at male and female cardinals flying from one bush to another. "The aspect of having a daughter could be a positive development, but I have to think that Cindy's trying to manipulate me in some way. Why would she insist that I donate a kidney? Cindy's kidney would be a better match. She's Nancy's mother, and she's younger than I am."

"Perhaps she has a health problem that bars her from being a donor."

"Or maybe she's trying to get me to financially support her daughter. I'll be doing some checking on her and her family."

Irma relaxed, seeing that Arthur had returned to his normal objective thinking and healthy suspicions.

CHAPTER 30 – PAPERS AND BROCHURES

Irma's digital photographs of the old papers offered improved contrast over the originals, but some of the written and printed documents were too light to image properly. Magnification of the images on the computer screen helped, as did comparison of a particular document with other related ones. As she studied them, Irma assigned subject matter codes to each item and added a code for the originator whenever that person was identified. She also made notes keyed to the document codes when she had to guess at faded or missing words and numbers.

While Irma worked on the miscellaneous documents, Arthur examined the travel brochures plus ticket vouchers and receipts. The bank's travel agency had specialized in cruises and bus tours, usually sold as lump sum purchases without individual item details broken out. The logic of this approach for legitimate travel bookings would be that it minimized the bank's accounting burden. The alternate logic that made sense for any fictitious money-laundering transactions would be the ease of slipping them into the records without having to conjure up detailed itineraries and expense details.

Arthur made lists of the bus lines and cruise lines, along with the names of the ships used for ocean tours. He noticed that most cruises had been booked on ships belonging to well-known cruise lines. He studied the receipts for cruises and discovered a pattern in their handling that he would discuss with Irma.

Arthur next tabulated all the travel brochures and other travel document images by destination. He observed that all the destinations were within the continental United States plus cruises to Alaska, Hawaii, Mexico, and the West Indies. He thought this was a bit odd for a travel agency that did not advertise itself as specializing in one type of trip or geographical area. However, he realized that it might have been a matter of keeping the side-business simple to operate.

When Arthur finished compiling his customer notes and tables of transactions, he gathered his papers and his laptop computer for a comparison of results with whatever Irma had discovered.

Irma looked up as Arthur entered the room. "This analysis has been productive and almost entertaining. I'm seeing some revealing patterns of transactions."

"Are they revealing enough to come to any preliminary conclusions?"

"Just one and it matches our suspicions. This bank was definitely involved in money laundering. It's too early to say whether it was the headquarters for the operation or merely one of several layers in the legitimizing process."

Arthur said, "Being the one of us more likely to make premature conclusions, I'll suggest that the bank was ground zero for the money laundering process. North Corner Savings Bank received sacks of money without any cover story for it. Then the bank staff developed layers of fake transactions to allow it to feed the cash back into circulation as normal currency. I'm sure one avenue for making the money look legitimate involved the travel agency, but I haven't yet learned how that part of the process worked. What have you found so far to convince you that they laundered money in the bank?"

Irma walked over to a card table on which she had stacked the original papers by category. She pointed to the two tallest piles of documents. "This tallest stack contains invoices and stubs from cashier's checks for payments made by the bank on behalf of its clients to the Suburban Vista Nursing Home. The second tallest stack contains the signature cards for the bank's safe deposit boxes. It appears to be a complete set because it has a card for every box number from 1000 to 1024, 2000 to 2024, 3000 to 3024, and 4000 to 4024. They had four modular racks of twenty-four boxes each, ninety-six boxes total."

Arthur put his materials on the table and opened up his computer. "I took photographs of the marks on the floor and the bolt hole patterns in the walls of that vault room. I want to check if they match your four modular racks." He brought up three photographs onto the screen and studied them one at a time. "It appears to me that they had four modules in the front half of the vault room, bolted to the outer concrete wall, and a fifth module across the room from the others, bolted to the internal concrete wall."

"Very good, Arthur. That confirms my next finding. All the checks made out to that nursing home were for the accounts of people who were not included in the signature card stack. Yet the bank copies of the checks had the annotation, *Cash Transfer from Safe Deposit Box per Durable Power of Attorney.*"

"Do you have the names of those people?"

"There were thirteen of them, five women and eight men: Sally Adler, Helen Barnes, Joyce Channing, Lynn Holmes, Karen Probst, Paul Burges, Harold Dawes, Joshua Leary, Bruno Malverno, Ralph McTavish, Benjamin Persky, Leonard Smith, and Stanley Wilcox."

Arthur looked at several sheets of notes he had made concerning cruises to the West Indies. "That list of names closely matches a set of names I took from cruise receipts in the travel agency operation. They also had the annotation, *Cash Transfer from Safe Deposit Box per Durable Power of Attorney.*"

Irma stared at Arthur. "How close was your list of names to mine?"

"I had every name except Wilcox. I may have missed that one in the receipts, or it may have been filed somewhere else before the bank closed."

Irma thought for a few seconds before responding. "The same people who were in the nursing home may have taken cruises. It would be natural for them to have used the same method of payment."

"You can't avoid classifying this as a suspicious coincidence that way. First, we've established that the funds came from safe deposit boxes that had no signature cards. I didn't tell you about the second point of coincidence."

"What's that?"

"Every one of the people common to both of our lists missed the cruise ship's departure. Every receipt for those people is marked *Passenger missed departure. Flown ahead to rejoin cruise in Nassau, Bahamas.*"

CHAPTER 31 – NEWS FROM HOME

When Renee Andrews answered the telephone, she received a greeting from Jayson's mother, Alberta Jones. Talking with Alberta had been difficult since Lawson's death because she usually had tears in her voice, but today she came across as cheerful.

"Hello, Alberta; you're sounding well today."

"Hi, Renee. I'm feeling well too. Continued thanks for letting Jayson live with you. Is he there? I need to tell him something."

"I'll get him for you."

Renee went to the top of the basement stairs. "Jayson, your mother's on the phone and wants to talk with you."

Renee's tall boarder took double-step strides up the staircase and nodded to her as he brushed by her on the way to the phone on the kitchen counter.

"Hi, Ma. What's up? I meant to call you last week but I've been busy with my two jobs. Do you need some money?"

"Don't worry about that today, Jayson. I have news for you, and it's finally something good."

"Has the bastard who shot Lawson gone to court yet?"

"Just to plead not guilty. My news isn't that good. The cops keep telling me they have a couple of people who might testify against him, but the witnesses are hesitating. They're afraid of gang vengeance. The prosecutors are trying to build a case that will stand up even if the witnesses won't testify."

"Well, if it's not about Lawson's killer, what's your good news?"

"I met a new guy, Terrell Martin, and I'm pregnant. I'm going to move in with him out in the suburbs, in Skokie. I'm getting out of this hell-hole for good."

Jay sat down on a kitchen stool. "Did you get pregnant right away, or has this been going on for a while? Are you going to marry this new dude?"

"We've been seeing each other for a while, and we've talked about marriage, but there's nothing definite yet. He's a widower. His wife died in an expressway shooting, so he knows where I'm coming from. Anyway, I'm going to have a girl baby, and I'm going to call her Lawra, spelled L-A-W-R-A, to remind me of Lawson."

"She can remind you of Lawson, Ma, but there's no way she'll take his place. Lawson was special. He can't be replaced by having another kid."

"I know that, but she'll be someone new to give me hope for the future. I can't keep living here, thinking about nothing but my dead son and all the others getting shot. Terrell Martin is giving me a way out of this. We'll be in a new place, and we'll have each other to lean on. Don't give me a hard time about this new chance, son. I need it. I've been praying for a way out. You'll like Terrell. I'm sure of it."

"OK, Ma, I'm happy for you. I got out of that neighborhood, and now you will too. Just do me a favor, and don't think of Lawra as Lawson born again. We're all different, and there'll never be another Lawson. Thanks for the good news. Keep in touch."

As he put the telephone handset back on its cradle, Jayson realized that he had just given his mother the same lecture that Sarah had given him. He had to be himself. Lawson was gone and couldn't be replaced by his mimicking his brother's lifestyle choices or by a new baby half-sister.

CHAPTER 32 - RUTH DALTRY

FBI Special Agent Ruth Daltry sat at her desk trying to make sense out of the DNA report she had received. Its subjects were the two bodies crammed into the so-called crypt behind the basement safe door of what had been the North Corner Savings Bank. According to the report, the male set of skeletal remains had been a US Army veteran who served in Vietnam. The female remains belonged to a woman who had a drunk-driving citation from 1991. At that time, she had listed her occupation as accountant. The Vietnam veteran had entered the military directly after high school, so they did not have an occupation listed for him. Perhaps these two had been employees or officers of the defunct bank. The technicians had found both loose and bagged currency in the crypt with them. Why had the killer of these two people not taken the money away? Had the cash been planted to convince police who might find them that they had died while robbing the bank? She smiled to herself over the amounts of money that had been left in the crypt of the bank basement and the tunnel on the other side of the crypt wall. It had been a case of buried treasure that no one knew was there.

The ringing phone interrupted her thoughts. She answered it with a crisp "Ruth Daltry."

"Hello, Ruth; Arthur Blake here. Do you have time for a short meeting today? Irma and I have some significant results from our analysis of the bank's operations, but we're not sure how to interpret them."

"Arthur, you probably won't believe this, but I'm in exactly the same bind with interpreting the findings on our crypt bodies. Come on over and we'll mull this out in our conference room. You suggested a short meeting. I think we'll be continuing through the dinner hour, so I'll make arrangements to have food brought in."

"We've been ignoring our DEA partner, Paul Garcia. Should he join us for this meeting?"

"You're a better diplomat than I am, Arthur. My gut feeling is that drugs aren't the key to the bank's activities, but I'll arrange for Paul to be at the meeting with us. Multiple points of view may help us figure out what they were doing."

When Arthur and Irma arrived, they discovered that Ruth had asked a younger dark-haired female FBI agent to join them. The introduction exchange identified this newcomer as Linda Higgins.

Arthur glanced at a sheet of scribbled notes taken from the bottom of his stack of papers. "Linda, are you related to Ted?"

"I'm his daughter, and one of my goals in joining the FBI was to discover what happened to him. Now that I know he was one of the two men trapped in that tunnel, I need to learn why he had to die so horribly."

Irma said, "Welcome to the team, Linda. I assume you lived with your mother while Ted was playing the part of Marco Locante during his undercover work."

Impasse

"I lived with her for most of my childhood. My mother divorced Dad because he insisted on taking dangerous undercover assignments. She wasn't willing to face long separations or to constantly worry about whether he would get hurt or killed while being Marco. After the divorce, I lived with Dad's mother. He remarried later on, but I didn't move back in with him and his new wife."

"You finally know what happened to him. Now we'll do our best to learn why he died and what was going on at that bank."

Ruth said, "Time for me to take control of my meeting, Irma. Your comment to Linda was a good summary of why we're here. Paul, thanks for joining us. I suspect that your DEA background will be useful in trying to sort the puzzle pieces we've found so far. At first glance they look unrelated, but I'm sure we'll eventually figure out how they fit together. I decided that Linda deserves to contribute to our analysis. Let's start by having Arthur and Irma report what they've learned."

Irma gestured for Arthur to present their findings. He stood next to the flip chart pad as he spoke. "The most interesting result of our studies is that although I studied the bank's travel agency business while Irma independently studied aspects of money laundering, we came up with closely related discoveries."

Arthur drew a diagram of the bank vault room, showing the locations of the five safe deposit box modules. "This was a neighborhood bank, so they had only five modules containing twenty-four boxes each. Four of those modules were on one side of the vault room, while one was bolted to the opposite wall. We found signature cards and rental receipts for all of the boxes in the set of four adjacent modules. There were no such records for any of the boxes in the other separate module. We think that the illegally-obtained cash to be laundered and made legitimate was divided and stored in the safe deposit boxes of the fifth module. They had an unusually large vault for a neighborhood bank, but we haven't yet discovered why they needed that much space or if the vault size is significant."

At this point, Irma joined Arthur at the front of the conference room. "I discovered that the bank made payments to a nursing home for thirteen individuals using undocumented cash from their safe deposit boxes in the fifth box module as payments for cashier's checks. I'm sure that nursing home represents the first layer in the money laundering process. If the FBI checks on that nursing home, you'll probably be able to connect the original cashier's check payments to expenditures by the home to a second organization. After some number of payment steps, you may be able to find the ultimate person or company that was behind the money laundering."

Ruth interrupted. "Irma, did you find something similar to the nursing home results in the travel business transactions?"

"I told you that the payments to the nursing home were made in the names of thirteen patients there. Arthur found that cash from the safe deposit boxes containing illegally-obtained money was used via the cashier's check process to pay for cruises for the same thirteen individuals that I encountered at the nursing home."

Paul Garcia said. "That sounds like a second branch in the money laundering process."

Arthur shook his head. "I disagree, because it's something more than that. All but one of the people on that list of thirteen paid for a cruise from Miami, but arrived late for departure and had to be flown to Nassau in the Bahamas to rejoin the cruise. Twelve coincidences like that do not happen. They are planned."

Ruth turned to Linda. "This case just ratcheted up to a higher level of importance. Linda, take Bob and Larry to check out the records of that nursing home that Irma identified. See why the people on her list were in there, when they were released, and what happened to them afterward. Also try to get a handle on how that home accounted for the extra money they received. Irma is probably right that it went on to the next layer in the laundering process, probably a fake vendor."

Linda said, "I'll get right on it, but what do you suspect?"

Ruth saw Arthur smile and nod. "Do you want to answer Linda for me?"

"Ruth and I both think that no one flew from Miami to rejoin a cruise in Nassau. Someone flew each person's papers to Nassau, and a foreign individual joined the cruise under that assumed identity. This was a true case of identity theft. Twelve unknown individuals took on American identities. If the people on Irma's list actually existed as patients in that nursing home, they may have been murdered shortly after their discharge from the home."

Paul asked, "Ruth, does this discussion impact your findings about the two bodies in the bank's hidden crypt?"

"The conversation about those bodies will have to wait for another time. We may have twelve people masquerading as Americans for more than twenty years, after killing the individuals they replaced. They could be the heads of terrorist sleeper cells or worse. Arthur, tell that construction boss to build his church. We have more important targets to investigate than that piece of real estate."

CHAPTER 33 – NURSING HOME

After obtaining from Irma her list of the thirteen nursing home patients whose accounts received payments from North Corner Savings Bank's *special* safe deposit boxes and the dates of those payments, FBI Agents Linda Higgins, Bob Marcus, and Larry Savage left to visit Suburban Vista Nursing Home. Linda would be the spokesperson, while Bob would examine any applicable accounting records and Larry would interview staff members with sufficient seniority to have memories of the patients on the list. They all realized that they were not likely to find many records remaining from patient transactions more than twenty years old.

When they arrived at the nursing home, Linda asked to see the administrator. The receptionist made a call, and upon receiving a positive response, led the visitors to a conference room. There, they sat for about ten minutes before they were joined by a woman, about thirty years old, wearing a beige business suit. She had dark hair, tied back in a pony tail.

Linda presented her credentials as she introduced herself. "Good morning. We're from the FBI. I'm Agent Linda Higgins, and these gentlemen are Agents Bob Marcus and Larry Savage. We'd like to have some informal conversation with you about some very old patients and their records. This is not a matter of your having done something illegal."

After shaking hands, the newcomer said, "I'm Doris Haden. I've been the administrator here for five years. Please pardon my being slightly out of breath. I'm a bit of a hands-on person, and I was sorting through some party decorations wearing jeans and an old shirt when the receptionist called to say you were here. I rushed to change my clothes before coming to see you. We've never had the FBI here before, so I didn't know what to expect. Help yourselves to coffee on the side table. If there's not enough there, I'm sure there's more in the lobby."

Bob and Larry went for coffee while Linda and Doris continued their conversation.

Linda said, "This visit isn't anything that should alarm you, Doris. We're here looking for historical information from more than twenty years ago."

"As I said earlier, I've been the administrator for five years. The current ownership group has run this facility for seventeen years, so you're interested in a period when a different set of people ran Suburban Vista Nursing Home."

"Do you have any employees who have worked here for twenty years or more?"

"That's unlikely, but I'll check. What is it that you're trying to discover?"

Linda doubted that she'd find anything useful but said, "We were hoping to find information about a few of your patients from back then, and we also wanted to study the old accounting system."

"In those days all the records were on paper. Suburban Vista was slow to computerize due to the small staff. Still, you might find something if you're willing to go through the catacomb."

"Catacomb?"

"That's what we call it. When our current ownership group took over the management of this place, we threw all the old ledgers and documents into an unused room in the basement. The intention was to retrieve each document and digitize it someday, but that day never came. You get so busy with the current day's problems that you fail to study the past."

Linda shook the administrator's hand. "Doris, if those old records are complete and useful, and if you'll give us full access to them, you will soon have them digitized for you by the FBI."

"That would be great, but the FBI would have to agree in writing that we would retain a complete set of our records. We wouldn't agree to give you access without a warrant if any of our historic files were to simply disappear."

"You're a good administrator, Doris, even if a young one. On behalf of the FBI, I agree."

CHAPTER 34 – ARTHUR AND RON

Ron Barabee sat at his desk in the office trailer feeling sorry for himself and his acute case of borestration. He had nothing better to do than play endless games of solitaire once he had completed his insurance claim paperwork. He was on the verge of starting to smoke again, even though it had taken a year and a half to kick that habit the last time. He was bored, but he was also frustrated by the probable loss of his best workers as they would inevitably find other projects that would pay for their skills immediately. The knock on his trailer door was a welcome pause for his train of thoughts. He called out, "Come on in. Misery loves company."

Arthur Blake turned the door knob and climbed into the trailer, carrying a grocery bag. With his free hand he waved to Ron. "Hello; sorry I haven't had time to stop in for a while. Is it too early in the day for you to join me for some champagne?"

"Does that champagne mean we have something to celebrate? Are you telling me we can finally get back to work here?"

"I believe I am. Let's drink to the new church that you're going to build for the bishop." Arthur pulled a bottle out of his grocery bag and set it on Ron's desk. Then he unwrapped two glasses cushioned in tissue paper.

"Arthur, let's have a party. I'll order a pizza for my share. I'll have to be careful that I don't drink too much, though. I'll be calling all the guys to come back to work, and I won't want to sound drunk."

"Ron, you've had more patience than I would. If I run into a stoppage on a case, I switch gears and find a different project to pursue."

"In a sense, I did. You can tell your bishop that we'll be able to make up a portion of the lost time. I looked up the Navy's PERT system – Program Evaluation and Review Technique – and I did some computer work to find the critical path for our tasks in building the church. If you do the jobs on the critical path first, you save time on the entire project. If we're diligent and lucky, we should be almost on schedule by the time we complete the building."

"Bishop Chandler will be happy to hear that."

"I'll drink to that, Arthur."

"I think the bishop will drink to that too."

CHAPTER 35 – CATACOMB

The uniform of the day for the FBI visitors to the nursing home was blue jeans and a flannel shirt. Linda, Bob, and Larry did not know what they should expect to find when they inventoried the so-called catacomb, but they would be prepared for anything. Their vehicle of the day was a rented moving van, and they had recruited several brawny assistants with wheeled carts.

When they entered Suburban Vista Nursing Home, Administrator Doris Haden greeted them wearing a dark blue business suit. She shook hands with Linda Higgins and said, "I wanted to have the roles reversed today. This time, you're in jeans ready for dirty work, and I'm dressed for business."

Linda smiled. "You made that catacomb in your basement sound so awesome that we brought a whole crew. We'll have to remove everything for sorting at our facility, and then we'll make digital records of all the papers. If you want, you may assign someone to inventory everything we take for documentation purposes."

"That won't be necessary. I'll trust you to do that. After you convert the various papers into data files, list them all, and I'll tell you which ones we want physically returned. Since your last visit, we had a board meeting and decided that for our purposes, we're generally better off with the data files. We're letting the FBI clean our house for us.

Thank you very much. I have plans for the space you're about to clear out."

"You make it sound as though the catacomb is quite large."

"I'll put it this way. You may need a second truck, and I'm planning to convert that space into a cafeteria for the staff and visitors."

After Doris removed the padlock from the gray-painted steel door in the basement, she opened it, releasing musty-smelling air into the hallway. She gestured with an outstretched arm at the challenge that faced the FBI movers and analysts. "It's all yours. We're more than happy to have data files and reclaimed space instead of all this."

Linda realized the job would be worse than she had guessed. The room appeared to be quite large, but there was so much stuff in it that she couldn't see the far wall. In addition to a large number of metal and wood filing cabinets, there were stacks of cardboard file boxes, and an array of old furniture, mostly bookcases and desks. She asked Doris, "Do you want us to take the desks too?"

"You signed up to check out everything in our catacomb. The desks were moved into this room immediately after we took over the nursing home. We upgraded all the facility's furniture and stored the old stuff without removing any papers or other property from the drawers. If you're searching for someone's personal property or criminal papers, you're more likely to find your objective in a desk than anywhere else."

"Doris, you've read too many melodramatic mysteries, and you're also using us to do your housecleaning."

"You're absolutely correct. We'll expect you to have this space cleared out by the end of the day, but just to show we're not rushing you, feel free to take up to three months before giving us the data files."

After Doris left, Linda called her office and asked her secretary to arrange for twice the warehouse space they had originally ordered and a second moving van. Then she gathered her workers and divided their tasks according to their physical capabilities.

CHAPTER 36 – ARTHUR AND IRMA

Irma's latest home improvement was a forensics laboratory in the basement of their old Queen Anne style house. She had initially planned to restrict her facility to analysis of small evidence samples, but after moving some of the basement contents to an unused room on the third floor, she decided there was enough room to expand her laboratory activities. She could now perform private autopsies when the circumstances made them appropriate. In the past, they had ordered a few such autopsies from Chicago practitioners, but she preferred to maintain her skills developed as a county forensic pathologist. Arthur suggested that the lab would also be suitable for the filming of horror movies in their home.

As Irma finished arranging some newly purchased chemicals on the shelves of a glass-fronted cabinet, Arthur arrived with a scientific equipment catalog from the morning mail.

"Here's your latest edition of Dr. Frankenstein's goodie book."

"You're jealous, because you don't have a playroom of your own."

"I don't need a playroom. I simply sit and play Hercule Poirot, using the little gray cells of my brain to solve problems and cases."

"What is your problem of the day?"

"Today, I'm ruminating over the possibility that I may have a fifteen year old daughter who needs my kidney for a transplant. That call from ex-wife Cindy disturbed my thinking process. I honestly don't believe that I could be that girl's father. Cindy and I had a long-running series of arguments about my work schedules at NASA. I was away most of the time, and on the few occasions when I was home, I wasn't in the mood to play bedroom games with her."

Irma perched on a tall stool and thought about her own feelings. "I should say that I'd be relieved if Cindy wasn't going to get involved in your life again, but I have mixed feelings. We talked about adopting a child, and then settled for our dog Rex. You took that as a great outcome, but I still felt cheated that we wouldn't have a child, adopted or not. The prospect of Cindy's daughter turning out to be your child intrigued me. She would be half yours, even more if you gave her your kidney."

Arthur sat on a second stool. "I didn't realize a child was that important to you. Let's get past the speculations and test me to see whether I'm her father and a compatible donor. How do we go about that?"

"Call Cindy and get the name of the hospital and the doctor there who wants to do the transplant. I'll contact that doctor to get DNA and blood sample test results for young Nancy Tillingham. After I receive that data, I'll be able to test you here to see whether you pass the preliminary tests for a compatible kidney donor."

Arthur relaxed. "It looks as though we're going to get some worthwhile use of this lab earlier than I expected."

Impasse

"That's good, but if the lab results show that Nancy isn't your daughter, I'd like to reopen the discussion of adoption possibilities."

CHAPTER 37 – BOBBY AND JAYSON

As Parkville Police Chief Bobby Andrews walked past the open door to the Records and Data room, he noticed Jayson Redshaw dozing in front of his computer. Bobby entered the room and tapped Jayson's shoulder.

"Time to wake up. You're supposed to monitor online communications, not let them sit until you're fully rested."

"Sorry, Bobby, but this is one boring job. Let me organize morning fitness sessions for everyone so that I get to use some muscles. That might help me stay awake during the rest of the day. I wasn't meant to sit and stare at a screen all day."

"That's not a bad idea for days when you have no specific assignment. What has Irma Blake had you doing lately?"

"I took part in exploring the basement of an old bank connected to a sewer tunnel where they found bodies. That was interesting, and I even contributed an idea or two, but now the FBI is the prime mover on that case, and we have to wait for their investigation results. Is police work always so hurry up and wait?"

"We have our ups and downs of activity as cases develop. Usually, we work on several cases at the same time to even things out. You wouldn't have many slow times if you worked for a major outfit like the Chicago Police Department, but we're a lot smaller and slower in our pace. It's a good thing for police when nothing terrible happens."

"Yeah, I know. Boring days mean things are going smoothly."

"How's your relationship with that gal from the State Police Lab coming along?"

"That's up in the air right now. Sarah wasn't too happy when I told her I was going to pattern my future based on my brother, Lawson's interests as well as my own. She said I can't bring Lawson back, and I'll have to be myself if I want her to be interested."

Bobby sat on the edge of a desk. "She's right. I once went to a religious meeting and a guy said that we're all unique unrepeatable miracles of God. It's that unrepeatable part that's the key here. You knew Lawson throughout his sixteen years of life, and you were very close. What you don't know is how he would have grown and changed in his more mature years, and you can't predict that either. You're here to be your own unique person. Imitating someone else doesn't work, and I know of many marriages that broke up because someone tried to imitate his or her spouse. Be yourself, and Sarah will run back to you."

"I want to, Bobby, but I don't want to forget Lawson and feel guilty about it."

"You won't forget him. Live your own life, and every once in a while, you'll feel Lawson looking over your shoulder, cheering you on. I felt the same thing after my dad died."

"OK, Chief, I'll take your advice. Now give me an interesting assignment."

Richard Davidson

"Here's one. See Sergeant Al Gomez, and tell
him you've been assigned to check out that rug we
bagged at the scene of that lawyer's office break-in
last week. Then take the rug to the State Police Lab
and ask Sarah Jackson to see what she can learn
from it."

"Thanks, Bobby; I'm sure she's just the right
person to study it."

CHAPTER 38 - LINDA HIGGINS

Linda's tension showed in her abrupt response when her secretary asked if she wanted more coffee. "I need something a lot stronger. We've been working on this junk from that so-called catacomb for two days now, and my coffee scorecard shows sixteen cups to date." She looked across the large warehouse space at the other fifteen people sorting through individual piles of documents and office furniture drawers. After studying each piece of paper the FBI worker fed it into a scanner on a wheeled cart alongside his or her workstation to generate a computer file for it. Once scanned, the document dropped into an open file box on the lower shelf of the cart. Other workers periodically exchanged file boxes containing the already-scanned papers for empty boxes. Linda had hoped that with enough staff they would find some worthwhile leads within one day. Twice that time had passed without any significant results. Perhaps this haystack didn't contain any needles. The investigation of the residue from the earlier nursing home regime's activities had been both painstaking and tedious, but not fruitful.

As Linda drained the last drop of her seventeenth cup of coffee, she saw a light out of the corner of her right eye. She swiveled her head to identify the source. The flashing signal light on Bob Marcus' cart indicated that he had found something that he considered significant. She walked toward Bob, and he turned off the light as she approached.

"What do you have for me, Bob? Did you find a smoking gun?"

"Let's say the gun is cocked, but not quite smoking. I noticed something earlier, and decided not to mention it until I had confirmation of my suspicion. I have now found seven documents showing extremely large payments to Mallinhardt's Auto Service for repairs to nursing home vehicles. The nursing home owned one van with a wheelchair lift, one pickup truck, and a sedan for the director's use. The average monthly payment for maintenance on these three vehicles was approximately nine thousand dollars. That's more than one hundred thousand dollars per year, which exceeds the price for buying those three vehicles brand new at that time."

"So, even if we find nothing else that's significant in all this catacomb stuff, we have clear evidence of money laundering and a new lead to investigate. Is Mallinhardt's Auto Service still in business?"

"I searched online, and they are still operating, although John Mallinhardt is well past the normal retirement age."

"That sounds promising. I'll put Larry in charge here, and we'll visit Mr. Mallinhardt after lunch. Write up your lunch receipt as a field investigation meal and I'll authorize reimbursement. You've definitely earned a free lunch.

Impasse

Mallinhardt's Auto Service occupied a large single-level soot-darkened brick building one block off Belmont Avenue on Chicago's north side. A dozen gentrified residences housing young upwardly mobile families shared the neighborhood with elderly deteriorating Chicago bungalows and small businesses. On this mild day, the front and rear garage doors at Mallinhardt's were open for improved ventilation. Linda parked on the street. Then she and Bob Marcus approached the open garage door. As they neared the building, they saw a single mechanic working on two classic Chevrolets from the 1950s. They entered the open doorway and saw an arrow-shaped sign labeled OFFICE pointed to the right. They turned and Linda knocked on the office door.

A loud voice responded, "Come in, but wipe your feet on the mat first. I want this rug to last a while."

Linda opened the door and saw a tall man with curly gray hair and a matching shaggy beard doing his best to force one more folder into the top drawer of a battleship gray metal filing cabinet. He looked at the visitors and gave up on his task, dropping the new file onto a desk cluttered with many piles of papers.

"Hello, folks. I never seem to win my battles with the file drawers. It's all kind of silly. I never look at the papers after they're filed anyway. If I did want a particular form or letter, I probably wouldn't be able to find it. What may I do for you today?"

Linda shook his hand. "Are you John Mallinhardt? I'm Linda Higgins, and this is Bob

137

Marcus. We're from the FBI." She and Bob held up their credentials.

John sat down and swiveled his desk chair to face them. "I didn't do anything wrong. I just accepted someone's generosity."

Linda kept her voice soft and free of emotion. "That would be when you received inflated payments from the Suburban Vista Nursing Home. What did you do with those payments?"

"First of all, that was a long time ago. At that time we weren't quite established here, and I needed all the financial help I could get. I went to the bank for a loan, and they said I didn't qualify for one, but they could help if I would work with one of their clients."

"Was this the North Corner Savings Bank?"

"Yes it was. You FBI people are really good at figuring things out. Anyway, they set up a procedure where Suburban Vista Nursing Home would pay more than was due for their car and truck service bills, and I would be required to use the excess to pay my rent, even if the surplus exceeded the rent amount that was due. The checks were always for larger amounts than my rent, so I had a period where I didn't have to come up with the rent on my own. I figured that it was like an interest-free loan from the bank for the purpose of helping my company get established during those lean years. We wouldn't still be here without that money."

"When did that procedure, as you call it, end?"

"Don't make me go into those file drawers to find an exact date. It was roughly twenty years ago."

"And where did you send this extra money?"

"To the property management company."

"What was the name of that company, and where were they located?"

"Now you are going to make me go to the files. They sent a statement and a self-addressed envelope. I just inserted my check, sealed it up, and put a stamp on it. The only thing I remember about their name or location was that it changed right around the same time that the nursing home procedure ended. That was OK, because by that time my business was doing well enough for me to handle my own payments. The timing worked out pretty well."

Bob Marcus stepped forward. "John, that's a very interesting story and procedure for getting your company to be self-sustaining. We're going to need the names and addresses of both of your property management firms. I sympathize with your comments about the difficulties of finding old papers, so I'll volunteer to find them for you if you give me permission to look in your file cabinet and give me a hint about where I should look."

"That's real nice of you Mr. Marcus. You have my permission to look, but those papers wouldn't be in this file cabinet. They're too old."

"Where would they be?"

"They'd be in one of the six file cabinets in the basement of this garage. If you do look down there,

Richard Davidson

take a good strong light, and be careful not to step
on one of my rat traps."

CHAPTER 39 – TEST RESULTS

As Arthur passed the open door to their basement, he heard Irma calling up to him. He answered her call. "I'm here. What do you need?"

"I need you down in my laboratory for a medical conference. I have your test results."

He descended the stairs rapidly, wondering whether the results would lead to a major change in his, or rather their lives.

"What do you have for me, Dr. Blake?"

"Thanks for that bit of formality, Pastor Blake. I'll start by saying that there were a few findings I didn't expect, even though I try to avoid predicting outcomes when I process data."

"Why don't you start with the DNA results – am I Nancy Tillingham's father as Cindy claims?"

"You like to plunge right into the pool, instead of testing the water with your toes first."

"You have it. Please drop the bomb on me. If I'm to have a sudden change in my life, so be it."

"Very well; I compared the DNA results I received from Dr. Rockman at Orlando Regional Medical Center with the sample I took from you, and the profiles show that you are definitely not Nancy's father. I have no doubt at all about that statement. How does that make you feel, Arthur?"

"I wasn't sure whether I wanted her to be my daughter or not. I'd say that my hopes were fifty percent each way. It does indicate that if Cindy's second husband, Tom Tillingham, was not Nancy's father, and I'm not either, then Cindy had another lover at the same time that both Tom and I were in the picture. My first wife cheated on me with at least two different men."

Irma didn't know whether to laugh or be sympathetic. "How does that affect your opinion of Cindy and your own ego?"

"I don't think it changes my self-image. When I was married to Cindy, I was so wrapped up in my space flight projects that I probably deserved to have my wife look elsewhere. I wouldn't have expected two or more elsewheres, though. That pretty much shoots down the validity of Cindy's story that she preferred a stay-at-home weatherman to an always-on-assignment engineer. She was after romance wherever she could find it."

"That comment's a bit harsh on Cindy. As your second wife, I might have to wonder whether you still care more about your work than you do about your wife."

"I suppose I had that coming. My rebuttal is that we work on investigations together, so work vs. wife doesn't apply. As to work vs. romance, I notice that your autopsy table is clear. Shall we have a mutual examination and experimentation session right now? I'm ready if you are."

"I'm sure you'd be the liveliest patient I've ever had on my autopsy table, but we have more test results to discuss."

"What more is there to consider, now that I know I'm not Nancy's father? I'll call Cindy and tell her she'll have to look elsewhere for assistance.

Maybe she's still in touch with that boyfriend she didn't marry."

"We need to discuss the analysis of your blood sample. You have type O blood. You can donate to anyone. You also match three out of six antigens with Nancy Tillingham. You aren't her father, but if you pass the cross-match blood test with Nancy, you could still be considered as a living kidney donor for her."

"She's Cindy's responsibility, not mine. Why isn't her mother, who's guaranteed to be a match, stepping forward?"

"That's something we'll have to find out, Arthur, but you should think about whether you would be willing to give Nancy one of your kidneys if that would be her only path to recovery."

CHAPTER 40 – BOB MARCUS

Agent Bob Marcus assumed John Mallinhardt had been kidding when he said his garage's basement was full of rat traps. Once Bob climbed down the rickety stairs with his high-intensity lights, he realized that the basement was full of both rat traps and rats that had learned how to avoid the traps. The smell of dead rats already in traps made him want to breathe as little as possible. He saw a dead rat that had been partially eaten by others. The periodic sound of scurrying rodents accompanied Bob's foot stamping rhythms as he examined the six file cabinets. His foot stamping was intended to scare the rodents away from his legs and feet. Bob hoped to locate the key documents before he gave in to his fear of rats. Snakes were his only greater taboo, and he couldn't guarantee that they weren't slithering around the basement too. The snapping of a rat trap reminded Bob to work rapidly.

The first conclusion he reached was that John Mallinhardt used his file cabinets as waste paper baskets. The objective was to have a place to stash papers without sorting them. This tactic would make it difficult to isolate items connected to the property management firms, but it would ease the selection of papers by the year in which they had been filed. Bob opened the top drawers of all six file cabinets and checked the dates on random papers. He decided that the fourth file cabinet from the right contained items that were between eighteen and twenty-two years old.

Having selected the single cabinet of greatest interest, Bob removed the front folder from each of the four file drawers. He found at least two property management statement copies in each of those files, each sheet having had the return payment slip cut from its bottom section. The older sheets bore the imprint of Ellsworth & Company, Management, while the more recent ones were under the name of Prop-It Management Co. Both companies used Chicago post office boxes as their return addresses, but they were at different post offices, as indicated by their zip codes. Bob spread the file contents on top of the cabinets to examine them side-by-side. He then told himself he had what he needed. After scanning the basement with his high-intensity lights to be sure he knew the locations of the rat traps and their furry targets, he stacked the lamps on top of the file folders and hustled up the stairs as fast as he could. He slammed the door behind him, but in his haste one of the file folders slipped out of the pile and got caught in the door. Bob opened the door enough to retrieve the folder and slammed the door a second time. In response, he heard three rat traps snap shut in the basement below.

CHAPTER 41 – BEGINNINGS AND ENDS

Irma Blake watched her husband draw a diagram on a large sheet of paper and then cross out several lines of that graphic. Then he sat looking at the altered result for several minutes without moving.

"What are you doing, considering all the possible people who might give Nancy the kidney she needs?"

"Nope; I'm back in the investigation business. I'm trying to get a handle on the money laundering operation. Here's a box representing the North Corner Savings Bank with a line leading into it representing the sewer tunnel used to deliver bags of cash. I've drawn a second dashed line connecting to the bank to indicate the two bodies we found in the wall compartment behind that safe door. We don't yet know the relationship of those individuals to the bank. I have a cash outflow line from the bank to a travel agency box. I have a second cash outflow line to a box marked Suburban Vista Nursing Home. The FBI is investigating where the unauthorized funds went after they reached that nursing home."

"I think I know the question that's behind your diagram. Everyone has been working to trace where the money went after it left North Corner Savings Bank. The unasked question is, 'Where did that cash come from before it reached the bank?'"

"Bingo! You have the key question, Irma. I suspect it's too early in the case for us to speculate on that."

"Meaning?"

"If we find the ultimate destination of the laundered funds, we'll either find the perpetrator or what he or she bought with the money."

"Keep in mind the fact that this happened about twenty years ago. We may not find anyone still living who was responsible for the money and the killings."

"Even if we don't find anyone at the end of the money trail, I want to learn more about those people who slipped into the country through the travel agency scam. It all has to be tied together. It could be a terrorist sleeper cell. If so we need to find them before they act on some master plan."

Irma reached over and drew a star next to Arthur's Travel Agency box. "You have a great idea. While the FBI traces the various money laundering steps, let's see whether we can trace the people who came into the United States through that travel agency cruise scheme."

CHAPTER 42 – CRUISING

Irma looked through her notes and found her list of the bank's travel clients who had missed their initial sailing but had supposedly rejoined their cruises in Nassau, Bahamas. All of these people had the same names as patients at Suburban Vista Nursing Home, and the consensus at the FBI investigators meeting had been that the passengers who boarded at Nassau were foreigners replacing their American namesakes. The thirteen listed names were: Sally Adler, Helen Barnes, Joyce Channing, Lynn Holmes, Karen Probst, Paul Burges, Harold Dawes, Joshua Leary, Bruno Malverno, Ralph McTavish, Benjamin Persky, Leonard Smith, and Stanley Wilcox.

A further check of her notes indicated that all of these people, with the possible exception of Stanley Wilcox whose travel details hadn't been found, sailed on cruises within a six-month period twenty years earlier. Irma prepared a summary sheet with this information and gave Arthur a copy.

Arthur studied the paper and said, "Finding these people won't be easy. We need a shortcut." He picked up the phone and called Ruth Daltry.

"Good morning; this is Special Agent Ruth Daltry."

"Hello, Ruth; Arthur Blake calling. Irma and I are working on locating those cruise passengers who might have assumed the identities of nursing home patients. Would our status as consultants to the FBI give us access to Social Security account information?"

"The short answer is no, Arthur, but tell me what you're thinking."

"We earlier commented that those unauthorized passengers boarding cruise ships in Nassau might have replaced nursing home patients who had been killed. If that assumption is incorrect, and those patients weren't killed, we might have two people using the same Social Security number in each instance. Our searches will probably reveal many people with the same name, but only our impostor and the original patient would have two people making deposits into the same Social Security account."

"That's clever thinking, but you do realize the substitutes may have changed their names after reaching the United States."

"I'm assuming that they boarded the ships using someone else's name and paperwork because they intended to continue to use those documents. Why complicate things by having to generate something totally different? Wouldn't you keep it simple, Ruth?"

"I suppose I would take that approach. I told you earlier that the short answer regarding access to Social Security records is 'No.' The longer answer is that I'll have you work with my assistant, Agent Jim Benson. Tell him what you want, and he'll be able to get the data for you. Just keep your requests specific. We can't authorize a fishing expedition."

"Thanks, Ruth; I'll email over the search specs. This may not work, but if it does, it will simplify finding those twelve suspects, thirteen if we include Wilcox."

Arthur ended the call and turned to Irma. "You heard that. What do you think about my guess that the nursing home patients whose identities were stolen are still alive?"

"I'd say that it's reasonable that they weren't harmed. Thirteen murders in a six month period might have blown the secrecy of a stealthy operation. Why attract attention to the names of your undercover agents?"

"Do you think the cruise substitutes were agents of an organization or country?"

"That would make sense, Arthur. What else is likely?"

"They might have been wealthy foreigners, buying their way into the United States, the way undocumented Mexicans pay *coyotes* to smuggle them across the border."

"Whatever they were, they won't be young now, twenty years later."

"Add that age point to our list of names for Agent Benson to check for Social Security anomalies. He should look for people with names on our list who are at least thirty-eight years old and have excessive or unusual payments to their Social Security accounts. If we're lucky, he'll find sets of two addresses or employers corresponding to instances of doubled deposits. Then we'll be able to trace both the nursing home patients and the cruise substitutes.

150

Impasse

Irma mumbled, "Unless those cruise substitutes changed their names after arrival here."

CHAPTER 43 – CINDY

They say your past comes back to haunt you, and it certainly has now. I wasn't sure whether Nancy was Tom Tillingham's daughter or Arthur Blake's. Now, the doctor tells me that Nancy's father wasn't either of them. He must have been that guy I met at Disney World. We had a party with his friends from Key West. It was a wild evening, and I don't even remember his name. He probably doesn't remember mine either.

Both Tom and Arthur now know I had sex with someone else while I was married to Arthur and seeing Tom. It's not a good situation. Nancy needs a kidney transplant and I can't be her donor. Thanks to my drunken father smashing our car into a tree when I was a kid, I have only one kidney. It didn't seem important when I was younger and indestructible, but it sure does now.

The doctor says that Arthur could be a compatible donor, but would he even consider it knowing that Nancy was fathered by someone I never told him about? Maybe I should have been more open and honest with my husbands, but I was afraid of losing them. Now I have no one but a very sick daughter. Even if she gets a new kidney, she'll have to fight possible rejection of it by her body, and who knows how strong she would get afterward?

Oh, God! I never thought of that. I may have to plan the rest of my life around caring for Nancy. I'm still young enough to find another husband, but who *would want to marry someone who comes with a medical care burden? I'll have to read up on the best guesses as to quality of life after this kind of transplant. I know a new kidney doesn't last a lifetime.*

Every time I think of something new about this situation, it gets worse. Now that Tom Tillingham is gone, we may not be covered by his health insurance. There's no way I could pay for a kidney transplant operation and all that follows it on my own. He sounded too angry for me to have a hope of convincing him to come back to us.

How am I ever going to get out of this mess?

CHAPTER 44 – PATIENTS

While Bob Marcus searched the file cabinets in the basement of Mallinhardt's Garage, Linda Higgins returned to the warehouse where FBI staffers continued to search through the papers and other materials from the catacomb at Suburban Vista Nursing Home. As she walked into the search area, she sensed that the people were more relaxed than they had been earlier. Had they found something useful, or was the difference due to their not having the pressure of her presence?

She scanned the room for reactions to her return and focused on Larry Savage. He was smiling. In keeping with his surname, Agent Savage almost never smiled. Linda approached his sorting station.

"How did the operation go while I was away, Larry? Did you find anything useful?"

The smile became a grin. "I think we hit the jackpot. We have the records for those thirteen people on your list. We found them in the file drawer of one of those old desks. That tells me that the person who occupied that desk was probably in on the money laundering scam. Otherwise, I would expect the records for those thirteen people to be scattered throughout this catacomb mess."

"Do we know whose desk that was?"

"I don't have a name, but I think it was the woman in charge of paying the bills. There was a file of paid invoices in one of the drawers."

"How do you know that person was female?"

"The desk had nail polish and a woman's ring in it. The ring was what they used to call costume jewelry, not valuable but decorative."

"How much information was there, Larry? I'd expect the accounting person to have details on patient charges, but not medical or personal histories."

"She had files on twenty patients, including the thirteen on your list. Those files included personal details. All twenty came here for rehab after knee, hip, or shoulder surgery, and all were under thirty years old when they were here. The listed thirteen are the only ones we've found who received payments to their accounts from that North Corner Savings Bank. They weren't all here at the same time. Their collective rehabbing took place over a nine month period."

"Did they have any unusual medical complications?"

"All twenty were in good physical shape except for needing to recover after surgery."

Linda took the stack of files from Larry. "If you've scanned these into the computer, I'll take them for the next meeting with Ruth and the others on the team."

"They're all backed up with digital files. We'll keep searching for more interesting records. I have the feeling that there's more useful stuff here."

CHAPTER 45 – MEETING

Ruth Daltry's FBI conference room was crowded and noisy as everyone waited for Ruth to complete a phone conversation in her office. Paul Garcia described unusual drug smuggling techniques to Arthur and Irma Blake, while Linda Higgins and Bob Marcus told Jim Benson about their exploration of the contents of the catacomb from the nursing home. Larry Savage, arriving late, brought an extra chair from the next office and coaxed a few people to move down the length of the conference table so that he could shoehorn the new chair into a small gap.

Everyone quieted down about fifty percent when Ruth came through the door, but kept talking at a lower level until she called for order.

"Thank you all for coming on short notice. I have the feeling that we have collectively discovered enough new facts about what happened twenty years ago and afterwards to justify this gathering. I suspect that Linda Higgins will have the most new information for the group, so I'll ask her to start."

Linda stood by the dry erase board, ready to list key points as required. She started by writing *catacomb* on the board. "The first thing I have to report is that we got very lucky. The current owners of Suburban Vista Nursing Home took control seventeen years ago. Their first step after taking over was to gather all the paper records, file cabinets, and other furniture from the previous administration into a large room until they could be examined and merged with the new regime's computer systems. It turned out that they never got around to converting the old documents for computer processing, so they were still in their original condition when we arrived on our fact-seeking mission. The administrator had christened the storage room as the catacomb, and it was an appropriate term. We moved everything from that cavernous room to a warehouse and assigned people to the task of analyzing it to learn all we could about the old owners of the nursing home. We have several findings to report today, but our search process, including conversion of documents to computer files, will continue until we have studied everything. Bob Marcus will cover our first discovery and where it led our investigation."

Bob walked to the board and wrote *garage/rats*. "I observed from papers in the catacomb that the old owners of the nursing home paid a ridiculously large sum each month to John Mallinhardt's garage for servicing the nursing home's three vehicles. John Mallinhardt is still in business, running the same garage. As soon as we presented our credentials, John stated that he didn't do anything wrong, but accepted the bank's generosity in helping him get his business established. North Corner Savings Bank arranged for Suburban Vista Nursing home to pay John too much each month for vehicle repairs and service, with the understanding that John would apply the extra amount to his rent and other lease payments and send it to the property manager. John regarded this as the bank giving him an interest-free loan to get his business started. I explored files in John's rat-filled basement and discovered that the property management firm at that time was Ellsworth & Company, Management. That firm has long been out of business, so we have not found the identity of the property owner who was hiding behind Ellsworth."

Paul Garcia said, "It's classic money laundering. The first layer was North Corner Savings Bank. The second layer was Suburban Vista Nursing Home. Then it moved to Mallinhardt's Garage, and on to Ellsworth & Company. Even if Ellsworth were still in business, we would have a hard time finding the absentee landlord for the garage because the business of property management firms is to hide the identities of the owners."

Bob Marcus said, "Thank you, Paul, for clarifying my point. It will be very hard to find the property owner hiding behind the management firm." Bob sat down.

Linda returned to the board and wrote *patients*. "All is not lost. Larry Savage will tell you what he and our other staffers found."

Larry Savage beamed as he announced, "We have found the personal and medical information for the thirteen people who are common to the nursing home and travel agency lists. We even have files on seven additional people in the nursing home that were grouped with the others even though they did not take trips through the bank travel agency."

Arthur Blake interrupted. "Are there any similarities among the groups of thirteen or twenty people?"

Larry leafed through the files for several minutes before responding. "I see your line of thought, Arthur. All of them were of similar age. Their rehab requirements were identical except for differences in the joint being exercised. The most interesting fact common to all of them was that none of these people had living relatives. That is too coincidental to be unplanned."

As multiple conversations erupted, Ruth called for order. "I think from Arthur's question and Larry's response we can conclude that these people were selected to be replaced by others, because no one would notice they were gone. They had spent enough time in rehab that even close friends might have moved on to other relationships."

Larry said, "That's covered here too, Ruth. The folders have a line for friendships, and they all say few or limited."

"That's it then. They were going to replace as many as twenty people, but for whatever reason, they stopped at thirteen."

Arthur stood. "To clarify Ruth's point for those of you who are new to this investigation, she's referring to twelve or thirteen former nursing home patients, there's a little confusion about one of them, who booked Caribbean cruises leaving from Miami and then missed their ships. The records show that these people individually, on different dates, flew to Nassau in the Bahamas and joined the cruise at that point. Our theory was that in each case, only the passenger's identity papers and tickets flew to Nassau, where a different person, using those papers, boarded the ship and became the original passenger. The replacement individuals then entered our American society as substitutes for citizens approximately twenty years ago."

Ruth continued. "Thanks for that clarification. To test our theory, Arthur asked Agent Jim Benson to check Social Security records for persons with the names of our thirteen cruise passengers to identify cases where two different people were paying into the same social security account. Did you find any of those situations, Jim?"

"I bought into the idea of two versions of the thirteen people and expected to find dual Social Security deposits, but I did not."

Irma Blake joined the conversation. "I see two explanations for Jim's results. Either the substitute individuals changed their identities once they arrived in our country, or our theory that only the identification papers flew to Nassau for the substitution is incorrect. The nursing home patients had no relatives. This was planning, not coincidence. I suggest that each of the former patients flew to Nassau and handed off his or her papers and tickets to the substitute who boarded the ship there. Each pair of people switched identities, with the former patient staying in the Bahamas or going to the counterpart's home country. I wouldn't be surprised if the pairs were selected because they had similar ages and physical characteristics. This was a sophisticated scheme."

Ruth nodded. "That makes sense, Irma. Why else would they have selected only nursing home patients without relatives? I suspect that the nursing home people missed their ships and switched off in Nassau so that other passengers wouldn't see two different people with the same identity. The plotters probably used some of the laundered cash to help our thirteen former patients settle into their new lives abroad. The patients committed no crimes that concern us in moving to other countries, but we need to find out why the substitutes came here and what they have been doing over the last twenty years. Jim, did your Social Security search locate them?"

"I located all people with the same names, but we'll have to check out every individual with those names to find the ones we want. We also don't know whether the women married and changed their names, or whether they all took on totally different identities."

Ruth agreed. "Jim has summarized our current situation. It's time to do major legwork to determine where the people on our list of substitutes are. We'll start by assuming they kept the names and backgrounds of the people they replaced and check out everyone in the country with those names. If we can find even a few of them, we may see a pattern that will point to the others. Thanks for coming today. Jim Benson will supply you with your name-checking assignments."

CHAPTER 46 – ARTHUR AND IRMA

As they drove home from the FBI meeting, Arthur said to Irma, "The FBI is properly trying to locate the thirteen substitutes who joined those cruises, but they're not doing much to find the killer of those people in the bank and tunnel twenty years or so ago."

"They're taking current threats first. That group could be a terrorist or espionage sleeper cell. It's also possible that finding the hidden thirteen may lead to progress on solving the murders. At least murder has no statute of limitations. I wonder about the missing money. The people in the tunnel delivered heavy sacks of money to the bank. They must have done this many times to justify their elaborate setup, but so far we've only identified money laundering for thirteen cruises and nine thousand dollars each month through the nursing home. What happened to the rest of the cash?"

"That's a great question, Irma, and as you implied the statute of limitations on theft of that cash has already run out unless the lawyers can find extenuating circumstances that keeps the possibility of prosecution open."

"Like what?"

"If the time available for prosecution starts when the crime is discovered rather than when it is committed, they might be in good shape. We haven't even discovered details of how much was stolen yet."

Impasse

"Arthur, I'm no lawyer, but the logic of that sound flimsy to me. It would be good to come up with a different approach to finding the killer or the missing money. We should move forward with our own investigation while the FBI does their *legwork* thing."

"I think that's an excellent idea, Irma, and I know the perfect place to start our independent inquiry."

"Where?"

"I think it's time for us to go to Nassau to follow some very cold trails."

"We're going to the Bahamas to track the people the FBI considers unimportant?"

"Yup."

"Will I have time to shop for a few new bathing suits and other outfits first?"

CHAPTER 47 – IRMA AND JAY

When Jay Redshaw answered his telephone at work, he heard Irma Blake's voice plus a lot of background noise.

"Hello, Jay, I have a combination of assignments and favors to request today. You may have to take some notes."

"Hi, Irma, are you having a party over there? It sounds pretty lively."

"Arthur and I are getting ready for a field trip, and we have some cleaning people here so that I won't have to worry about the condition of the house while we're gone. We don't know how long we'll be away, so I need you to drive over here and take our dog Rex to stay with you at Bobby and Renee's house. I've already cleared it with them. You'll find our spare house key in the flower pot to the right of the front door. Once you use the key, take it home with you. I may ask you to get something else here later while we're gone."

"Rex and I are friends. I'll be a good dog sitter."

"He'll enjoy his vacation. Your assignment while we're gone will be to contact Special Agent Ruth Daltry at the FBI and tell her that Arthur and I were called out of town, but you don't know where we are or how long we'll be away. Tell Ruth that I asked you to check on the DNA test results for the bodies found in the bank basement crypt. I believe that the FBI has come up with names for our basement victims, but very little background information.

Impasse

While we're away, I'd like you to search the internet and any other sources you can find for details about those people. I think their identities will be essential to understanding what happened at that bank and finding the killer, even after all this time."

"Where will you be? Will I be able to contact you?"

"This may sound strange, but I'm not going to tell you so that you'll be able to honestly tell Special Agent Daltry that you don't know. If you need to contact me or Arthur, send an email. I'll be able to pick that up from anywhere. If I need to contact you, I'll do the same. You'll be operating independently for a while, but I'm sure you're up for it. Your work will be very important to solving this case."

CHAPTER 48 – NASSAU

The plane settled on the Nassau runway with only the slightest of bumps. Irma made a mental note to thank the pilot as they filed out.

Once into the terminal, Irma and Arthur collected their luggage, passed through Bahamas Customs, and then located the bus for the Orange Hill Beach Inn, on the Atlantic coast, not far from the airport. After settling into their room, they changed and swam first in the hotel's swimming pool and then descended the rock-lined stairs to test the ocean experience. They found the surf relatively calm but much colder than the pool. After swimming they walked on a smooth stone shelf just below the surface in one area. Then, following a stop at the honor bar for two bottles of beer, they returned to the lounge chairs by the swimming pool.

Irma leaned back in her chair and smiled at her husband. "Thank you for not mentioning our investigation yet. I want to relax and enjoy this place first."

"We won't work until tomorrow. This case is over twenty years old. Another day or two won't hurt anything. After you're through with soaking and sunning, we can either check out the hotel food or look up a fancier place to eat."

"Let's stay here for the first evening. I have a feeling we'll have enough fancy dining once we get back on the case."

The next morning, Irma awoke to find Arthur dressed and sitting at the desk, studying the local telephone book.

"You're up early. This is vacation."

"I'll call it workation. I decided that a good first step would be to see how many people in Nassau had the same names as those former nursing home patients."

"Don't tell me you found them all in the directory. I need our vacation to last a little while."

"I won't tell you that because I haven't found a single one of them. Even if I restrict my searching to their last names, I found only one name that has more than a single entry."

"Which one?"

"I couldn't find Lynn Holmes, but I found eight people with the Holmes surname."

"You may have found one or more of her children. If our thirteen nursing home patients remained in Nassau, they could have adult children by now. Of course, it's likely that they moved somewhere else or changed their names."

"There's also the question of whether Lynn Holmes would have had a different last name after marriage. Either way, it's a place to start looking."

Arthur made a list of the Holmes names, addresses, and telephone numbers. Then he went to the hotel desk, purchased a prepaid Bahamas cell phone, and sat by the pool to make his calls. His first call reached a woman who thought he was a bill collector. The second, third, and fourth calls drew polite responses that the person on the line had no knowledge of Lynn Holmes. The fifth call was to an Erik Holmes.

When the phone was answered, Arthur asked, "Is this Erik Holmes?"

"Yes, who's calling?"

"My name is Arthur Blake, and I'm trying to reach a woman named Lynn Holmes. Would you happen to know her?"

"Why are you looking for her?"

Arthur hesitated while he attempted to respond to Erik's unexpected question. He knew he should have prepared better. "I'm a church pastor trying to reconnect with her from a long time ago."

"You'll have to do better than that. She hasn't gone to church since she was a child."

"Then you do know her. The truth is that I want to talk with her about something that happened many years ago when she was in a nursing home for rehabilitation after an operation."

"Why should I help you? What's in it for me?"

"I'd be willing to pay a finder's fee to you for connecting me with her."

"I'll need one thousand U.S. dollars to set things up."

"That's awfully steep. I'm willing to pay five hundred dollars."

"This isn't a negotiation, Mr. Blake. If you don't pay me one thousand dollars, you'll never find Lynn Holmes because that's no longer her name. I need to know how important this introduction is for you."

"Where would we meet for the payment, and how do I know I'd actually get to talk with her after paying you?"

"Meet me at Bahamian Cookin' Restaurant and Bar on Trinity Place in downtown Nassau tomorrow afternoon at one o'clock."

"I can do that, Erik, but again, I'll need a guarantee that you won't take my money and run. How do you know Lynn?"

"I need to know how important this is to you, so go to a bank and get me the cash. After I receive it and discuss your interest with Lynn, you will meet her if she's willing. I can assure you of that because I am her son."

"What if she's not willing to talk with me?"

"Then you're out one thousand dollars. If she thinks you're a threat, you will not meet."

"I'll be at the restaurant at one o'clock. How will I know you?"

"Look for the only person with a Sherlock Holmes pipe on the table in front of him."

CHAPTER 49 – ERIK AND LYNN

Trinity Place turned out to be much narrower than its name suggested. The Bahamian Cookin' Restaurant and Bar featured a high ceiling and black tables topped with black and white mosaic tiles. The establishment apparently catered to tourists, because most staff and patrons were white. One of the few dark-skinned exceptions sat at a table underneath a hanging white globe light with a curved-stem large-bowl pipe in front of him.

Arthur and Irma approached the owner of the pipe. "Erik?"

He stood. "You must be Arthur, and who is your companion?"

"This is my wife, Irma. We would both like to meet your mother."

After they sat, Arthur withdrew an envelope from his inside jacket pocket and handed it to Erik. That would-be Sherlock took it, folded it in half, and put it into his back pocket without checking the contents.

Erik smiled. "The food here is quite good. Shall we eat or talk first, or perhaps you wish only some refreshing drinks?"

Irma said, "We should get to know each other. We came to learn about your mother and her associates. Food encourages friendship. What do you recommend?"

"This restaurant is well known for their conch fritters, if you don't mind eating fried food."

Impasse

When the waiter took their orders, they all ordered conch fritters in different quantities accompanied by Kalik beer. Erik, being an enthusiast for conch fritters, ordered the most. Then the casual cross-examinations started.

Erik said, "You appear to be tourists, but you are acting like police. Tell me more about yourselves."

Arthur looked at Irma, and she nodded for him to respond. "We have no official police connection, but we find ourselves investigating unusual events on a regular basis. By background, I'm an engineer and a United Methodist pastor, while Irma is a doctor specializing in forensic pathology. Our interest in your mother actually stems from problems involved in building a new church. I'm afraid it's a long story, but we encounter events and then try to learn why they happened or what problems they might cause."

Erik turned to Irma. "You do post mortems on people after they die?"

"I do, but no longer in an official capacity."

"We have something in common. I work for a veterinarian, and I sometimes assist in animal surgeries. Once in a while we do post mortems on working animals like horses, but people don't want us to invade the bodies of pets that have died."

"Sometimes, you have to use diplomacy to get permission for a human autopsy as well. You appear to be well-educated, Erik."

"I have had my years in the classroom and two apprenticeships. Before I worked for the veterinarian, I apprenticed as a video recorder repair technician. Now I am trying to learn more about computers."

Arthur tried to steer the conversation toward Erik's mother. "Does your mother have friends who came to the Bahamas from Illinois where she once lived?"

"That's something you will have to ask her when you meet."

The food arrived, accompanied by aromas and tastes that were new to the Blakes, but savored by Erik. They toasted each other with the Kalik beers and then paused their discussion while they ate.

Arthur had eight conch fritters and Irma four, both orders accompanied by peas and rice, while Erik had twelve conch fritters with coleslaw. After the meal, Erik Holmes took out his telephone and keyed in a number. When the call was answered he said, "They look essentially normal, Mom. Come join us at Bahamian Cookin'." He sat back and relaxed. "She'll be here in about ten minutes."

Twelve minutes later, Erik rose and beckoned to a woman as she entered. Arthur and Irma noted that the new arrival was white, indicating that dark-skinned Erik was the product of a mixed marriage. She had graying hair peeking out from under a red flowered kerchief. Lynn was taller than Erik, suggesting that his father was short.

"Pastor and Doctor Blake, I'd like you to meet my mother, Lynn Cooper."

They exchanged greetings, and Lynn sat with them after ordering a fruit punch from the waiter as he walked by. Erik and Arthur ordered beers, and Irma decided to also try the fruit punch.

Impasse

Once the drinks arrived and they were on a first name basis, Arthur asked, "Are we correct in assuming that you were offered a new life here in exchange for your identity papers?"

"That was a very long time ago, but you are essentially correct. If I hadn't wrecked my knee skiing, it never would have happened. I had my right knee replaced, and a man at the nursing home gave me this unbelievable proposition while I was in rehab. I would have to agree to live in the Bahamas as a different person in exchange for free transportation to my new home and a lifelong annuity to support me. I was in my twenties and had no relatives requiring me to live near them, so I accepted. I felt as though I had won the lottery."

Irma asked, "What name did you have to assume?"

"I became Emily Everett. I didn't like that name, so after five years I had my name legally changed back to Lynn Holmes, pretending that it was a new name for me. I was a single mother to Erik, so I legally changed his name too. I had to work through a lawyer because my annuity payments continued to arrive at the bank payable to Emily Everett. A few years later, I married Frank Cooper, so I've had a whole bunch of names."

Irma made notes in her pocket notebook as rapidly as possible. "We might not have found you if you hadn't changed your name back to the original version. Lynn, have you been in touch with other people here who have had the same identity change experience?"

Lynn stared at Irma. "What do you mean? Did someone else get the same offer and arrangement I did? I thought my situation was unique, so the answer to your question is no. How many others were there?"

"We think there were a total of twelve or thirteen, including you."

"That's the wildest thing I ever heard. I guess a whole bunch of people won the same lottery I did. Erik, have you heard any gossip about other people with name changes?"

"I haven't, but once you changed us back to the original family name, I stopped thinking about the subject of people with new names. Do you want me to put something on Facebook or one of the other social media outlets?"

Lynn shook her head slightly. "No, that wouldn't be fair to people who were content with their new identities. You folks have found me. I'm proof that the exchanged identities happened. Does it change anything for anyone?"

Arthur said, "I'm not sure yet, but tell me what your citizenship was as Emily Everett."

"I was a British citizen, United Kingdom, but I became a citizen here, so now I'm a citizen of the Commonwealth of the Bahamas and a subject of the Queen. It does get confusing because I gave my American citizenship to someone else."

Irma asked, "Are you happy here, Lynn?"

"Of course I am. This place is beautiful. I have a fine son and a loving husband. Hopefully, that son will soon have a family of his own."

Impasse

"Mom, stop nagging me. I'm happy being single."

CHAPTER 50 – FEEDBACK

The telephone was on its third ring as she rushed into the office. "Special Agent Ruth Daltry."

"Hello, Ruth, it's Arthur Blake calling from paradise."

"I heard a rumor that you had gone on vacation. Where exactly are you?"

"To be precise, I'm sitting in a lounge chair by a swimming pool in Nassau."

"That's what they call an enviable position. What may I do for you?"

"Please take notes. I have some information for you and your legwork people."

"Go ahead; I'm ready."

"Each person on that list from the nursing home was flown to Nassau where the identity exchange was made. The nursing home individual received an annuity for life under his or her new name. There were no further contacts or stipulations, but the annuities were handled through a Bahamian bank, so it was most convenient to continue to live in the Bahamas."

"Got that. Have you located the thirteen nursing home patients?"

"I located one of them, Lynn Holmes, because she decided after five years to legally change her new name back to the original, without revealing her history. The interesting aspect of the case is that Lynn had no knowledge of any other identity switches. She thought she was the only one."

"Who was her tradeoff partner?"

"The person who became Lynn Holmes in the United States was Emily Everett, a citizen of the United Kingdom. If you check her background, you may get a better idea of what's going on in this conspiracy."

"Great! What else do you have?"

"This afternoon, I'll email you the name of the bank that handles Lynn's annuity. She didn't remember it offhand, so she'll look it up and call me with the information. It would be better if the FBI contacts the bank to put some official pressure on them, but I'm betting that all the annuities flow through that same bank. I think they'll either have addresses for the other twelve switched people, or you'll be able to contact them when they go to the bank for their monthly payments."

"You're doing a pretty good job for a guy on vacation. I'll attach an authorization letter to my next email so that you can check that bank for annuity records. You're already there, so let's save costs over sending someone else. Our nearest office is in Barbados."

"Being an amateur, I don't have any jurisdiction problems."

"Much as I hate to admit it, Arthur, you're far beyond an amateur at this investigation business. We may want to discuss your status someday."

"How are you folks doing at locating the identity switchers who are masquerading as American citizens?"

Richard Davidson

"I'm still waiting for results. We have a meeting scheduled for tomorrow. I'll email the summary. So far, you have the most useful data."

"I have information on replaced people who are no longer important. Let me know what you find out about Emily Everett."

"Will do, and thanks."

CHAPTER 51 – CINDY

Nancy's getting worse. So much time spent at the hospital for dialysis. The swelling of different parts of her body is getting worse. She doesn't look like herself. She's weak and won't eat much at all. Something has to be done, but what? If I had leveled with Tom and Arthur about her birth I might have a chance of Tom staying with me and Arthur donating a kidney. I kept telling myself that I didn't know who Nancy's father was. That one-night stand should have meant nothing, but it screwed up all our lives. I didn't even want a child back then. Now I'll do anything to save Nancy. ANYTHING!

She's so calm about it all. If I were in her shoes, I wouldn't be able to live for today and not worry about tomorrow. I've always been a worrier. That's why I had to have someone else when Arthur got so tied up with his work. I needed security. No excuse for that one-timer who turned out to be Nancy's father. That was simply caused by my drinking too damn much. I was really blue that night, and I needed someone right there and then. At least he never knew about fathering Nancy. He wasn't a keeper at all.

I must be falling apart. I can't even remember the doctor's name. It's something like Bannerman, but that's not quite right. Anyway, Dr. Bannerman or whoever he is says that the next few weeks will be critical for finding a transplant organ. He's trying to find one through the organ bank, but they have such

Richard Davidson

long waiting times. I've heard several stories of people dying before an organ became available. Maybe if I put Nancy's story online on social media, I'd get volunteers ready to be tested for a living transplant. I'll try that. I have to do something.

CHAPTER 52 – EMILY EVERETT

Arthur Blake read aloud the email from Ruth Daltry. "Find out whether Lynn Holmes became Emily Fiona Everett or if she had a different middle name."

Irma said, "That's a reasonable request. Emily Everett is a probably a common name in Britain, so the FBI needs to narrow their search by learning the middle name that Lynn used after she switched identities with Emily."

"That's one way of interpreting the message, but I take it to mean that Emily Fiona Everett is someone special and significant. They want to know whether the Emily who took part in the identity exchange was this important person or someone else."

Irma made the call from her poolside lounge chair. "Hello, Lynn. It's Irma Blake. We need to know whether, as Emily Everett, you had the middle name Fiona, or if not, what was it?"

Arthur couldn't quite hear Lynn's response. He hoped Irma's continuing conversation would reveal it.

"Is that so? Did you actually meet her, or did some intermediary give you her papers without her being present...? I understand, and that makes sense.... Somebody professional planned ahead.... Thanks for the information.... Yes, we'll be here for another week, and we'd love to get together again. Let us know when and where you want to meet."

Irma put her phone on the table, closed her eyes, and relaxed against the back of the lounger.

"Are you going to pretend I'm not here? Tell me what she said."

"You are impatient, Arthur. Everything fits together. Lynn did become the highlighted Emily Fiona Everett. They never met, but each was given the identity papers of the other, revised to show the matching photograph and appropriate personal description. Somewhere in Nassau there was or is an outfit that specializes in counterfeit identification papers. The rest of my conversation should have been obvious. Before we leave, Lynn wants to get together with us on a social basis, without any reference to the investigation. Can you be off duty long enough to handle that?"

"Yes, I do know how to relax at the appropriate time. Right now, I have to send an email to Ruth, giving her your very intriguing results. By the way, that bathing suit looks great."

"Thanks, but no thanks. You were supposed to be dazzled by my appearance in this suit when we first arrived. It's taken you altogether too much time to react. When we go out for dinner, I'm ordering the most expensive item on the menu."

Arthur returned to the pool area after exchanging emails with Ruth Daltry. Irma was sleeping, so he tilted the umbrella closest to her to shade her from the sun. As he finished, she woke up.

"I'm here for sunshine, not shade. What did you learn from Ruth?"

Impasse

"Emily Fiona Everett is or was the heir to her British industrialist father who made a fortune designing and manufacturing powered floor-cleaning machines for institutions and wood-working machines for furniture makers. She was also a leader among Brits who believed in UFO events and visits to Earth by creatures from other worlds."

"Why do you have trouble deciding whether to use 'is' or 'was' in referring to her. Did she die?"

"No one knows. She hasn't been seen in public since 1997, but she always avoided publicity and rarely left her estate. There's still staff activity at that location, and her businesses are doing quite well. Some UFO enthusiasts think she was abducted by aliens, but our investigation suggests she is now living somewhere in the United States, having exchanged identities with Lynn Holmes. She may be living her new life for privacy reasons but still running her business interests through a manager.

"The FBI will have to locate and interview her before we'll know for sure what she's doing. They're concerned that Emily Everett may be organizing a political movement designed to undermine the U.S. government. It wouldn't take much to have Americans mistrust the two-party political system and look for something else to replace or alter it. What do you think she's doing, Irma?"

"It has to be something very important to her. She's been working on it for at least twenty years. How old is she?"

"She was thirty-three when she disappeared in 1997. She would be fifty-three now."

Irma stood and draped her towel over her shoulders. "I've had enough roasting in the sun for now. I'll dress while you call Lynn for the name of the bank where she picks up her annuity payment. We're still waiting for that information from her. Then you may take me out for lunch on the way to interviewing the bank manager."

CHAPTER 53 – JAYSON AND SARAH

Jayson looked at his notes from calling the FBI, and said, "They gave me a brief identification of the two bodies in the old bank crypt. I have a name for the man, Kenneth Shea, and the fact that he was an Army veteran who served in Vietnam. They identify the female remains as belonging to Mary Lowry who had a ticket for drunk driving and worked as an accountant. That's not enough information to give us a feeling for what was important to them and how they lived their lives. I need to – pardon the expression – learn enough to put some flesh on those bones."

Sarah wrote down the two names. "I'm not sure how much we can learn about people who died so long ago, but I'll help as much as I can."

"Thanks, that's all I can ask. Let's start by saying that both names sound Irish. They had some connection to North Corner Savings Bank. They probably also knew each other."

Sarah said, "Their connection to that bank could have been minor. They could have been random customers or bank robbers."

"The bank robber idea might be worth considering. If the bank was doing something criminal, they might have wanted to get rid of the robbers rather than report them to the police."

"The FBI said the woman was an accountant. She may have worked there."

Richard Davidson

"That's good thinking, Sarah. Let's check Google and the State Police files to see whether we can get some facts about those two people to take us beyond conjecture."

"That's fine with me, but don't expect too much, Jay. They died a long time ago. We might not find anything on them. Add to that the fact that Kenneth Shea and Mary Lowry are common names. We'll have trouble deciding whether information we find applies to those two bodies at North Corner Savings Bank."

"All of that's true, but I feel challenged to find out as much as we can about those two. Their stories may turn out to be important for solving this case."

CHAPTER 54 – CENTRAL BANK

Having received contact information from Lynn Holmes Cooper, Arthur and Irma visited the Central Bank of the Bahamas and requested a meeting with Sidney Morris, Lynn's contact there. Arthur carried the FBI Contractor Identification document emailed to him by Special Agent Ruth Daltry. Mr. Morris came out to greet them wearing a custom-tailored blue suit that managed to look both conservative and tropically informal at the same time.

"Good morning to you both. It is my pleasure to welcome you to Central Bank. How may I be of service to you today?"

After exchanging handshakes Arthur said, "We're here in connection with your dealings with Lynn Holmes Cooper. Is there a room where we may talk privately?"

Sidney Morris nodded, smiled, and led them to a nearby private office. He closed the door after they entered. "We have a conference room upstairs, but we use this small office for loan application discussions because it is more convenient to the lobby area. Are you here on Mrs. Cooper's behalf?"

Arthur focused on Morris' eyes, to detect any unusual reaction to his next statement. "Actually, we're here on behalf of the FBI. We're contractors to that agency, and I have an authorization document to show you relating to this discussion. Our FBI letter is accompanied by a second memorandum from the Royal Bahamas Police Force requesting your cooperation." Sidney Morris showed no reaction beyond a slight increase in the warmth of his smile.

"Wonderful. We always appreciate official visits so that we may demonstrate the efficiency of our bank. What information do you desire?"

Irma opened her notebook. "We know that you are the contact for processing payments to Lynn under her annuity."

"That is correct, and we have never had a delayed payment to her."

"Our interest today is in other annuities you may process. I have a list of people who may also have annuities processed by your bank. We would like you to confirm the ones who are your clients for this service."

Sidney gestured his request for a brief pause by holding up his forefinger. Then he opened the laptop computer sitting on the desk and keyed his identification and password into it. As the screen lit up with the bank's logo and then its home page, Sidney said, "I'm pleased that you have a list of specific names to check. In the absence of names, I would not be able to examine our files for you. We have a fiduciary responsibility to our clients to keep their affairs private in the absence of a specific government inquiry. Now, what people are the subjects of your search?"

Irma read the list slowly to give Sidney time to check each record. "Sally Adler; Helen Barnes; Joyce Channing; Lynn Holmes we've already discussed; Karen Probst; Paul Burges; Harold Dawes; Joshua Leary; Bruno Malverno; Ralph

McTavish; Benjamin Persky; Leonard Smith; and Stanley Wilcox."

Sidney searched through his files for several minutes, making notes on a pad of paper and occasionally shaking his head negatively as he worked. When he finally looked up, he had a bewildered expression.

"I have searched the names on your list, but before I say anything about my results, I would like your assurance that none of our clients will be in legal trouble because of the information I will share with you. It would be bad for our business to have clients' file data used against them."

Arthur agreed. "I understand your misgivings. We are here to obtain information for the FBI to use in a case based within the United States. Your clients are connected to that case, but they are not suspects in anything criminal at this time. I can't guarantee that their status will remain the same, because this is an ongoing investigation. We would appreciate your cooperation in giving us the details you have found without the need to obtain a judicial search warrant."

Given the suggestion that the bank might face a search warrant, Sidney Morris decided to summarize his findings informally. "The files on most of the people you have listed do exist, and they are quite unusual. I will comment on them, but I am not willing to let you examine our records before we are ordered to do so by the judiciary. Will that be sufficient for today?"

After exchanging glances and nods with his wife, Arthur said, "We will work with whatever information you choose to share for now."

"First of all, I must indicate that we have no file involving one of your names, that of Stanley Wilcox. All the other names are involved in our files."

Arthur asked, "What do you mean by saying they're 'involved in' your files?"

"All except Mr. Wilcox have annuities processed through this bank. Those funding instruments bear the names on your list. However, each was individually signed over to a person with a different name. I do not feel comfortable with releasing the second name to which the annuity was assigned because that would be confidential information. In the case of Lynn Holmes Cooper, the funds were transferred to another name and later transferred back to Lynn Holmes. Her payment name was later changed to Lynn Cooper after her marriage."

Irma said, "It would be a big help to the FBI if you gave us those assigned names."

"I'm sorry, Dr. Blake, but just as you have to honor confidentiality of medical records, I must do the same with our financial files. I have given you most of the data you requested. I hope it will suffice. I also must request that we end this meeting, so that I may be present at an important loan evaluation conference which has already started."

Arthur and Irma realized that they had reached the limit of Sidney's cooperation, so they agreed to end their meeting without saying anything that

Impasse

might make them unwelcome on a return visit to the bank. They thanked Mr. Morris and left.

CHAPTER 55 – EVALUATION

The flight back to Chicago was uneventful until its final stages. A narrow band of thunderstorms passing through the O'Hare International Airport area made takeoffs and landings temporarily unsafe. Air Traffic Control required all incoming flights to circle within a holding pattern until the weather cleared for landings. Despite the air turbulence which threatened to spill their drinks, Arthur and Irma used the extra flying time to evaluate their progress on the case.

Arthur withdrew a folded sheet of paper from his inside jacket pocket. "My notes aren't as neat as yours, but they diagram our findings. Our biggest success was finding Lynn Holmes Cooper and getting to know her to some extent. I consider her to be a normal, optimistic person who stumbled into this identity exchange and adapted to it. Her new life has nothing to do with any criminal conspiracy."

"I'll second that, Arthur. Lynn is so naively normal that she grew tired of being someone else and legally converted her new identity back to her original name. Without admitting to anyone that she was living under a false identity, she restored her own image. I think she's smart and creative."

Arthur referred to his diagram. "Our second success was learning that twelve of the thirteen people on your list of nursing home alumni who booked trips through the old bank's travel agency are still living in the Bahamas, supported by annuity payments processed through the Central Bank of the Bahamas. We failed to get information about Stanley Wilcox, the thirteenth person, and we failed to get the new identities of eleven of the twelve people transplanted in the Bahamas."

Irma said, "That's not really a failure. The FBI has Lynn's exchanged identity, Emily Fiona Everett. If they find her, she may provide the other names. They could also get a search warrant for the files of Central Bank of the Bahamas to find the names of the other individuals."

Arthur circled a name on his list and put an asterisk next to it. "I'm intrigued by the person we didn't find, Stanley Wilcox. As they used to say on the children's television show, Sesame Street, *one of these things is not like the others*. I'd like to find out what makes him different."

CHAPTER 56 – RUTH DALTRY

Ruth took notes as she sat across the conference room table from Arthur and Irma. "You two have done well in the Bahamas. I hope you managed to fit some fun as well as work into your schedule while you were there. I want you to know that the official members of our investigating team have been busy also. I originally added Paul Garcia to the team because I thought we needed someone from the Drug Enforcement Administration for money laundering expertise. Paul played a hunch and searched the files of people with controlled substance prescriptions. He suspected that a woman with all the pressures of remote management of British businesses would have some medical problems. Paul discovered one Lynn Holmes who is the correct age has several active prescriptions. She lives in Orlando, Florida. We had our people take several old photographs of Emily Fiona Everett and age them by about twenty years. Our agents compared the photographs with the woman living as Lynn Holmes in Orlando and they match closely."

Irma asked, "When are you planning to visit her, and will you give her advance notice or just appear on her doorstep?"

"We're going to be a bit cautious before we visit. Agents are tracking her movements and reviewing her telephone call history. There are eleven or twelve others who came here as part of this scheme, so we want to find out whether she has stayed in contact with them. She won't elude us if she tries to move away, but I doubt that will happen. We'll visit her within the next two weeks. Would you two like to come along?"

Arthur turned to Irma. "If you want to be there go ahead. I have a couple of other matters that will keep me busy for at least two weeks."

Irma gave no indication that she had been surprised by Arthur's response as she told Ruth that she would indeed like to visit Emily Everett.

As they were preparing to leave, Arthur asked Ruth, "One more item, did you find out whether Stanley Wilcox took his cruise and returned, or did he also remain in the Bahamas?"

"We checked that one. He probably shouldn't have been on your list. Wilcox took a return cruise. He didn't stay in Nassau."

CHAPTER 57 – CONNECTION

Sarah Jackson had looked forward to sharing coffee and a pastry with Jayson but found that for the first time since they started their joint project at the Illinois State Police Forensics Laboratory, he hadn't arrived on time. She didn't know whether to expect him to come in late. Perhaps he decided to do some work for Chief Andrews in Parkville, but didn't tell her in advance. She decided to discard her diet and eat Jay's half of the pastry as well as her own.

By the time Jay arrived, two hours late, Sarah had started work on a DNA analysis from a rape and murder on the Tri-State Tollway alongside a disabled vehicle. She fought back a shudder as she visualized the circumstances of that crime. The victim had been a housewife on her way home after attending her uncle's funeral in Chicago.

In the middle of Sarah's meditation Jay appeared in the doorway of her laboratory. "Hi – sorry I'm late, but I had to check something on my computer in Parkville. It's linked to the prison system records in Massachusetts, and I thought I remembered something about Albert Rivers, one of the guys who died in that tunnel to the North Corner Bank. My search struck gold. It confirmed that our victim from the bank crypt, Mary Lowry, was listed as Albert Rivers' next-of-kin. She was his sister."

"Good work, Jay. Maybe the other body, Kenneth Shea, was her boyfriend."

"I think I told you that someone had cut the wires to the tunnel ventilation system and manhole cover actuator, trapping and killing Albert Rivers and his partner."

"The partner was FBI Agent Ted Higgins, playing the part of Marco Locante?"

"You have a good memory, Sarah. Anyway, if someone from the bank murdered them, and Mary Lowry was Albert Rivers' sister, the killer probably wanted to get rid of Mary and her boyfriend or protector. She may or may not have worked at the bank, but someone at least arranged for her to be there."

"Super work. You have both an identification of Mary and a motive for killing both her and Kenneth Shea."

"Now all we have to do is figure out the identity of the murderer twenty years or so later."

CHAPTER 58 – EMILY FIONA EVERETT

A tall, middle-aged woman with an almost-military bearing answered her front door to find four people standing on the porch. She had one of the few homes in Orlando with a porch, and she enjoyed having a group of people within its embracing railings.

"Good morning; you appear to be a delegation of some kind."

The leader held up her credentials. "Lynn Holmes? I'm Special Agent Ruth Daltry of the FBI, and these are my associates, two from our agency plus one civilian." She gestured toward Irma. Ruth introduced each member of the team to Lynn.

"You're quite welcome here. May I assist you with something? Would you like to come inside and talk? I prefer the porch myself. There are plenty of seats."

"The porch will be fine, unless you prefer to have privacy."

"I have nothing to hide. Why would I need secrecy?"

"Perhaps because you're not really Lynn Holmes; you're Emily Fiona Everett."

She responded without hesitation. "Oh, that's not important. I prefer to be Lynn Holmes though. Too many people expect me to give them money if I use the Everett name."

Ruth looked puzzled. "Don't you realize it was a crime to enter this country using someone else's name?"

"I don't believe the exchange of names was a crime, or at least not a serious one. With regard to illegal entry, I qualified for that and had a green card as an EB-5 immigrant investor under my original name. I have established several companies in the United States that have created many jobs."

"What about your other associates who did the same thing?"

"You know about all twelve of us, do you? If you'll pardon the expression, we're all in the same boat, wealthy Brits who were granted that EB-5 status. We brought large amounts of capital to our adopted country, even though we were cheated out of a substantial amount of it."

Irma interrupted Ruth's questioning in the hope of making their conversation less formal. "Lynn, or Emily, would you like to tell us your story from the beginning instead of answering specific questions?"

"I'd be happy to do that, but would anyone like a drink or a snack first?"

The visitors all declined, but Emily went inside to get some iced tea for herself. When she returned she said, "It's pleasant to have a group gathered on my porch. My friends and I meet here frequently. Getting back to the beginning of my story, we're all quite wealthy, and we have one thing in common. We all believe in UFOs, unidentified flying objects, and are convinced that they are visitors from other worlds. We got hooked on these beliefs after the events at Redlesham Forest in Suffolk, England during 1980. Did any of you read about them?"

Irma nodded. "I did. As I recall, several US Air Force people at a base in Suffolk said they saw lights in that forest and a craft landing in a clearing, but that the object moved away from them when they approached. I think their commander wrote something confirming the sightings. The problem is that I also read articles explaining away the lights as being from a lighthouse on the other side of the forest and from a meteor burning up in the atmosphere."

"You have a good memory, Irma. I was only sixteen years old at the time, but I've relived Redlesham in my mind many times. You get opposite viewpoints when unexpected events happen. Someone witnesses something, and two sides of the story quickly emerge. Some, like my friends and I, want to believe we had an alien contact, while others feel threatened by that possibility and try to explain the evidence away as naturally occurring phenomena. We're well-educated and sophisticated, but we came down on the side of believing."

Ruth asked, "What do UFO incidents have to do with your coming to the United States in such an unconventional way?"

"I'll get to that. The problem is that if you believe some things, you tend to accept others as extensions of the first. We believe that aliens have visited us, so it doesn't take a great leap of imagination to ask whether it would be possible for us to visit them."

Ruth said, "NASA is working toward interplanetary travel in the future, Emily, but they're far from achieving it, except with unmanned probe vehicles."

"Anything is possible if you're a believer. That's what got us into trouble. In 1996, we were approached by a very persuasive man named Albert Rivers. He said he was an associate of an American inventor who was preparing to launch a manned exploration vehicle to Mars. The inventor would accept us as passengers for one million dollars each, payable in cash, but we would have to keep the project secret because NASA had not given the trip its blessing. We gave our money to Mr. Rivers, but the voyage to Mars was either a hoax or was technologically deficient at that time. In other words, Albert Rivers took us collectively for twelve million dollars."

Ruth interrupted Emily. "Most people who get cheated out of a large amount of money lament their losses and commit to keeping better control over their money in the future. You and your friends stayed here and took little notice of your losses."

"I have two responses to your comments, Ruth. First, we were all very wealthy, so even with the loss of a million dollars, we weren't hurting. Second, we were committed to our beliefs about visitors from other worlds, and we had pledged our lives to finding an opportunity to be part of the space program. Many of our investments here have been in companies that are subcontractors to NASA and

SpaceX. Besides, if we do manage to fly to Mars or some other planet, we won't need our money there."

"Do you think SpaceX will make good on their promise to take people to Mars and establish a colony?"

"I do, and we may be part of that effort. Two people in our group have already given SpaceX deposits toward being on board their second or third passenger trip around the moon and back to earth. The rest of us have signed up with both Blue Origin and Virgin Galactic to take brief trips to the edge of Earth's atmosphere. We are taking steps toward going into space. The Mars voyage may not happen before we're too old for it, but several in our group are raising children who will be prepared to go when the technology is ready."

"Are their children as committed as you are?"

"They're not only committed. They're excited to be in the generation that finally gets to expand society to other planets."

Irma had waited patiently for a gap between Ruth's questions and Emily's responses. She interrupted. "I have to ask; why did you come here using the bizarre procedure of exchanging identities with people who had no families and spending money on annuities for them in the Bahamas?"

Emily laughed. "We are a bit over the edge in our belief in alien contacts. That was our expensive inside joke. Did you ever see the movie, *Invasion of the Body Snatchers*? We were the international aliens taking the place of existing citizens the way the outer space aliens did in that movie. It made us think we had accomplished a little bit toward our goals, and it gave those twelve unfamilied Americans pleasant and economically comfortable lives in a beautiful country. I told you that we are all quite wealthy. We had no problem affording their annuities and expenses."

Ruth asked, "You keep mentioning the twelve people in your group. We had thirteen people on our list of American passengers who took part in those identity exchanges in Nassau. Was Stanley Wilcox part of your group?"

"No, but I remember his name. He ran the bank travel agency. He was in Nassau to make arrangements with the man who altered the photographs and our travel documents to match our exchanged faces and personal characteristics."

"Did you meet the man who altered the identification papers?"

"No, but I think Wilcox referred to him as Murray or Murphy or some similar name. It was too long ago for me to be certain."

CHAPTER 59 – ARTHUR

Arthur appreciated Irma's not questioning his begging off from the visit to Emily Everett. He didn't know whether she had guessed what his priority project was, but he wouldn't have been surprised if she had. Important personal decisions lay in his future, and it was time for him to get the knowledge he would need to face them. He needed to go to the hospital where fifteen-year-old Nancy Tillingham was being treated. He wanted to talk with her doctor and also meet Nancy without her mother, Cindy, being present. Soon, he would have to decide whether to take the final tests and donate a kidney to Nancy if he qualified. He wouldn't make that decision unless he first met her and determined whether they could relate to each other well. If he were a saint, relationships wouldn't matter. A saint would simply do his charitable duty for a person in need. Arthur knew he fell far short of sainthood and couldn't give up something as important as a kidney without a very good reason. Nancy was not his child, and Cindy had cheated on him with at least two other men while they were married. He had already decided that he wouldn't give up one of his kidneys just because Cindy had requested it. He had to meet Nancy and see her as someone with whom he felt comfortable sharing part of himself. He would meet her as a stranger, so that her reactions to him would not be biased by his past relationship with her mother. He had the contact information for the doctor and hospital from Irma's laboratory files. It was time for him to visit that specialist and arrange a meeting with Nancy as a mysterious stranger.

Two mornings later, Arthur arrived for his meeting with Dr. Louis Rockman promptly at nine o'clock. They shared an elevator to the third floor without talking, but their identities became obvious when they both walked toward the same office door.

"Dr. Rockman? I'm Arthur Blake, your nine o'clock appointment."

"I had a feeling that I was supposed to know you when we walked down the corridor together. You're Irma Blake's husband."

"That I am. She's in charge of bodies, while I care for souls."

"That's right. She said you're a pastor. Come on into my office, and sit down while I ask my secretary to get us a couple of coffees. You look like a man who likes it black, correct?"

"Perfect. That shows that you're either very astute, or Irma mentioned it, and you have a good memory."

"I'm not sure why, but it came up during my conversation with Irma about your possibly being a suitable donor for my patient, Nancy Tillingham."

"I'm afraid my love for coffee is part of my basic chemistry."

Dr. Rockman left the room to talk with his secretary. When he returned, he suggested that they sit at his side table. "If I sit at the desk, I always have the feeling that I'm claiming a superior position. The table is more of an equalizer."

As they settled at the table, Dr. Rockman's secretary returned with their coffee and two foil-wrapped chocolates."

"As I understand it, Arthur, you're here because you want to meet Nancy. By the way, call me Louis or Lou so that we're on an equal footing."

"Equality appears to be important to you, Lou. May I ask why?"

"Too many people feel that the word of a doctor is sacred, and they don't question it or supply enough background information. Without going into details, I had a patient a few years back who followed my instructions to the letter on treating one illness, but was too timid to volunteer that she had a second condition that I didn't know about. The treatment for one condition was incompatible with the second, and she almost died. I now use questionnaires and informal meetings to be sure I know everything I can about a patient's background before I recommend a specific treatment."

"That's a good approach, and it touches on my reason for being here today. I was Cindy's first husband, but I didn't even know about her daughter Nancy until a few months ago. It now appears from the test data that you and Irma exchanged, that I'm a couple of tests away from qualifying to be a suitable living kidney donor for Nancy. I will need to get to know Nancy before I could consider such a donation, but I don't want Nancy to know I was her mother's former husband, and I don't want Cindy to know I came here. Would you be willing to set up a *blind* meeting between me and Nancy?"

"That's almost like one of our standard double-blind drug tests. The patient doesn't know whether he or she is getting the experimental medicine or a harmless placebo. You don't want a former relationship to color your discussions with Nancy. I think your request is a reasonable one. She's scheduled to be in today for a three hour dialysis session. I could have her see me in this office afterward. You'll be in the background wearing a white lab coat as an observer. Someone wearing a uniform is usually looked upon as being impartial and/or invisible. The only question I have concerns how to introduce you. Nancy may know your name from her mother."

"Introduce me as Richmond Peterson. That's a stretch without being a complete lie. The town I grew up in is Richmond, Illinois, and my father's name is Peter, so I am a Peterson. You can call me Rich as a nickname."

"Fair enough, Rich; you do realize you may have to reintroduce yourself to Nancy later under your real name."

"That won't be a problem. I'd like to have you introduce us and then say that my job is to interview her about how she has been feeling during the whole kidney failure and treatment process. That will allow me to steer the conversation wherever I feel it should go."

"I like that approach, but to keep this ethical and useful, send me a summary of your interview results for her file. You can sign it Richmond

Richard Davidson

Peterson in case Cindy sees it at some point. We'll start your session with Nancy at two o'clock."

"Thanks, Lou. I'll be back this afternoon."

CHAPTER 60 – NANCY TILLINGHAM

Dr. Rockman introduced Nancy to Rich Peterson and then left them together for his outlook interview. Rich was the first to speak.

"Nancy, I know that you've been through many phases of your ongoing ordeal, but I want you to relax as we discuss a variety of things. Do you think you can do that?"

"No problem Mr. Peterson; I've been tested, measured, poked, and prodded so many times that this is all old hat to me. As they say, it comes with the territory."

He admired her pluck and willingness to face her condition as one of those adverse things that happen in the course of life. Nancy was an outgoing teenager, her appearance only slightly marred by her current skin discoloration and bloating. She leaned back in her chair as he talked.

"I know that you've just completed a dialysis session. How do you feel after that procedure?"

"When I first started having dialysis, it was both painful and scary, because I didn't know what to expect. It's still pretty uncomfortable, but it's become part of my routine, so I can handle it. Right now, I feel better than I did before that session."

"Prior to your illness, were you athletic?"

"I wasn't into any team sports, but I handled gym classes well and liked to go hiking with my dad, even though it turned out he isn't really my dad. Sorry about adding that remark. We have a screwed-up family."

"Do you get along well with your mother?"

"Sure. Mom's been real supportive in trying to find a living kidney donor for me. She says and does all the right things for me, but sometimes I feel she's talking about me rather than to me. I've become more of a cause than a person to her. I assume that will change once they find a donor and I have my operation, but who knows?"

"If the operation were behind you, what would you like to do with your future?"

"Well, I know I'd have to plan on taking serious medications for the rest of my life to avoid rejection, and I'd probably need to find a second donor in fifteen or twenty years, because transplants don't last forever; but having said that, I'd like to become a stand-up comedian."

"Do you consider yourself funny?"

"I certainly see all the gyrations I've been going through as funny in a sick kind of way. I also think it's funny that you're interviewing me in disguise, Arthur Blake. I have your picture on my wall because I collect photos of all members of the family, past and present."

"You caught me, Nancy. I wanted to meet you and get to know you without having to tell you I was once married to your mother. I thought we'd react to each other differently if I started with the relationship."

"You're supposed to be a great investigator from everything I've read online, but you blew your cover because you underestimated your interviewee."

"Yes, I did, and now I know you're comical, because you use funny words like 'interviewee.'"

"I'll get even with you, Pastor Arthur Blake. It's my turn to interview you."

"Go to it."

"When you preach a sermon, do you feel everyone will understand your message?"

"Paraphrasing Paul in the Bible, he said that he wanted to be all things to all men, that he might save some. I'm like a comedian. I usually start with a joke to try to get the congregation tuned in to me. Then I make eye contact with as many folks as possible to let them know that I expect them to listen. I've even been known to continue talking while I approach someone I see sleeping, and then speak very loudly next to him or her."

"I get it. You preach a serious message, but you have fun doing it."

"Now tell me how you're going to handle being a comedian talking about the funny side of all your health procedures."

"Bingo! I'll preach a serious message, but I'll have fun doing it."

"It's been great meeting you, Nancy."

"Don't rush off without giving me a hug, Arthur. I need all the loving I can get."

CHAPTER 61 – HOMEWARD BOUND

Emily Everett and the others in her group had settled in the Orlando, Florida area to be near the Cape Canaveral space launch complex. Nancy Tillingham was being treated at the Orlando Regional Medical Center because she and her mother still lived in the same house that Cindy had lived in with Arthur when he was a NASA Engineer at Cape Canaveral. Accordingly, Arthur called Irma and arranged to fly home on her flight following their separate field trips. Once on the aircraft, they relaxed until they had reached cruising altitude. Then they compared notes on their missions and interviews.

Arthur spoke first because he hadn't told Irma in advance about his visit to the Orlando Regional Medical Center. "I expect you feel I was being mysterious when I didn't tell you where I would be while you were with the FBI people."

"Nope, I know you too well. I expected you to be in or near Orlando. You visited your ex-wife Cindy, went to see Dr. Rockman about your kidney compatibility tests, or visited Nancy Tillingham. How did I do with those guesses?"

"You were correct with two out of three of them. In baseball that would be a .667 batting average. Very good. I met with Dr. Rockman, and then I spent some time with Nancy. I introduced myself as an interviewer for the medical center, but Nancy saw through my disguise right away. She said she had my photo on her wall at home from the time when I was married to Cindy."

"She sounds like a bright girl."

"She is, and despite all of her medical problems she wants to become a comedian when she gets well. She has a positive outlook."

"That sounds as though she impressed you."

"Speaking of that, how did Emily Fiona Everett impress you? Is she a criminal or an eccentric?"

"Some might consider her eccentric, but I see her as someone with great wealth who wants to do something no one else has done in the past. She and her friends want to go to Mars. They're UFO believers who want to make a return visit to someone else's planet or at least the moon or Mars."

"I spent my years with NASA working toward sending people to the moon and beyond, so Emily and I would probably get along well together."

"You undoubtedly would."

"How did she explain coming to the U.S. as Lynn Holmes?"

"She said it was their very expensive joke. They played *Invasion of the Body Snatchers* complete with giving all those replaced people annuities for life. She also said that Albert Rivers, who died in that sewer tunnel, was a con man who took each person in her group for a million dollars, promising a trip to Mars twenty years ago. That's where all the laundered money came from, a total of twelve million dollars in cash."

"We have a large portion of that money to track, and we have the four murders in the bank tunnel and vault to solve, but I wonder if the FBI will give this case lower priority now that they know Emily Everett and her friends aren't terrorists."

Irma took out her pocket notebook and wrote a brief version of his question. "I think the answer is that the FBI will keep working hard on all aspects of our puzzle. They're going to want to check Emily's story. Then they'll get the names and addresses of the rest of her group and examine their activities over the last twenty years. However, the main reasons they'll keep the effort going are that they're charged with looking into bank fraud, plus the fact that Ted Higgins who died in the tunnel was an undercover FBI agent and a former love interest for Ruth Daltry."

"You're right. They lost one of their own and won't rest until they catch his murderer."

Irma put her hand on Arthur's arm. "Just to show that you missed a valuable interview, we have a strong candidate to be that murderer."

"Who?"

"Stanley Wilcox – it turns out that he worked for North Corner Savings Bank as the head of their travel agency, and he may have had another title as well. He flew to Nassau to work with the document counterfeiter on matching original photographs and descriptive details to the travelers' new identities. Then he returned to the United States as himself."

"How do we locate him after twenty years?"

"Why do you think it will be difficult?"

"If he murdered those people, he would have obtained new identity documents for himself along

Impasse

with the sets he generated for the folks from England."

CHAPTER 62 – JAY REDSHAW

When Arthur and Irma opened the front door of their house, they heard the telephone ringing. Irma answered and heard Jay Redshaw's excited voice."

"Hi, I've been calling from time to time for the last two days, hoping that you and Arthur would be back from your field trips. I hope you're both back. Anyway, I've made some progress on our case while you were away, and I'd like to share it with you and Chief Andrews. I'd like to do a presentation at the Parkville Police Department at ten o'clock tomorrow morning. Do you think you can fit it into your schedule?"

"Well, hello to you too, Jay. I guess I'm guilty of having thought of you as an assistant, rather than an independent investigator. We'll definitely make it to your show and tell session. I won't press you for any advance revelations, but I wonder whether your findings should be shared with Ruth Daltry of the FBI. I'll leave it up to you to decide whether she should be there."

"That's a great idea. I'm now going up the chain of command, giving my results to you and then depending on you to share it with the FBI."

"Fair enough. We'll do it the traditional way. I'll make all the arrangements, and we'll see you in Parkville tomorrow morning. I'm looking forward to learning about your research procedures as well as your results."

Impasse

After hanging up the phone, Irma found Arthur in the kitchen. "I thought you'd be getting your coffee. We have an appointment tomorrow morning at ten o'clock at the Parkville Police Department. Jay Redshaw made some progress on our case while we were away, and he wants to do a presentation there."

"This isn't the first time that one of our young associates came up with a key to solving a case."

"I won't prejudge the value of his findings, but he's excited by them."

"Good. I'll look forward to that meeting. In the meantime, I'm going to find myself a quiet corner and try to think of a way to find Stanley Wilcox after twenty years of his living under an unknown assumed identity."

CHAPTER 63 – PRESENTATION

They gathered at ten o'clock the next morning in the Records and Data room of the Parkville Police Department. Jay had set up a refreshments table with pastries and both hot and cold drinks. Chief Bobby Andrews attended, accompanied by a friend from the Chicago Police Academy who would evaluate Jay's investigative results and presentation skills on an unofficial basis. Ruth Daltry took a seat in the back to avoid making the young speaker nervous because of having an FBI Special Agent present. Arthur and Irma took the opposite approach and sat in the front row so that Jay could focus on friendly faces. Several Parkville police officers were also present to gain on-the-job training credits.

As Jay was preparing to begin, Arthur nudged Irma. "I'm surprised Sarah Jackson didn't come down from the State Police Lab. They've been working together on some aspects of the case. It must have been too long a trip to fit into her schedule."

"Look out the window. She's getting out of her car, along with two other people from the Rockford Lab."

Once Sarah and her associates came inside and sat down, Jay began his presentation.

"Thank you all for coming. For anyone who doesn't know me, I'm Jay Redshaw, and I'm currently working part time for Chief Andrews in this Records and Data facility and part time for Dr. Irma Blake on private investigation research. I have a few new findings to share."

Irma stood and turned to face the audience. "To give you background, our case involves a defunct bank in a northwest section of Chicago. I asked Jay, with the assistance of Sarah Jackson from the Rockford State Police Lab, to use DNA comparisons to identify two bodies found in a sewer tunnel leading toward the bank vault. I later asked him to check further on two bodies found in a locked compartment in that bank's vault. Those bodies had been identified by the FBI, but we needed more information about those individuals. Please continue, Jay."

"Thanks, Dr. Blake. The two men who died in that sewer pipe tunnel were Albert Rivers, who served time in a Massachusetts prison for fraud, and Ted Higgins, an FBI undercover agent operating as Marco Locante. In order to learn more about Albert Rivers, we had the computer in this room modified and qualified to gain access to Massachusetts online prisoner and administration files. That is why we're meeting here today. The two people whose bodies were jammed into what we've called the crypt compartment of that bank's vault were identified by the FBI as Mary Lowry, an accountant, and Kenneth Shea, a Vietnam War veteran. Mary Lowry's name sounded familiar to me. I decided that I had seen it while doing an online check on Albert Rivers time served in Massachusetts. I rechecked that database and discovered that Mary Lowry was listed as next of kin for Albert Rivers. She was his sister."

Arthur flashed a thumbs-up approval sign at Jay. "If Mary was Albert's sister and she was an accountant, she probably worked at the bank where we discovered her body."

Jay agreed. "I came to that same conclusion, and then Sarah suggested that if Mary had a connection with Albert Rivers, Kenneth Shea, the other person found in that vault crypt might have been linked to Rivers also. I did some more searching of the Massachusetts files and discovered that Kenneth Shea worked as an assistant to the warden in the prison where Albert Rivers was confined. His personnel file was off-limits to remote browsing by someone like me, but his resume showing his education and job qualifications was accessible. Kenneth Shea took online courses in physics, astrophysics, aeronautical engineering, and astronomy during the period when Albert Rivers was in the prison where Shea worked."

Chief Bobby Andrews said, "I know only a little about this case, so please tell me whether the courses Shea took are significant."

Ruth Daltry stood in the back row. "I'll address that question if you don't mind, Jay."

Jay nodded his affirmation and sat down. The group turned in their seats to face Ruth.

"Albert Rivers was in prison for fraud. He was a confidence man. After he got out of prison, he swindled a group of wealthy people in England by promising to connect them with an American inventor who had developed a spaceship that would be taking passengers to Mars. To convince those people to invest money in the venture, Rivers needed a scientist and inventor. Jay's discovery of that online course work suggests that Kenneth Shea played that part. He was the great innovator that Rivers paraded before the likely investors."

Jay responded. "Thanks for finding my results convincing. I'll add one more piece to the analysis. If we question coincidences, it's significant that Kenneth Shea quit his job approximately one month after Albert Rivers was released from prison. They had an arrangement to work together."

Arthur stood and faced the audience. "The creative aspect of a gathering like this is that we feed off each other's thoughts and conclusions. If we accept Jay's findings and Ruth's comments, we can take the next step and reach a conclusion about motive. The person who killed Albert Rivers and Marco Locante in that sewer pipe tunnel plus Mary Lowry and Kenneth Shea in the vault crypt was trying to eliminate anyone connected to the swindle of those British investors who thought they were buying passages on a journey to Mars."

Irma said, "More than one murderer might have been involved, Arthur."

"I don't think so. Why eliminate everyone who can connect you to a crime, only to involve another individual who would be a witness to the murders you've committed?"

Ruth Daltry stood and faced Jay. "This has been a valuable meeting. Thanks to you all, especially Jay. The perspective of the murderer being the one remaining individual involved in the journey to Mars swindle will guide the FBI efforts toward finding and apprehending Stanley Wilcox, the manager of the travel service at North Corner Savings Bank."

Ruth placed her notebook in her briefcase and left. As she did so, Arthur stage-whispered to Irma, "All they have to do is find him after twenty years of living under a different identity."

CHAPTER 64 – CINDY

Cindy Tillingham needed to do something to give her daughter a future. She was certain that Arthur Blake wouldn't give up a kidney for someone who wasn't his daughter and was the product of a dalliance by his cheating wife. She had screwed up her life in so many ways. Her loneliness during Arthur's long work sessions with NASA had led her toward stability with Tom Tillingham. She had undermined that second marriage in one drunken orgy with a stranger who had planted the seed that grew into her daughter. Now she faced a lonely future with the responsibility of caring for a daughter who might not live long or might survive with limited health and hope. She had tried praying, but it either hadn't worked, or she wasn't good enough at it.

It was time to do something.

Cindy went into her garage carrying her tablet computer. She put it on the front seat of her car. Then she removed the hose from the shop vacuum cleaner and used duct tape to connect one end to her car's exhaust pipe. She put the other end of the hose through the open rear side window and raised the pane of glass to hold it there. Then she added more tape to block the opening above the glass.

Cindy sat in the driver's seat without doing anything for about five minutes. Then she prayed that her final act would win her some points with God. She sent an email to Dr. Louis Rockman:

Richard Davidson

URGENT! ASAP look for me in my garage.

Give my remaining kidney to Nancy and harvest my other organs for others.

Tell her I love her and I want her to make the most of her life.

Thank you for kind words and Nancy's transplant.

I feel better already.

Cindy laid the tablet on the car seat and started the engine. She wondered how long it would take.

CHAPTER 65 – MEMORIAL SERVICE

Following the harvesting of her organs, Cindy's body had been cremated. Her ashes were stored for a memorial service to occur after Nancy recovered enough to attend following her transplant operation.

At the memorial service, the minister preached a sermon bemoaning and condemning the act of suicide to end a life, while at the same time honoring Cindy's decision as one full of love. It was a verbal tightrope act that simultaneously confused and soothed those in attendance. Arthur Blake gave thanks that someone else was presiding over this service.

As Cindy's first husband, Arthur sat in a front pew, reserved for family members. Irma sat with him, but he wondered how she was reacting to that arrangement. Tom Tillingham, husband number two, was absent, as was any message of sympathy from him. Apparently, Tom had closed the book on the *Cindy* chapter of his life and moved onward.

Nancy, not yet completely recovered, sat next to a nurse who had become her friend during all the time she had spent at the medical center. Nancy showed little emotion during the service, but wiped her eyes when it concluded. The minister called on her to say a few words about her mother. When she spoke, the congregation became completely silent, wanting to hear every word, but many broke into tears when Nancy described her awe at living with a portion of her mother inside her body. Many had trouble remembering that Nancy was only fifteen years old. Her bearing and delivery as she addressed the congregation showed unusual maturity due to the many hardships she had faced during her health ordeal and the loss of her mother. There wasn't a dry eye in the congregation when Nancy made a final pledge to her mother's spirit to live a life that would be worthy of that final organ gift.

Following the service, the minister carried the container of ashes to the memorial garden behind the church, with Nancy and most of the people following him. Once there, he said a final prayer and scattered about half of Cindy's ashes. Nancy had decided that she would keep the other half of the ashes as a symbol of her shared existence with her mother through the transplant.

After most of the other people left, Arthur and Irma approached Nancy for a private conversation.

Arthur rested his hand on her shoulder. "I don't know how much thought you've given to your future, but we'd like to be part of it. How would you like to live with us?"

"For how long?"

Irma said, "Let's rephrase that. We'd like to adopt you, Nancy. If you could find room in your life for us, we'd like you to be part of our family."

"You're not saying this just because Mom's memorial service made us all shed a few tears?"

"Arthur and I started to discuss your future right after your mother died. Even if you don't want us to be your adoptive parents, we'd like you to live with us until you become an adult. We wouldn't want you to face the anguish of being placed with strangers by a state agency."

"I might turn out to be difficult to live with. Would you kick me out if I have problems settling in with you?"

Arthur laughed. "An adoption isn't a marriage, but it's still for better or for worse. We'd be taking chances on both sides. You might not like Irma's autopsy laboratory in the basement."

"I'm sure I could put together a comedy routine about that one. Irma, did Arthur tell you I want to be a comedian?"

"He did. If you've written any routines, I'd like to hear them."

"That sounds like a deal. I'll be your daughter, and you'll be my test audience."

"Great! You get another bonus, a golden retriever named Rex."

"I always wanted to have a dog, but Mom was allergic, and then I got sick. I'd like one other bonus. Could I change my name to Blake instead of Tillingham? Then I could sit in the front of the class instead of the back."

Arthur asked, "Do they still alphabetize classrooms? Blake it shall be. Would my new daughter like to give me a hug to seal the deal? Better yet, let's make it a group hug including all three of us."

CHAPTER 66 – MISSING PERSON

Three weeks after Jay's presentation, Arthur called Ruth Daltry.

"Hi, Ruth; Arthur Blake checking in to find out whether the FBI has any good leads for locating Stanley Wilcox, our person of interest in those old bank killings."

"We don't have anything yet, despite having tried many of our usual techniques for locating a missing person. He apparently changed his identity immediately after returning from his cruise to Nassau twenty years ago. No income tax or Social Security taxes have been paid since that time for the original Stanley Wilcox identity."

"Can you simplify your search by looking for new Social Security and IRS accounts that opened at the time that the Stanley Wilcox accounts went inactive?"

"Large numbers of accounts open and close all the time. He may have become a person who was about to die, so that he could take on the continuation of a real person's accounts."

"That last statement includes the possibility of his having killed an additional person in order to take his place."

"That it does. This guy covered his tracks well, but we'll find him eventually."

"Did your undercover associate, Ted Higgins, leave any records of his investigations prior to his death in that sewer tunnel?"

"We haven't discovered where he was living, and as you know, that was a long time ago. If he was renting space, his landlord would have cleared it out within the first year of Ted's disappearance and found a new tenant. You're asking many of the questions that we've asked ourselves, Arthur. Keep asking, though. Maybe you'll come up with an angle that we missed."

"What about searching your National Crime Information Center databases?"

"NCIC has huge amounts of data, but to trace an individual through it, you need at least one reference point. We don't have his current name, Social Security number, date of birth, or anything else. We found no current vital statistics. This guy knew what he was doing to disappear."

"I have no more questions or suggestions, Ruth. Your FBI people have covered all of the normal approaches. If I come up with something abnormal that might work, I'll let you know."

CHAPTER 67 – SETTLING IN

Nancy's first impression of her new home as a Blake was pure awe. The century old but recently renovated Queen Anne house was spacious, having three floors above ground plus a basement. As Irma led Nancy from the long porch through the front door, Nancy's eyes focused on the elevator next to the staircase. Its walls consisted of ornate brass scrollwork which was different on each side.

Irma saw Nancy's concentration. "That elevator will make life here much easier for you while you're still recuperating from your transplant operation. You may choose a bedroom on either the second or third floor without having to worry about long flights of stairs. Later, when you're strong enough to use the stairs you may prefer a second floor bedroom."

"Why do you have that beautiful cage? It's a big surprise when you first see it."

"We bought this house from a woman who was in her nineties, Midge Drinkwater. Her deceased husband, a banker, had installed the elevator so that she would have access to all parts of the house without much effort. He selected that design to match the age and style of the building. After we bought the house, Midge stayed on as a tenant for a while."

"I hope she didn't die here and leave her ghost behind."

Impasse

"No, Midge was still quite lively when she moved out, and we're not haunted in any way that I've discovered. Rex would chase any ghosts away if they did show up."

"Rex is a beautiful dog, Irma. Would you mind if he slept in my room to keep me company. We never had a dog. Mom claimed she was allergic, but I think that was her excuse for not wanting any pets around the house."

"Rex has the run of the house, so if he chooses to be your roommate, that's fine. If you're smart, you'll select a bedroom with a large bed, because Rex may want to jump in with you."

"Wow; that would be great. I've never slept with a dog before. If he likes me, I'll take over his grooming. Would that be OK?"

"Keeping Rex groomed is a big job. He sheds on a continuous basis. If you feel up to that challenge, I'll gladly give you the grooming job."

"Speaking of jobs, I hear that you and Arthur investigate mysteries. Would I be able to get involved in that work?"

"Let's take one step at a time, Nancy. First, you'll have to complete your rehabilitation, following your doctor's orders. Then, we'll get you registered in our local school so that you'll catch up with studying you missed due to medical treatments and meet some new friends. After that, I'm sure you'll be questioning us about our current cases on a regular basis. Just remember, mystery lover; you're Nancy Blake, not Nancy Drew."

"Thanks for reminding me, Irma. I like to hear people call me by my new last name. Speaking of names, I may call you and Arthur by your names for a while before Mom and Dad feel comfortable to me. Will that be alright with you?"

"Call us whatever feels more natural to you. Names don't build relationships; love does."

CHAPTER 68 – STANLEY WILCOX

After receiving an email request for an urgent meeting, Arthur and Irma Blake arrived at Ruth Daltry's FBI office twenty minutes before the appointed time. Arthur used the extra time to locate Agent Bob Marcus.

Arthur knocked on the cubicle wall. "Hi, Bob; I assume you're going to be involved in Ruth's urgent meeting. Can you tell me what it's going to be about?"

"At this point it's hush-hush, but I'll tell you that it will be intense enough for you to need more than one cup of coffee."

"That must mean that your people found something significant."

"No more hints. You'll have to be patient."

Ruth started the meeting promptly at ten o'clock. Five people were in the conference room: Ruth Daltry, Linda Higgins, and Bob Marcus for the FBI plus Irma and Arthur Blake. In her opening comments, Ruth stated that Paul Garcia of the Drug Enforcement Administration would no longer be part of their investigative team.

She continued. "We've taken this case through several twists and turns to the point where we concluded that the twelve unconventional immigrants from the United Kingdom did not pose a terrorism threat. By process of elimination plus feedback from those Brits, we concluded that

Stanley Wilcox was either the killer of the people in the bank tunnel and vault, or he was a significant person of interest in those crimes."

Arthur said, "We agree with those statements, but I notice that you've worded them carefully. Are you about to tell us those conclusions are wrong?"

"Not exactly, Arthur, but you'll have to be patient. Bob Marcus will describe the problem we're facing."

Bob turned over the cover sheet on his flip chart pad to reveal a wide angle photograph of the warehouse area where FBI staff had been searching the so-called catacomb contents from the Suburban Vista Nursing Home. "As you can see from this image, we had a tremendous assortment of documents and artifacts gathering dust in that nursing home catacomb from just after the time when the bank murders were committed. Our initial goals were to find out about money laundering and those people who were patients at that nursing home and then took cruises arranged through the North Corner Bank Travel Agency. Once we had that information, we could have quit, but our staff members are trained to be as thorough as possible, so they continued to search the contents of the catacomb. Although they have not completed their assignment, they discovered additional information that affects our outlook for the remainder of the investigation."

Arthur put a ten dollar bill on the table in front of him. "I'll bet ten dollars that you're about to mention Stanley Wilcox."

"I won't take your bet, but what's the logic behind that statement?"

"It's not bizarre or magic, Bob. We learned from Emily Fiona Everett that Stanley Wilcox was the manager of the travel agency they worked with at North Corner Savings Bank. We also learned that he arranged for their identity change identification papers as they acted out *Invasion of the Body Snatchers*. Irma and I have assumed that Wilcox arranged a new identity for himself while he was getting counterfeit documents for the others. During the presentation by Jay Redshaw, we concluded that Stanley Wilcox was the one party to the Mars voyage scam who was still alive. Therefore, even though you are discussing old materials from the nursing home, you will now mention Stanley Wilcox."

Bob said, "I have two five dollar bills in my wallet. If you'll give me your ten, I'll replace it with the two fives and split the bet with you. You are half right. I am going to mention the name, Stanley Wilcox, but I am not going to mention the individual we are seeking who went by that name."

Irma laughed. "If you two boys will quit playing games, I'd like to learn what Bob and his associates discovered. Please get us back on track, Bob."

"Thanks, Irma. Arthur did have a good line of thinking, but we discovered he couldn't be completely correct. We knew that the original connection to the nursing home was that it was a vehicle for laundering some of the scam proceeds. They picked on that particular nursing home because Stanley Wilcox had once been a patient there when he was rehabbing after knee replacement surgery. We assumed that during the period when Wilcox was at the nursing home, he made friends with the management and talked them into making extra money by participating in his scheme."

"So, what did you discover to change that thinking?"

"What we discovered, Irma, was that Stanley Wilcox died in that nursing home during a second period of rehab there following shoulder surgery. He was working out on an exercise machine, and it electrocuted him due to a defect."

Linda Higgins added, "A very suspicious defect."

Bob said, "The data we found is incomplete, but it looks as though Stanley was in there following knee surgery two years prior to all of those cruises, and he was back in there following shoulder surgery the following year."

Ruth Daltry had sat silently during the last several exchanges, but she felt it was now time for her to join in. "You've now reached the *Aha!* moment. As I see it, Wilcox approached a person in nursing home management to see if he wanted to make extra cash through the money laundering scheme. That person, who may or may not have been one of the owners of the home, got greedy and decided he wanted to take over the whole scam. He arranged for the defect in Wilcox's machine, quietly disposed of the body, and took the place of Stanley Wilcox. My guess is that they would have been somewhat similar in appearance."

Arthur interrupted. "We have no picture of either one, but I'll go along with your speculation."

Ruth continued. "The replacement Wilcox had to get rid of his co-conspirators, who would know he was an impostor and who may have also served as officers of North Corner Savings Bank. He murdered Albert Rivers and the man he thought was Marco Locante in the tunnel by trapping them there and letting them die of asphyxiation. Then he killed Mary Lowry and Kenneth Shea and stuffed their bodies into the vault crypt. He probably fired any other bank employees by mail or telephone and hired new people to replace them. Then, he sold the bank to a larger organization that would not want to continue operations in the existing small building."

Bob Marcus turned to Arthur Blake. "So, you were correct in saying I would talk about Stanley Wilcox, but the criminal we're seeking is a different person from the original Stanley Wilcox."

Irma said, "Finding him is going to be close to impossible. We had thought we were looking for Wilcox, who may have been using a different identity for the last twenty years or so. Now, we're saying that the Stanley Wilcox whose name was on the bank sale papers was actually someone else. Where do we even start?"

After a pause of several seconds, Arthur said, "I may have a place to start."

They all looked at him.

"Emily Everett said that Stanley Wilcox was in charge of the travel agency at North Corner Savings Bank. Irma found a box of papers in the basement of that bank. We took them home, and my job was to look at the travel side of the operation as reflected in those papers. My pile included a couple of hundred travel brochures of several types. Those brochures were printed on glossy paper. If either or both of the individuals claiming the name of Stanley Wilcox handled those brochures, even twenty or more years ago, we may have latent fingerprints that the FBI Laboratory could enhance, record, and identify."

CHAPTER 69 – PLAN B

The FBI Laboratory people picked up the travel brochures and other documents from the Blakes' home, being careful to avoid deteriorating any prints that might have survived twenty or more years in a rubble-sealed basement plus more recent handling by Arthur and Irma. The technicians also took impressions of the Blakes' fingerprints so that they could be eliminated from any array of prints collected from the documents.

Once the technicians had left, Arthur, Irma, and Nancy ate their lunch and, due to Nancy's prodding, discussed the investigation.

Nancy said, "It's hard to believe that you're trying to solve murders that happened roughly twenty years ago. I haven't been alive that long."

Irma smiled at her newly adopted daughter. "Twenty years isn't long at all for such a forensic effort. Scientists are still debating whether French Emperor Napoleon Bonaparte's death in 1821 was caused by arsenic poisoning."

"How do they hope to find out?"

"One group analyzed hairs removed from Napoleon's head after death and found that he had arsenic levels seven to thirty-eight times higher than normal and concluded that he must have been murdered using poison."

"That sounds convincing."

"Another group disputed that finding, because they analyzed hairs taken in 1805, 1814, and 1821 while Napoleon was still alive and found that all three sets of hairs also had very high levels of arsenic. They said that if arsenic killed him, Napoleon would have been dead in each of those years when he was still alive."

"Those results are weird."

"If you think that's weird, there's another group that thinks that the British stole Napoleon's body and replaced it with someone else's corpse. They want to have him dug up and tested with DNA sampling to see if the body matches his hair samples, but the French government said that the body will not be disturbed. The whole point is that crimes can still be successfully investigated long after they occur. That's one of the reasons why, in U.S. law, there's no statute of limitations for murder. There have been many cases where evidence shows up long after the killing."

"Are you going to let me watch you do an autopsy someday?"

"Probably, but you'll have to think long and hard about your attitude toward death first."

"That's an easy assignment. I thought about it every day when I expected that I'd never get a kidney transplant in time to save my life. I'm definitely a realist about death. I haven't seen many dead people, but I was around the hospital several times when people died and the staff discretely spirited them away from their fellow patients."

Arthur entered the discussion. "I like your use of the term 'spirited them away.' It fits with the Christian belief that the spirit or soul continues to function after the body dies. I haven't asked before,

Nancy, but how active have you been in church attendance?"

"I'll be a challenge for you, Arthur. Once you were out of the picture, Mom stopped going to church. At times I wanted to go with my friends, but Mom somehow thought she was getting back at you by keeping me away from religion. She knew you had moved into the ministry. I'll be open to catching up with my lack of religious background, but that's just one obstacle I'll face in starting over with you."

Irma and Arthur discussed Nancy's comments after their new daughter walked Rex outside for the last time and then took him along when she rode the elevator up to bed.

Arthur said, "She's very bright and curious. It may be a challenge for us, but we're going to have to start thinking like parents."

"What's the difference between the way a parent thinks and the way we thought before Nancy came into our lives?"

"We should ask her to think about what she wants to study and what she wants to do for a career."

"Arthur, you already told me that she wants to be a stand-up comedian, based on your conversation in the hospital."

"That's a whim, not a serious long-term career consideration."

"Congratulations!"

"Why are you congratulating me, Irma?"

"You've achieved your goal. You're thinking like a conventional parent who wants his child to do something he can brag about."

"I did sound like that, didn't I?"

"Yessir. You and I both know that we'll expose Nancy to many of the things we do, including autopsies and religion; she'll learn about common careers in school; and then she'll get some ideas of her own, including comedy. All we have to do is be there for her, in the sense of supporting whatever she wants to do. Her career will be her choice, not ours. That's what I feel thinking like a parent is, or at least ought to be."

"Wow. I do like your parenting course. I'll probably turn out to be an overly-protective parent. Please be my compass and keep me from looking stupid as we try to guide Nancy. As you probably guessed from all the stalling I did every time we discussed adopting since our wedding, I thought I would never have a child, and I wasn't sure I could handle parenting."

"Well, you now are an official parent, Arthur, and I know you'll be a good one, so don't sweat it. All it takes is love and tackling problems one at a time."

"That and commitment. You can put me down for being the second kidney donor for Nancy many years in the future when she needs a replacement, assuming I pass the final matching tests."

"I thought you'd eventually come to that decision. Let's not discuss it with Nancy just yet. Her first transplant is barely behind her, and she might be bothered that you didn't reach your decision in time to keep her mother from committing suicide. You can announce your willingness to give up a kidney in fifteen to thirty years, when she'll need that next transplant. Let's take things one step at a time."

"Speaking of a step-by-step approach to problem-solving, shouldn't we consider our next step in the bank murders investigation? The FBI Laboratory will look for old latent fingerprints to identify. While they're doing that, we should develop an alternate approach to finding the killer in case fingerprint evidence isn't retrievable. The FBI Lab is pursuing the Plan A approach. We need to generate a Plan B that has some chance of success."

"How about using our time machine to go back to Nassau twenty years ago? We could interview the person who created the false identification documents."

"I know you have some fancy gear in your basement laboratory, but I didn't know you had a time machine."

"That was a slight exaggeration, but the approach might have some merit. I'm sure you'll be able to come up with something to serve the same function as a time machine."

"This wouldn't have anything to do with your wanting to go back to Nassau, would it?"

"That's a great suggestion, Arthur, but you can do any traveling that might be required. I'm committed to getting Nancy settled here."

"I hate to admit it, but your idea of going back in time has some merit. We can't physically do it,

Richard Davidson

but we might be able to refresh some memories. I'm going to work on a way to do that."

CHAPTER 70 – IMPLEMENTATION

Erik Holmes finished his phone conversation and walked into the kitchen. "Guess what, Mom? I'm going to finally act like the Sherlock version of my name."

"I didn't know Sherlock's middle name was Erik."

"That's very funny. You must be in a good mood."

"I'm in a good mood when you are. So, what did Arthur Blake say to you?"

"I didn't say I was talking with Blake. How did you know?"

"You're not the only Holmes in this family. If you're going to play Sherlock, you had to be talking with someone who could authorize that. How many people doing detective work do you know? Just one and his name is Arthur Blake."

"His wife Irma works with him on investigations, but you're basically correct."

"How much is he going to pay you? You've never done anything for free."

"He's giving me a base amount, and then we'll negotiate my final pay, based on what I find out."

"That's fair enough. What are you supposed to do?"

"I'm going to start by interviewing you. I told him you have a very good memory, and he said that would be important."

"Start interviewing, Erik. I'll help if I can."

"Arthur wants to learn more about the guy that generated the identification documents when you became Emily Everett and she became you."

"That was a long time ago. I'll try to pull up memories. What do you want to know?"

"Emily Everett says she remembers the identification papers guy as something like Murray or Murphy. Do you know what his name was?"

"He didn't use his real name because counterfeiting money or documents is illegal, but he called himself Mercury when he worked with clients."

"Why Mercury?"

"He called himself that because it described how quickly he could disappear when the cops came to check up on him."

"Mom, you have a great memory. I can hear the jingle of the cash register as my pay increases with useful results."

"Go ahead and jingle. Mercury wasn't his real name. I have no idea what it was."

"That won't matter if people know him as Mercury. Do you know if he's still alive and in the papers business?"

"I saw him from a distance when I was down by the docks last year. He's older and slower. He doesn't move like Mercury anymore."

"I'll check with people down there who might know of him. I'll also pretend I need a new identity. I'll try to contact the younger people who are in that business now."

"I wouldn't recommend that Erik. Some of those counterfeiters are tough customers. I also wouldn't give up on the possibility that Mercury is still doing his thing in competition with the young guys. I'll say this for him; the one time I met him, he acted like a gentleman."

"I'm surprised you think he might still be a paper merchant more than twenty years after he worked with you. I figured he'd be too old to copy logos and seals."

"Thanks, Erik. First of all, they do most of that work using a computer now. Second, he's not ancient; he's my age."

CHAPTER 71 – THE DOCKS

Erik Holmes picked the early afternoon for his first foray into the dock neighborhoods. He wore a flowered shirt and shorts to look like a tourist. Large crowds of cruise passengers meandered past the rows of tour vendor stalls near the Cruise Terminal and on Prince George Wharf. Most of the booths sold locally crafted souvenirs augmented by mass-produced trinkets from China. Here and there, local people sat or stood in the paths of the tourists looking to strike up a conversation and suggest the purchase of more exciting but less conventional goods and services. Erik casually studied a middle-aged woman who might have been informally operating on the wharf for many years. As he neared her, she left her seat and approached him.

"You look like a man who likes to party. I know where there are nice local girls."

Erik kept a serious expression on his face. "I am looking for services, but not that kind. I have a slight problem with my travel documents that I need corrected. I heard that such services are available here. Someone told me to ask for a man named Mercury."

"I haven't heard anyone ask for him in a long time. Are you some kind of cop? Wait – I know you. You work at the veterinarian's. I take my cat there – she's a beat up old gray thing. You gave her a shot last time I went there."

Impasse

Erik wasn't happy that his tourist disguise had been penetrated, but he responded as the cool guy he thought himself to be. "I remember now. You're Mrs. Ginty. You thought your cat was on her way out, but I told you I thought she was good for another three years."

She squinted at him as though she was examining him in fine detail. "Now tell me why you're looking for Mercury."

"He once did a favor for my Mom, and now I want to see if he'll do one for me." It wasn't quite the truth, but it was close enough to be believable.

Mrs. Ginty took a step backward and relaxed her expression. "If I tell you where to find Mercury, will you forget you saw me here and what my job is?"

"Forget what job? I'm sorry, but I don't know your name."

"That's good enough for me. Mercury works at the shell jewelry shop near the far end of the row of vendors on Prince George Wharf. He does his private business in the back room there. One more thing."

"What?"

"The next time you disguise yourself as a tourist, lose your Temple Christian High School class ring."

CHAPTER 72 – MERCURY

The sign on the store said *Seashells She Sells*, but when Erik entered he saw two men behind counters displaying jewelry made from seashells. The *she* person was nowhere to be seen. He approached the older of the two men.

"Do you call yourself Mercury?"

"Who wants to know?"

"My name's Erik Holmes. About twenty years ago, you did some identity papers for my mother, Lynn Holmes."

"That was a long time ago."

"Do you remember what you did back then, or do you have records with details?"

Mercury relaxed back against the wall. "I might, for a price."

"I'm just a poor Nassau kid. I can't give you much."

Mercury chuckled and high-fived Erik. "Well played. I started out as a poor Nassau kid too, but I soon learned that there are others with money who pay Nassau kids to get or manipulate information for them. Who are you working for?"

Erik did his best to minimize his pause for thinking before he answered. "I'm doing a favor for a preacher in the States. He's helping a parishioner straighten out the details of her family tree."

"That might be a true answer, and it might not. Tell me the information you want, and then I'll tell you whether I might have it and how much it will cost."

"My mother, Lynn Holmes was one of a group of twelve or thirteen Americans who came here about twenty years ago to meet cruise ships they had been scheduled to travel on. You provided identity papers and exchanged photos for a matching set of people from somewhere else who became those Americans, while my mother and the others in her group remained here in Nassau using the names of counterparts in the foreign group. Does that ring a bell with you?"

"Indeed. That was my biggest single job ever. Information about that job would be very expensive. I keep my records because it is always better to sell something more than once than it is to get paid only a single time."

"Mercury, I don't need data on the whole group. I'm looking for the identity work you did for the thirteenth person, the one who arranged for you to process papers for the whole group. Surely, that little bit of information can't be that expensive."

"Don't try to con a con man, Erik. It won't work. Tell your sponsor that he'll have to pay ten thousand U.S. dollars for those little details."

Erik realized that he'd have to ask for a higher amount so that he could make something for his efforts too. "This guy's a preacher, he won't have huge sums of cash, and I need to hit him for something too. How about a special price for a Nassau kid? You're getting older. Someday, you may need a favor from me."

That got a laugh out of Mercury. "I like the way you look at life. I'm not as old as I look to you, and I intend to be functioning for quite a while yet. Even so, Little Brother, I'll give you credit for trying. I'll drop my price to ninety-five hundred, so that you can get five hundred bucks out of this."

Erik knew it was time to stop pushing. He told Mercury that he'd be back with his client's best offer. As he left the wharf, he waved to Mrs. Ginty, and she waved back.

CHAPTER 73 – ARTHUR AND RUTH

The FBI receptionist called Ruth Daltry to say she had Arthur Blake in the lobby asking to see her. Ruth checked her calendar to confirm that they hadn't set a meeting for today, but told the receptionist to have him escorted to her office. This was a subtle reminder to Arthur that she didn't care for unexpected callers. Blake had a contractor pass, which gave him some freedom of access at FBI Headquarters, but Ruth's request for an escort indicated that he shouldn't push frequent appearances on her doorstep.

When Arthur arrived at Ruth's office door, she waved him to a chair, but held up a finger to indicate she needed to make a call first. He waited while she called Bob Marcus and asked for a status update. Then she stood to greet Arthur.

"Hello, Arthur; I assume you're here to learn whether we retrieved any fingerprints from the brochures and other old bank papers you gave us. Bob Marcus said the lab people are still working on a couple of experimental techniques, but they weren't successful using our normal methods. That may put our killer of Stanley Wilcox and the bank people beyond our reach, at least for a while."

"It's interesting that you've gone beyond thinking that the death of Wilcox was suspicious, and now attribute his death to the same person who killed the people in the tunnel and the bank vault."

"I took that leap of logic because it would be unnaturally convenient for Wilcox to have died accidentally just as the killer was looking to take over the bank scam operation."

"Fair enough, but I didn't come here to check on the fingerprint effort. I'm hoping that you'll authorize my spending of some FBI money, and I decided that a face-to-face meeting would be warranted for me to argue my case."

Ruth leaned back and drummed the fingers of her right hand on the desktop as she considered his request. "Arthur, you and Irma are consulting with us because of your successes on unusual cases and initially as a buffer to keep your Bishop Chandler from constantly complaining about delays in building his church. I don't feel it's appropriate to give you access to our budget for major expenditures."

Arthur stood. "That's fine, Ruth. If determining the killer's identity isn't important enough to spend some money, I'll be patient and wait until we figure it out by conventional procedures." He took a step toward the door.

"Hold it, Arthur. You didn't say what you wanted the money for."

"You didn't ask."

"Touché. How much is it going to cost, and what will I get for it?"

"My man in Nassau ..."

Ruth interrupted. "You have a man in Nassau? Our nearest office is Barbados."

"My man has located the individual who prepared the counterfeit identity papers twenty years ago, and that person says he will give us names and details for the identity switches involving the bank travel agency for ten thousand dollars. One month of agents in the field and sitting around conference tables would cost you much more than that. Will you spend money to save time on this investigation?"

"I have all the names for Emily Fiona Everett's group. She gave them to us. We'd be paying to get the original name and the switched identity for the perpetrator of the scheme."

"And that individual is likely to be your killer."

Ruth hesitated. "Let's just say that my earlier comments applied to you and Irma as individuals. Since you function as an agency with representatives in various locations, we would be justified in purchasing services from you, as we would from any other company. I'll authorize you to spend ten thousand dollars for informant fees and investigation expenses."

"You'd better make that eleven thousand five hundred dollars, to include the recruiting fee and commission for my operative in Nassau."

"I'll do you better than that, Arthur. I'll make it fifteen thousand dollars, but I want you, not your agent, to question the identity counterfeiter."

CHAPTER 74 – NASSAU

Erik met Arthur as he got off his plane at Lynden Pindling International Airport and led him to the airport Starbucks for coffee plus a strategy discussion. As they walked, Arthur asked about the large number of smaller planes lining the taxiways.

"Are the smaller aircraft mostly charters and air taxis for island-hopping, or are they owned by individuals?"

"Some of each. We have a fair number of freight and passenger airlines serving all the islands. Generally, they use two-engine types. Most of the personal planes belonging to rich guys have only one engine. I'm not a pilot, but if I were, I'd want two engines. There's a lot of ocean between the Islands."

At Starbucks, Arthur ordered his coffee large, strong, and black while Erik opted for an iced coffee.

Erik asked, "Do you drink hot coffee during hot weather?"

"Oddly enough, I enjoy it in all kinds of weather, even when it comes without the caffeine. I want to thank you for tracking down Mercury. His records will get us past a big roadblock we've been facing, in trying to identify a murderer."

"You're saying that the guy who arranged for my mom to live here in paradise is a killer."

"Unless we learn something completely unexpected, it looks that way. He wouldn't have been dangerous to her or to eleven other people similarly resettled here, but so far, we think he killed at least four, and maybe five, people twenty years or so ago. Once we track him down, we'll check to see how much damage he's done more recently."

"I hope he's stayed away from our islands."

"He's probably somewhere where there are big money and power opportunities. Tell me about Mercury. What's his outlook, and how should I approach him?"

"He's a clever guy who's proud of having started out as a Nassau kid with ambitions. He had talents for art, and later, computers. Mercury considers himself a persuasive con man and a good salesman. He's tough, but he wants to appear gentle. That's one reason why he runs the *Seashells She Sells* Shop, even though he doesn't have a female partner. He and one other guy design and manufacture their seashell jewelry. Mercury has kept up his art skills even though, with computers, he doesn't have to do hand artwork anymore."

"Does he still create and manipulate identification documents?"

"I've heard that he does that work in the back room of his shop, but I don't know for sure."

Arthur finished his coffee. "Well, now that I've had my drink and your input, I think we're ready to visit Mercury. When we get there, introduce us and then take a walk outside. I won't want him to think we're ganging up on him.'

"One thing I have to tell you. Mercury backed off the ten thousand price and said he'd take ninety-five hundred dollars."

"That's good negotiating. That extra five hundred dollars is yours, along with an additional five hundred I planned to give you."

"Thanks, Arthur; I hoped you'd pass along the reduction, and the extra amount is a bonus. Let's see what we'll get for the money."

Thirty minutes later, after a brief stop at a bank, Erik and Arthur walked into the seashell jewelry shop and stood off to the side while Mercury completed a sale to a female tourist who appeared to be about fifty years old, but dressed as though she was fifteen years younger. Then they approached Mercury, Erik leading the way.

Mercury had altered his position so that he watched them while he completed his jewelry sale. "Hello again, Erik. Is this your client?"

Erik introduced them. "Mercury, meet Pastor Arthur Blake. Arthur, this is Mercury, who has only one name."

Mercury laughed. "I actually have a first name, a surname, and several baptismal names, but we won't bother with any of those today. I must admit to being surprised. When Erik said his customer was a preacher, I thought he was bullshitting me. Is it just a title, or do you really run a church?"

"I did have a United Methodist congregation, but now I'm mostly a consultant to our bishop when I do church work. I hear that you're very talented and have an excellent memory."

Erik took that statement to be his cue to leave the scene, so he edged his way out the open doorway. He would find Mrs. Ginty and chat with her during the negotiations.

Mercury signaled to the other salesman to take over, and he led Arthur through a door into the back room. There, a rather elaborate computer and printer setup plus a specialized drawing table dominated the small space.

"Welcome to my second business place, Pastor Blake. If you have current documentation needs, I'll be pleased to serve you. Otherwise, we can get right to your interest in events that happened some twenty years ago."

"Will you be working from memory, or do you have the details recorded?"

"The information I will be giving you is reliable. I document all my transactions, although I will not reveal the form of that recording. Do you have the payment I agreed to?"

Arthur retrieved a folded envelope from his shirt pocket. "This envelope contains a cashier's check from a local bank for ninety-five hundred U.S. dollars."

"How is it made out?"

"It's made out to CASH. I didn't think your official business affairs would use the name Mercury. You may endorse it any way you wish."

Mercury examined the check and nodded his agreement. "I understand that your primary interest is in the individual who purchased the modified identity documents for the twelve people who took the cruises and journeyed to the United

States plus the documents for the twelve Americans who were to remain in Nassau under exchanged identities."

"That's correct. I'll even guess that that individual's name may have been Stanley Wilcox."

"Your guess is incorrect. My client for these services was Gary Wilcox. In addition to the twelve sets of exchanged credentials, I updated his background to add an industrial design college degree. I also prepared for him a set that gave him the identity of his brother, Stanley Wilcox, and a second set that proved him to be Stephen George Ackerman."

"Who was the older brother?"

"Gary was older by one year, but they looked quite similar. At one point, I inadvertently switched their photographs, and Gary made me redo his Stanley credentials."

"Do you still have those pictures?"

"I can give you copies marked with the correct names on the backs, but they are twenty years old and may not be very helpful."

"They'll be of some value. Did Gary say why he wanted the industrial design degree status? How was he to work with?"

"Gary played his cards close to his vest. For every fact he gave me, I suspected that he was concealing two more. He was not the type I would ever consider accepting as a friend or even an ongoing business associate. He did everything that was required of him, but not one bit more."

"I'll need the addresses, social security numbers, and other information on his documents."

Mercury handed Arthur a large envelope. "Copies of his two sets of new credentials are in here, along with a copy of Gary's genuine documents that I used as a template and his updated version. I've also included copies of the credentials for the twelve people who remained in Nassau. They may have moved on or changed their names by now."

Arthur opened the envelope and studied its contents. "Your manufactured credentials look quite genuine. These copies contain more information than I expected to get. Thank you very much."

Mercury smiled. His two gold teeth reflected brightly. "I said before that Gary Wilcox was not the type of person I would accept for an ongoing business relationship. You, Pastor Blake, are easy to deal with. I am being complete in what I give you, because I hope that you will have the occasion to require my services again. If you need me, have your local Nassau boy, Erik, call on me. He also shows promise for the future."

Arthur shook hands with Mercury. "I agree that he does show promise. It has been a pleasure dealing with you."

CHAPTER 75 – NANCY

Irma paused as she passed by the elevator that hugged her staircase. She heard unusual sounds coming from somewhere upstairs. A scrollwork elevator shaft acts like an ear trumpet, channeling sound along its length, but allowing a little to spill out through each filigree opening. She climbed the staircase stealthily, listening to discern the source and nature of the sounds. When she reached the second floor, Irma realized she was hearing crying, coming from the third floor. At the third floor landing Irma saw that Nancy's bedroom door was partially open. Rex sat outside the door with his ears pivoted to hear the sounds coming from within.

She knocked on the door. "Nancy, are you alright? Is there anything I can do for you?"

Nancy left her bed and opened the door all the way. As she turned and walked back to her bed, she blotted her eyes with a tissue. "I'm just tied up in knots as I think about Mom killing herself so that I could have her one remaining kidney."

"She loved you very much."

"She loved me, but she also felt she had screwed up her own life. I was the blunder that came from her screw-up. I've had to realize, once we found out that I wasn't a biological Tillingham, that my whole life was a mistake my mom made at some drunken party. I shouldn't have been born in the first place. That hardly makes me feel great. I think that part of Mom's motive in committing suicide was to do something good for me to offset what she considered bad or stupid things in her past. She was helping me but also trying to bribe her way into heaven."

"But you appreciate her sacrifice, or you wouldn't be sitting here crying."

"Irma, I'm also crying because I want to call you Mother, but I can't, at least not yet."

"Give it time. I'm here for you, no matter how long it takes, and the name isn't important."

"It is to me. I need a fully functional family. You and Arthur are offering it to me, but I'm too mixed up to accept it."

"You love Rex, and he loves us all unconditionally. Learn to love like a dog. It will come."

"He is a good morale booster. Come here, Rex. You need to be scratched behind your ears."

Rex walked over to Nancy and sat with his head cocked at angle, waiting for her massaging fingers.

Irma said, "To be fair, I should tell you that Arthur and I have to learn how to be a family for you too. We've never had children, and sometimes feel as though we're not handling the process very well."

"You're doing great. I've never had so much attention. At times, I used to feel I was a piece of furniture at home, rather than one of the family members. I'd get an occasional 'Hello' and 'Goodbye', but not much else. One time I told Mom I was taking a train to New York City for the weekend, and she said, 'That's nice.'"

"You won't be doing much traveling here until you're fully recovered from your transplant operation, but after that, we'll take some trips together. We want to take you to Richmond, Illinois to meet Arthur's parents, your new grandparents. You're their only grandchild, and they're looking forward to your full recovery and visit. Speaking of traveling, you have less than a year to go before you're old enough for a driver's license. Once you're back to normal and in school, you'll have to register for a Driver's Education course."

"Don't think that hasn't crossed my mind. All the legal stuff hasn't been sorted out, but I'll probably inherit my mother's car. At that point, I'd like you to take me to a dealer so that I can trade it in on something different. I won't drive the car my mother died in."

"I agree with that viewpoint. You don't need any extra creepiness. You can do practice driving with me in my Mustang once you get your learner's permit."

CHAPTER 76 – FBI MEETING

At the start of the meeting in her conference room, Ruth announced, "Arthur and Irma Blake are with us today to show us how amateurs can sometimes get more information than our agents."

Bob Marcus said, "You probably expect us to object to that statement, but I've seen several instances where people were afraid of FBI agents but would talk with civilians. When Arthur walks in with his pastor title, most folks react to him as being non-threatening."

Linda Higgins indicated her agreement with a nod but didn't say anything.

Arthur's reaction was to stand, go to the dry erase whiteboard, and write: Stanley Wilcox. Then he turned to face the others. "We earlier pegged Stanley as our killer because we saw him as the mysterious thirteenth cruise traveler and, per Emily Everett's input, the manager of the North Corner Savings Bank Travel Agency. Then Bob Marcus found evidence that Stanley Wilcox had actually died at the Suburban Vista Nursing Home before he was supposed to have worked with the document counterfeiter in Nassau. That Nassau individual, who is known as Mercury, would not have talked with the FBI. No one could have said that he was withholding information if he simply said that he couldn't remember details of events that happened twenty years ago."

Richard Davidson

Ruth said, "I certainly couldn't, and I consider my memory to be good."

Arthur continued. "Mercury is artistically talented, a computer whiz, and a savvy businessman. He didn't rely on his memory. He kept detailed records, but I have no idea where they are or in what format. Mercury planned ahead, looking toward future opportunities to sell the transaction information to third parties like me. He's an opportunist, so it's likely that he would also consider blackmail if he found one of his former clients to be in a sensitive position. He appears to be a simple vendor of tourist items, but he is much more than that. Frankly, I like the man."

Bob Marcus smiled. "I'd give a lot to receive an endorsement like that."

Linda Higgins spoke for the first time. "I take your comments to indicate that you trust the information you received from him. What do you know now that you didn't know before?"

"I knew going into my meeting with Mercury that Bob earlier came up with the discovery that Stanley Wilcox died while a patient at Suburban Vista Nursing Home and that Ruth concluded that someone on the nursing home staff who resembled Stanley took his place. My conversations with Mercury revealed who that replacement person was." He walked over to the dry erase board and wrote: Gary Wilcox. "Gary was Stanley's one year older brother, and they could have passed for twins."

Linda said, "Gary murdered his own brother?"

Irma said, "That's taking sibling rivalry too far."

"Continuing, Gary showed up in Nassau, traveling under his own name and identification papers. He bought two sets of documents from Mercury. One identified him as his brother, Stanley Wilcox, and the other set proclaimed him to be Stephen George Ackerman. He also showed a touch of ego by adding extra academic background to his own resume. My guess is that he became Stanley until he disposed of his brother's business partners and sold the bank. Then he probably became Stephen George Ackerman and disappeared with all the profits."

Bob checked his notebook. "According to my records from the catacomb search, there is no record of a Gary Wilcox having worked at Suburban Vista Nursing Home. That may mean that Gary manipulated the files there to keep people from finding him and linking him to his deceased brother."

Ruth stood and faced Arthur. "You were correct. Your trip to Nassau was a worthwhile investment for us. Thank you. Now we know the original identity of our murderer. We should be able to find which name he is currently using by taking his three identities and finding the one with a currently active Social Security account."

CHAPTER 77 – ASSESSMENT

Bob Marcus knocked on Ruth Daltry's open door and waited for her to wave him into the office.

"What's up, Bob?"

"I have good and bad news for you."

"That sounds familiar. Give me the good news first."

"We contacted the Inspector General's office at Social Security, and they gave us the addresses that correspond to the Social Security numbers for the three identities we're searching: Gary Wilcox, Stanley Wilcox, and Stephen George Ackerman."

"That is good news. Now, what's the bad news?"

"The bad news is that all three of those Social Security accounts are active. Our suspect is either covering his tracks by having others deposit Social Security taxes for his unused names, or he is pretending to be three different people at the same time."

"That's more than slightly weird. Maybe he gets alerted if we contact one of his extra identities, as in an early warning system."

"We have the three addresses. We can do simultaneous raids."

"Hold off for a while. Put surveillance on each address for two or three months to check for activity, and get photographs of everyone at each location. We'll need to compile three evidence files and see what they have in common. We could be looking at immigration fraud or human trafficking.

Look closely for interactions among the three identities."

"I'll say one thing for this case, Ruth. It has its bizarre aspects."

"I see that too, but I'm determined to solve it, because I owe that to Ted Higgins."

"Undercover work is always dangerous. That's why I never volunteered for it. I want to work with the organization backing me up. I'm not cut out to be a lone wolf."

"Off the record, that difference in outlooks had a lot to do with why Ted and I split up."

"If it's alright with you, I'll run one of the surveillance teams. I'll assign Linda Higgins and Larry Savage to cover the other two identities."

"Are the locations of the three Social Security payers close to each other?"

"They're in three different states."

CHAPTER 78 – STEPHEN GEORGE ACKERMAN

According to Social Security records, Stephan George Ackerman lived on Shore Drive in Mukwonago, Wisconsin. When Larry Savage and his team of agents arrived at the indicated point alongside Lower Phantom Lake, they discovered that the address corresponded to a home that had burned. The remainder of the building had later been torn down as a safety hazard. Larry checked with the Mukwonago Police Department and found that the fire had occurred two years earlier. The police listed the cause of the fire as careless use of fireworks. They had no indication of a current address for Mr. Ackerman. Larry asked an agent to check for a forwarding address at the Post Office, and she returned with the information that Stephen George Ackerman had rarely received mail, and he hadn't filed a forwarding address when he moved following the fire. Additional local inquiries indicated that all the neighbors assumed Mr. Ackerman had been retired. Prior to the fire, he stayed home most days. He had been cheerful with neighbors, but he didn't mingle on a regular basis. They didn't remember seeing Ackerman later than the cleanup period following the fire. During that period he had been properly emotional about the loss of his home.

Larry wondered whether Ackerman had deliberately destroyed his home in order to eliminate evidence and obscure his trail. He decided to leave one agent in town to question local residents, but hoped that one of the other identity checking teams had greater success. Larry had no idea why the Social Security file on Ackerman was active or who was handling the deposits to it.

CHAPTER 79 – STANLEY WILCOX

Linda Higgins had mixed emotions as she approached the farmhouse outside Kankakee, Illinois. Someone calling himself Stanley Wilcox lived here, and she couldn't be sure whether he was the person suspected of killing her father in that old sewer tunnel or if she was about to meet someone who had just assumed the Stanley Wilcox name. The preliminary surveillance report had indicated nothing unusual about this farm. She knew that some evidence indicated that Stanley Wilcox had died in a suspicious nursing home accident, but how completely could you trust documents more than twenty years old? One of the agents working with her walked to the back of the house in case the suspect tried to escape through the back door.

Linda rang the doorbell. It was answered after a minute or so by a muscular man wearing a red plaid shirt, red suspenders, and blue jeans. She guessed that he was approximately thirty-two years old. "Good morning. I'm from the FBI, and I'm looking for Stanley Wilcox. Does he live here?"

"I'm Stan Wilcox. What is this about?"

"We're looking for a Stanley Wilcox who was associated with the North Corner Savings Bank in Chicago about twenty years ago. Would that be anyone in your family?"

The man noticeably stiffened. "Aren't you people ever going to leave me alone? Were you sent here by the Internal Revenue Service to harass me on their behalf? Enough is enough! You government people have been bugging me for close to those twenty years you mentioned."

Linda was confused by his words, but wanted to calm him down before he did anything violent. "I'm sorry if my inquiry upset you. I believe we're looking for someone older than you who worked for that bank I mentioned. You're too young to be the individual we wanted to interview. Do you have an older relative who has your name?"

He relaxed slightly. "You're almost showing common sense. I've never understood why the IRS thought I made money off a bank sale when I was ten or eleven years old. Even they should understand that the only bank I owned at that age looked like a pig with a slot in his back."

Linda began to understand and changed the subject. "Do you live here alone?"

"Except when my fiancée joins me, but that's no business of yours. I grew up on this farm. My mother died after a struggle with breast cancer when I was thirteen years old, and Dad died in a tractor accident two years ago. Now I'm trying to keep the farm going and to pay the bills without any assistance from this bank money they think I have, which is ridiculous."

"What was your father's name?"

"He was William. He was so tired of Wee Willie Wilcox jibes and jokes that he fought my mother's desire to make me his junior and named me Stanley."

"Well, Stanley, I think I understand how the Internal Revenue Service mistook you for someone who owed them tax money. We won't bother you any further today, and I promise I'll talk with someone at IRS and tell them that you are not the party they think you are."

"Thank you, Agent Higgins. If you can get them off my back, I'll be forever grateful."

Linda gathered the FBI team together and told them that the owner of this farm was not their suspect. That individual had used the Social Security number of a child with the same name on his fake credentials. She hoped that the other search teams were having better luck.

CHAPTER 80 – GARY WILCOX

Following the preliminary surveillance period, Bob Marcus drove into the picturesque Iowa village and parked in front of the woodworking shop. As Bob climbed out of the SUV, he looked up and down the main street at the many tourists, some going in and out of various shops and others sitting on several of the rustic wooden benches, talking to each other. *If you want to hide from the law, why would you operate a business in a tourist mecca like the village of Amana in the Amana Colonies?*

He climbed the four steps and opened the front door of the shop, which occupied a compact old blue wood frame house. A bell rang announcing his presence. He stood for half a minute, seeing no one, but hearing a machine in the background. He could smell freshly cut wood. Then he heard a shout from behind a curtain.

"I'm in the shop. I'll be out in a minute. Hilda's out to lunch."

A few minutes later, an unusually tall man walked out from behind the curtain, wiping his hands on a cloth. He put the cloth into his back pocket and finished wiping his hands on the well-worn thigh portions of his jeans. He extended his hand as he stepped toward the man waiting in his front room.

"Good afternoon; I'm Gary Wilcox. Pardon the sawdust. Sorry you had to wait. We're short-handed during lunchtime. Hilda goes first, and then I sneak a bite later. Are you interested in wooden toys or animal carvings?"

"Actually, I'm interested in you. My name is Bob Marcus, and I'm an FBI Agent. Here are my credentials."

Gary pulled over a stool and sat. He gestured for Bob to take a matching stool.

"What may I help you with, Bob?"

"First, you may tell me whether you've been Gary Wilcox from birth, or whether this identity is a relatively recent incarnation." Bob turned on the audio recording function of his phone.

"I'm the genuine original Gary. There's no doubt about it."

"Have you been Gary all along, or did you take some time out to be Stanley Wilcox and Stephen George Ackerman?"

"Stanley was my brother. He died about twenty years ago. I don't know the Ackerman fellow."

Bob made a show of consulting his pocket notebook. "That's funny. I have evidence that you had extra identification papers made in the names of Stanley Wilcox and Stephen George Ackerman. If you have always been Gary Wilcox, why did you need new papers?"

Gary saw that this conversation would require time. He walked to the front door and switched the customer greeting sign from *Open* to *Closed*. Then he returned and straddled the stool. "I needed to briefly assume Stanley's identity and amplify my qualifications in order to complete a transaction that was pending when my brother died. The Ackerman name was something I did on a lark. It was just in case I someday wanted to be someone totally different. I never used that identity."

"Someone did. Even the impersonation of your brother could be considered fraud."

"If so, it would only be on a misdemeanor level. Many people claim better grades in school than they actually had, or take an online degree and pass it off as something much more prestigious."

"Would this transaction you mentioned have been the sale of North Corner Savings Bank in Chicago?"

"Yes, that was it. Stanley died just before that deal was to have closed. I was a minor shareholder, but Stanley owned most of the stock. I was his only heir. I simply took his place in order to close the sale quickly. I would have been the owner of his shares through normal estate processing anyway, but I sped things up."

"That was probably because the buyer would not have waited for *normal processing* but would have bought another bank instead."

"That was a consideration. In any event, that all happened about twenty years ago. The statute of limitations on fraud is much shorter. I believe it's five years in Illinois and seven years when federal rules apply."

Bob watched Gary's expression carefully. "There's no statute of limitations for murder cases."

Gary showed no change of expression or demeanor. "That's an interesting fact, but what does it have to do with the sale of that bank?"

"At the time of the sale, the North Corner Savings bank contained two dead bodies in a compartment within the vault and another two bodies in a sewer pipe tunnel leading from the parking lot to an access hatch in the vault's rear wall."

This time, Gary's face showed shock. He was either genuinely surprised or an outstanding actor.

"You're kidding. Are you saying that when I closed the deal on that bank, I sold the new owners four dead bodies as well? How did they get there?"

"We suspect that either you or your brother Stanley killed them and left them there to rot. Would you like to comment on that prospect?"

"I know nothing about dead people. If they were there, they must have been there before I took over the sale negotiations. I didn't spend much time in the building, and I didn't have access to the vault. The out-of-town buyers didn't care about the building because they were going to tear it down and move their local headquarters elsewhere. It was all just a business strategy to let a bank from a different state enter the Illinois market. Bank employees handled the physical aspects of the building closure."

Bob tried a different approach to see if it would rattle Gary. "Before the sale occurred, why did you eliminate all evidence of your having worked at Suburban Vista Nursing Home? We have all their records from the period of your employment there, but your data is missing."

"I didn't do anything like that. I did leave quite suddenly. If there are no remaining records, my bosses must have gotten rid of them so that no one could give me a future recommendation. They were angry with me for my sudden departure."

"How long have you had this shop?"

Gary visibly relaxed at the change of subject. "I've been butchering wood here for almost five years. I did everything myself until a few months ago, when Hilda came on board. I should have added someone earlier. With her up front, I can concentrate on the creative parts of the job. You should take a stab at running your own business someday, Bob. It gives you real freedom, so long as you can pay the bills."

Bob was pleasantly surprised by Gary's willingness to talk without legal representation. It was either due to true innocence or a brazen ploy to claim virtue. In either case, Bob knew that he wouldn't learn much more by continuing to question Gary. He turned off the recorder.

"That's all the discussion I need right now, Gary. I won't take up any more of your business day. We'll want to talk with you again, so please stick with your normal routines and don't change your identity again."

"I'll be right here when you want me. Here's a carving of a monkey, on the house. He's a good luck symbol."

"I'll have to do without that good luck, Gary. We're not allowed to accept gifts." *I wonder if he's suggesting that he made a monkey of me while I questioned him.*

CHAPTER 81 – REPORTS

Ruth summarized the three reports she had received to an audience of Larry Savage, Linda Higgins, Bob Marcus, Arthur Blake, and Irma Blake. "As I interpret your reports, it should be easy to pinpoint the date of sale of the North Corner Savings Bank from both transaction reports and the date when the IRS began pestering the young child namesake of Stanley Wilcox for overdue taxes. If we have that date and can find how much earlier the adult version of Stanley died, we may be able to determine whether Stanley or Gary Wilcox killed the people in the bank and in the tunnel."

Bob said, "That would be a good approach, but our fragmentary discoveries about Stanley Wilcox dying at that nursing home don't include any date information."

Arthur gestured to Ruth for attention. "We're convinced that the killer of the men in the tunnel was quite tall. What are the heights of the two brothers?"

Bob shook his head. "That won't work as an approach. Gary is about six feet, three inches tall, and we have notes that describe Stanley as closely resembling Gary, to the point that some people confused their identities."

Irma said, "That may be the key to why Gary thought he could take the place of his brother for the bank negotiations."

Impasse

Ruth held up her right index finger. "My mother would shake her finger at me when I stated something as fact that I couldn't prove. I'll do the same for you. Be cautious about discussing the case as though everything a suspect said is true. We already know that Gary lied to Bob. He said that he never used the fictitious identity of Stephen George Ackerman. We know that someone calling himself by that name lived in Mukwonago, Wisconsin until his house burned down. Larry, did you get a description of Mr. Ackerman? Was he tall?"

"He was, and I have a newspaper photograph to prove it. The *Mukwonago Chief* ran a photograph of Ackerman with some of his neighbors outside the Castaway restaurant on Phantom Lake. It was a charity special event, and he is the tallest person in the group."

"Bob said, "Let me see that picture." He reached across the table to take the photo from Larry's outstretched hand. "Ackerman is definitely Gary Wilcox. That means Ruth's premise is correct. He lied to me about never using the Ackerman identity."

Irma gave a thumbs-up sign to Ruth. "You caught me believing his story. That makes me wonder what other lies he told Bob, but it also raises the question of why Ackerman's house burned down. Was it simply Ackerman's convenient exit strategy? He could have been destroying evidence there?"

Ruth said, "I consider it unlikely that he would torch the house to get rid of twenty-year-old evidence. That's out of proportion to any benefit he would receive. He lived on a lake and could simply give anything he desired a watery grave."

"Your choice of words may be the key."

"What do you mean, Irma?"

"You said 'watery grave'. What if he wasn't trying to hide anything from his old crimes, but was getting rid of a new body by burning it and then throwing the remains into the lake?"

"We'll leave that as an open possibility, but the local fire department didn't find anything suspicious, and we don't know that Gary, or Ackerman, had a candidate for murder. Let's leave a question mark on that fire for now."

"Fair enough, Ruth."

"I'll summarize by saying that we want to continue looking for any records that indicate when the bank and tunnel victims died relative to the date of sale of the bank. That timeline would give us a better understanding of whether Stanley or Gary Wilcox should be our most likely suspect."

CHAPTER 82 – JAYSON

Chief Bobby Andrews enjoyed his second mug of morning coffee and a piece of his wife's apple pie while he basked in the thought that nothing unusual had occurred to interfere with his routine for ten whole days. Recent police matters had become almost trivial, but if trivial meant peace and civility in his village, he would enjoy it. The telephone rang, disrupting his daydream.

"Chief Andrews speaking; how may I assist you?"

"Chief, this is Sergeant Max Casper of the Illinois State Police. I've been working with the State Police Merit Board on recruiting matters, and we've come up with a new program for civilian employees. I'd like your permission to discuss it with your man, Jayson Redshaw."

"I'll need to know more about this program, and you should know that Jayson shares his time with Arthur and Irma Blake as a private investigation associate."

"We probably couldn't do a three-way split on his time, but here's what we're thinking. Jay has the height and probably the skill of a decent basketball player. If he's interested, we would train him to be a basketball coach. We're looking to set up local basketball programs around the state in urban areas to keep kids off the street and competing peacefully. If he qualifies, Jay would be doing some good work for us, and might work into a trooper slot later on."

"That sounds like a good deal for him, but his brother was killed on the south side of Chicago, and we're trying to keep him away from gang activity areas."

"I did know that, Chief. If he signed up, we'd put him somewhere else. Like Rockford. He would do some traveling with his team if they got into playoff games."

"You have my permission to talk with him. Don't sugar-coat the risks of working with gang kids."

"I won't, and thanks."

Jay smiled to himself as he walked across the lobby of the Rockford State Police Laboratory and saw Sarah talking with the receptionist. He walked toward her.

"Surprise!"

"What are you doing here? I don't have any forensics job orders with your name on them."

"I'm here for a meeting with State Police Sergeant Max Casper. He said he would be in the main conference room."

"I don't know him. He must be based somewhere else. Is this something secret, or can you tell me about it?"

"It's not secret, but let me take you to lunch and tell you about it afterward. Can you buy into that approach?"

"I'll buy into it, but it'll cost you. I plan to be steakhouse hungry for lunch."

"That's a deal. I'll meet you in your lab after my meeting."

Sergeant Casper was seated and studying a file folder when Jay entered the conference room. He stood to shake hands.

"I've been looking forward to meeting you, Jay. Grab some coffee or water, and we'll get right to it. I was surprised to see that you already have a file folder as a consultant to this laboratory."

"Thanks, Sergeant. That consultant label is slightly incorrect. I've worked with this lab seeking services for the Parkville Police and the Blakes."

"They opened this file after your presentation in Parkville, where some State Police people learned a few things from you."

Jay smiled and nodded. "I understand from Chief Andrews that you're wondering whether I can play basketball. I'll give you a yes to that if you're talking about the schoolyard variety of ball. I worked two jobs and didn't have time for my high school team, so I'm a novice when it comes to setting up team plays and strategy."

"I see from your file that you took a one-on-one course in DNA analysis with Dr. Irma Blake. We'll set up a similar course with a college basketball coach if you decide to work with us."

"Give me the overall picture of what you want."

"Our goal is to minimize violence in this state. We share that goal with every local police department, but our jurisdiction is the whole state. We're planning to set up a statewide set of basketball leagues based in cities with urban violence problems. There would be a separate league structure for Chicago because its population is so much bigger than any of our other cities. The idea is to keep young people off the street doing something they enjoy. We'd like to have the coaches be only a few years older than them so that they'll communicate well. What do you think of that plan?"

"It sounds good, but lots of fights break out at basketball games, and sometimes players and fans carry their grudges out to the street."

"We'll have troopers and local cops there to minimize conflicts. What else?"

"Would this be a part-time thing, so that I could keep up at least one of my other jobs?"

"We'd want you to be full time during the period when you'd be learning how to coach. Then it would be part-time, but it would be more than half-time. Later, when your team gets organized and plays, you might have to add time for counseling players with problems."

"I wouldn't want to be in Chicago."

"We're thinking Rockford."

"Would you pay for me to take some classes? I couldn't do counseling without training. I'm also thinking of applying to be a trooper in the future, and you require some college background or military service. I don't have the military, so I'll need some courses."

"Your long-term interest is great. I'm sure I can swing some education money. I'll also arrange for you to get credit for your DNA Analysis course with Dr. Blake. What do you think? Do we have a deal?"

"Let's say that I'm leaning your way, but I'll have to run the proposition past the Blakes and

Chief Andrews. They've done a lot for me, and I wouldn't want to drop out on them without giving them a chance to voice objections."

"Grapevine has it that you'll want to talk it over with Sarah Jackson too."

"I'm taking her out for lunch after we get done here. How did you hear about our friendship, Sergeant Casper?"

"Everybody in this laboratory knows about it. They informed me when I arranged for this meeting room. Your friendship with Sarah might also have something to do with my recommending you for assignment to the Rockford league."

Jay took Sarah to Outback Steakhouse despite her plea that she was only kidding when she demanded an expensive lunch earlier.

Once they settled into their booth he said, "This is a tentative celebration."

"What are you celebrating, and why is it tentative?"

"I've been offered a post coaching basketball for the State Police. I'd be part of a league aimed at keeping kids in the gym instead of on the street."

"That sounds super. Why is it tentative?"

"I'm giving you, the Blakes, and Chief Andrews the chance to talk me out of it."

"Wow! Is my opinion that important to you?"

"Of course it is, and it's getting more important all the time."

"Where would you be assigned?"

"Oddly enough, Rockford."

Richard Davidson

"I vote that you should take that job ASAP. I may even be able to save you some rent money on your own place."

"Hold that very tempting thought. I'm not sure you're ready to have me around all the time."

"Are there going to be girls at those basketball games?"

"Of course there will."

"Then I definitely want you with me all the time."

CHAPTER 83 – FBI MOVES

Ruth Daltry discovered that Irma's questioning why Stephen George Ackerman's house burned bothered her more and more as time passed. She decided to send Bob Marcus and Linda Higgins to check the building rubble and the adjacent lake for anything suspicious. The preliminary surveillance in Amana, Iowa ended after Bob Marcus' interview with Gary Wilcox. She assigned a new surveillance team to Amana to keep track of Gary Wilcox's activities and be sure he didn't leave town. She would personally take on the job of determining when the North Corner Savings Bank had been sold.

After issuing the assignments to her field teams, Ruth began her survey of the bank merger records. She had learned in her earlier introductory study that Illinois was one of the last states to allow branch banking. Prior to 1990, Illinois banks could only have one location and had to be Illinois entities with very few exceptions. In 1993 branch banking limitations in Illinois were finally eliminated, but the only way an out-of-state bank could enter the Illinois market was by buying a bank with an Illinois bank charter that was at least five years old and then merging it into the purchasing bank to become its first branch within the state. This was the formula when Third Texas Bancorp acquired North Corner Savings Bank in 1995. The purchased bank was merged and renamed Third Star Bank to remove possible bias against the inclusion of Texas in the name. The existing location was abandoned in favor of a near-north Chicago site that was in an upscale neighborhood. Then, six months later, Third Star Bank was itself purchased and merged into a larger interstate banking group.

Ruth drew a horizontal line on a pad of paper. *We'll need to develop a timeline to figure out which Wilcox brother is more likely to have been our murderer. The bank sale took place in 1995.* She labeled the right end of the line 1995. *Ted Higgins went undercover as Marco Locante in 1992.* She marked the left end of the line 1992. *Can we find more events that happened during those three years? The most important one would be the date of Stanley Wilcox's death in that nursing home. I'll ask the crew searching the so-called catacomb materials to concentrate on finding that timing.*

As Bob Marcus and Linda Higgins drove toward Mukwonago, Wisconsin, Bob steered the conversation toward a sensitive topic. "Linda, during all those years when your father was among the missing, did you hold onto hope that he was still alive, or did you conclude that he had died, but you didn't know the circumstances?"

"I didn't know anything about his guise as Marco Locante, but to me Ted Higgins was Superman. I grew up knowing that my father could do anything, and I was certain that sooner or later he'd come back to me with his jaunty walk and big smile. He did that several times during my teen years after having been gone for months at a time. I kept telling myself that his last mission was just a longer one and that I would someday see him again."

"It must have hit you like a ton of bricks when we identified one of the bodies in the tunnel as being his."

"It would have shattered my world if so much time hadn't passed before that discovery. I kept telling myself that he would come back alive, but I really didn't believe my own thoughts. I was being faithful to him by keeping hope alive, but the flame of that hope had died down to flickering embers many years before he was found. Now, I simply want to close the books on the bastard who killed my father and in the process to prove to his memory that I'm a good FBI agent too."

"Don't worry about that last point. I'll vouch for your being one of our best."

"Thanks, Bob. Your endorsement means a lot to me." Her thoughts tentatively considered the thought of a romance with dependable but colorless Bob.

They rode on silently, each absorbed in personal thoughts, until they came to the site of the house that had burned alongside Lower Phantom Lake in Mukwonago, Wisconsin.

CHAPTER 84 – CATACOMB REVISITED

Sandra O'Brien, Sandy to those who knew her well, had inherited supervision of the FBI crew searching through the catacomb documents and artifacts from Suburban Vista Nursing Home's earlier owners. The job had gone down in priority following its hectic opening weeks, but Ruth's phone call earlier today had relit everyone's urgency fire. The new goal was to learn when Stanley Wilcox had died in the exercise equipment accident. Sandy instructed one pair of searchers to find equipment maintenance records. She charged a second pair to look at OSHA accident records. She would look for Stanley's death notice outside of the catacomb materials in published funeral records.

For two days everyone worked with renewed vigor, but by the status meeting on the third day, the group's enthusiasm had waned.

Sandy opened the meeting with her own progress report. "Given the efficiency of today's search engines, I expected to find Stanley's death notice quite easily. I forgot that data wasn't computerized as frequently twenty-some years ago. Search engines don't do a good job of finding local paper records. We don't know where Stanley was buried. He could be far away in another state. Do we have any clues from the maintenance records?"

Amanda Celli stood. "I'll speak to that one. We couldn't find a date, but we did find a handwritten note indicating that several pieces of exercise equipment were discarded because they thought they were unsafe or worn out. The note indicated that the marketing department wanted new-looking exercise units because potential patients frequently choose their rehab facility based on the appearance of the equipment."

"That note may not be tied to the time of Stanley's accident. They could have decided to upgrade their facilities at any time. What do we have from the OSHA reports to the government?"

Nick Calhoun stood and looked at his clipboard. "Don't get your hopes up on the OSHA front. Every report in the files is identical. They all indicated that they never had an accident or injury in the nursing home. That administrative group was shady and wasn't going to invite federal inspectors to visit them. Don't forget, we got interested in Suburban Vista because they were laundering money for that fraudulent bank."

Sandy nodded. "Thanks for reminding us, Nick. We've been looking for records that a proper institution would have kept. That description may fit the nursing home under its current ownership, but the earlier people were both devious and sloppy in their record keeping. That's why the new folks threw everything into the catacomb room instead of auditing their predecessors' paperwork."

"I suggest that you give the results we summarized in this status meeting to Ruth Daltry. We're not going to find any more information. Those old paper-pushers wouldn't admit to any accidents at all." Nick sat back in his chair and threw his

Richard Davidson

clipboard onto the table, making a loud noise to
add finality to his statement.

CHAPTER 85 – DISCOVERY

Bob Marcus rented a boat and trailer and launched the craft from Stephen George Ackerman's property. As he did so, he wondered whether the land still belonged to Ackerman or if he had sold it after the fire. No sign proclaimed that it was currently for sale. Bob opened the canvas bag of tools that he had purchased at the home improvement store. As he did so, he watched Linda Higgins using a rake with a charred handle to sort through the house rubble that hadn't been completely cleared after the fire and demolition. They had decided to divide their search responsibilities with Bob exploring the lake bed while Linda checked the remains of the house.

Bob lowered two large rope-mounted three-pronged hooks into the water behind his boat, being careful to tie the ropes to cleats well clear of the propeller blades. He started the engine and kept it at low speed, easing the boat forward. The towed hooks did not snag on anything immediately. That probably meant that the lake bottom was mostly sand here. Bob continued forward until he passed several lots with houses on them. Then he gradually turned the boat leftward, turning around in a wide arc so as to avoid tangling his ropes or swinging them too close to the propeller. He was halfway through his circle, directly in front of the Ackerman property, but well out from the shore, when he snagged something. Bob cut the engine, put on his work gloves, and started to drag the object to the boat pulling the taut rope hand over hand. At first, it resisted his efforts, and he found that he was pulling the boat backwards toward the snagged item. He began to think he had hooked onto a sunken log, when the object popped free of the mud and started to move toward him as he pulled. After five more minutes of pulling, it drew close enough for Bob to realize he had captured an old construction truck tire. He started the engine and towed his prize to the shore so that he wouldn't snag it a second time.

While Bob battled the oversized rubber doughnut, Linda methodically cleared one small section after another of the space where the house had stood. She considered herself lucky to have found the rake with the charred handle among the rubble. She had black hands, but an optimistic outlook as she continued to search the destroyed house's footprint in a grid pattern. The wooden floor had burned completely, so Linda realized she was raking through both the debris from the house and anything that might have been in the crawl space beneath the floor.

Linda looked up from her efforts to see Bob wrestling a large tire onto the shore. She wondered what the lakebed would look like if all the water were drained. It might even reveal the truck that had once borne that tire. Somehow, the tire made her feel like Don Quixote, jousting with a windmill. After all this time, they weren't apt to find anything significant here. Even so, they would complete their assigned exercise.

Impasse

Two hours later, Bob's tire had been joined on the shore by an old bicycle, a trash barrel, and a section of the wood picket fence that had once surrounded the Ackerman house. Linda had only small items like screwdrivers and kitchen gadgets to show for her efforts. As she looked down, she noticed that her blue jeans were black where she had wiped her hands on them. Linda was approaching the final square in her grid search pattern when she saw a piece of canvas with a leather carrying handle attached to it. She cleared the space on the ground around it and saw that the object was half buried. After several minutes of digging with the end of the steel rake head, she pulled the item free. Then she carried it to the shore, scrubbed it in the water with an old cloth, and waved her rake in an arc to attract Bob's attention. Once he saw her, she gestured with her hand for him to bring his boat closer.

Bob nosed the boat into the shallows, jumped out, and dragged the craft onto the shore. "What's up? Did you find something?"

"I did, and it makes all this work worthwhile. I found a money bag, and after washing it in the lake, I can read *North Corner Savings Bank* stamped in black ink on the canvas."

CHAPTER 86 – DECISION

After Bob and Linda returned to the Chicago office, Bob reported their findings to Ruth Daltry. She was elated. "We have Gary Wilcox now. If he only negotiated the sale of that bank, there would have been no way for him to have that money bag. We have his recorded statement that he hardly went into the North Corner Savings Bank building at all and had no access to the vault. I'm ready to arrest him, but just to be on the safe side, Bob, check the bag you two found at Ackerman's place against those found in the sewer tunnel and in the vault crypt. If they're all similar, our case gets stronger."

"You know that Gary's defense team will claim that he's guilty of nothing but fraud in pretending to be his brother when selling that bank and that he took the money bag as a souvenir. They'll claim that Gary's brother Stanley committed the murders before he died."

"Bob, every time I get enthusiastic about something, you give me a counter-argument. I need you to back me up more. Maybe I am rushing things. I'll go along with you and hold off for a while, but you're going to have to help me build a really strong case. This guy has to pay for those murders."

CHAPTER 87 – IRMA AND NANCY

Nancy walked Rex around the grounds, down the driveway hill to the road, up to the next intersection and back again. Irma watched them return from the porch couch.

"Come on up here, you two."

Nancy climbed the steps to the porch and released Rex to lie down. "That was a good walk. I've been making it a little longer each time we go."

"How are you feeling? Did the driveway hill bother you when you climbed it?"

"Nope. I declare myself fit again, and it's a lot higher level of fit than I've had for a very long time."

"That means it'll soon be time to get you back on a regular school schedule instead of my picking up assignments and tutoring you."

"I realize that, and I'm more than ready for it. No offense, but I need to get with kids my own age again, even though they'll all be strangers at first." Nancy sat on the couch next to Irma.

"You'll make new friends here. Have you kept in touch with your old friends in Florida?"

"Just a few of them. When I spent so much time in the hospital, before and after my transplant, some kids I rated as close friends drifted away."

"That's a natural process. How would you like to visit some of those who are still on your friend list?"

"That would be great. What's up?"

"I think you deserve a vacation before you go back to school full time. I thought we would head to Florida in the Orlando area, get you together with some of your old friends, and then head for Disney World."

"That sounds cool. Would I be able to stop by the old house while we're there?"

"Sure. It's up for sale, with the proceeds aimed at paying your remaining medical bills plus your college education, but it hasn't sold yet."

"Will Arthur go with us?"

"Yes and no. He wants to visit some people down there who are part of our current case, so we'll probably travel together, but he won't go with us to Disney World."

"Well, if we do go there, I'll be your guide. I've been there so many times, I know where all the secret cast entrances are hidden, and I even know some people who work there."

"If you've visited Disney World so much, would you rather go somewhere else?"

"No. At this point that place will feel more like home than the old house. I've turned the page, you're my mother now, and you're stuck with me forever. Arthur's my father, and Rex is my shaggy brother." She reached over and hugged Irma. "Sometimes I'll call you Mom and sometimes Irma. Will that be alright, Mom?"

"More than alright. I've been waiting my whole life for someone to call me Mom."

CHAPTER 88 – FLORIDA

The Blakes flew together to Florida because it was their first family trip that included Nancy, but separated once they reached the Orlando Airport. Irma and Nancy would stay at the Caribbean Beach Resort at Walt Disney World, be tourists, and use the Disney bus service. Arthur would rent a car and stay in Orlando.

After he checked into his room, Arthur called Emily Everett. He thought of her by that name even though she was living under the Lynn Holmes name, because he had befriended the original Lynn Holmes Cooper in Nassau. He would just have to live with the confusion the two names caused.

"Hello, Lynn Holmes speaking."

"Hello, Emily, it's Arthur Blake calling. I missed visiting you earlier because of scheduling problems when my wife, Irma, and the FBI people were there. I'm in Orlando, and I'd like to visit you and also arrange a field trip to Cape Canaveral and the NASA facilities for you and your eleven associates."

"I'd certainly like to spend some time with you, Arthur, without those FBI people along. We have taken the tour of the Cape several times. You know that space travel is our Holy Grail."

"You may have taken the public tour, but I worked as an aerospace engineer for launches there, and I'd be able to show and tell you many things that would be new for you."

"By all means, come out and tell me more. I'll have lemonade and fresh cookies for you when you arrive."

"I'm on my way. I'll see you shortly."

When Arthur arrived, he found Emily sitting on her porch with her pitcher and platter, as promised.

"I hope you don't mind my calling you Emily. It's easier for me, because I know the other Lynn Holmes."

"No problem, Arthur; sometimes I think of myself as Emily Everett when I'm discussing people or things from my old life. Why are you really here? The tour idea is great, but you wouldn't have come all the way from Illinois just for that."

"Now that you mention it, I would appreciate some additional details about the things that happened more than twenty years ago. I'm sure you remember some things from having been there that we can only try to reconstruct."

"Now your visit is starting to make some sense. Have some cookies first, and then you can get me into a remembering mood. It may take a bit of effort though. I haven't thought about those events for a long time."

"These cookies are good. I'm not sure I can identify everything in them."

"I have a secret recipe. I can tell you that they include favorite things from England, Florida, and a few other places. Now, give me your first comment or question."

"Tell me more about Albert Rivers. He must have been awfully persuasive to convince you and your group to part with so much money."

"It was quite a lot. Albert was one of those rare individuals who could convince you he was doing things for you, while you were actually doing things for him. He came along with a convincing story of having seen and photographed UFOs, when we were longing to prove they were real. We believed what he told us because it was what we needed to hear."

"What did he tell you?"

"He said that he had been a pilot in the US Air Force and that he had seen and chased a UFO, but couldn't catch it. He showed us a picture of what he had seen that looked very real."

"That must have impressed you."

"It certainly did. We invited Albert to a series of parties so that he could tell more people about his experience. During those parties, we told him about our dream of someday traveling out into space. We kept saying that if others could come here, then someday we ought to be able to go away from our home planet too."

"That's what I was working toward when I worked for NASA. It sounds as though you weren't willing to wait for national and international space agencies to solve the problems of space travel."

"Of course we weren't. We figured we'd be long dead by the time those outfits tried to go somewhere beyond the moon. We needed someone who would shortcut the process. Look at Elon Musk and SpaceX today. They're doing things on their own that are pushing NASA and the other agencies to speed up their programs. That's what we were looking for twenty-some years ago."

"I can understand that outlook. Back then, you were ripped off by a con man. If you gave your money to SpaceX today, you'd be making a wise or at least forward-looking investment."

"You have to admit that SpaceX and the other private firms aiming at space travel are shaking up the established agencies and governments."

"That's true, Emily, but they're not perfect either. They have occasional mission failures and take risks beyond NASA's standards."

"Arthur, tell me what you think of our group of twelve space enthusiasts from the UK."

"That's a tough assignment because you're the only one in the group I've met. Given that fact, I'll bet that you're a bunch of icebergs."

"What do you mean by that?"

"I think there's a lot more in each one of you below the surface. Despite the length of time you've been in this country, you haven't revealed very much about yourselves."

"Alright, tell me who you think we are."

"Each one of you has a lot of wealth. You hardly blinked when Albert Rivers swindled you out of a million dollars each. Without any evidence, I'll bet that each of you earned the bulk of your wealth even if a bit of it was inherited. That means that you're all talented individuals. Given the fact that you're all hoping to go to Mars, I'll bet that your collective talents would mesh together well for surviving there. After all, you've been chasing this dream for a long time. You must have thought through the requirements for interplanetary travel."

"As they say in the space game, you have the right stuff, Arthur. You summed up our group very well. We have doctors, scientists, engineers, and survival specialists. Our companies in both the UK and here are pursuing their appropriate business interests, but they're also doing research and development on devices that would be useful for planetary immigrants. We're definitely not just a group of eccentric rich people, although we don't mind if others view us that way. It's fun to have people underestimate us, and sometimes it's a great advantage."

"What happens if you don't get to go because of delays in getting a Mars mission ready?"

"In that case, we'd reveal the technology and devices we've developed and sell them to the space agencies. We'll either get to go, or we'll stay here but know that we've made contributions to the expedition that will go someday."

"And you'll get wealthier because of your foresight."

"It's going to happen, and we intend to be part of it in some way, preferably by making that journey ourselves."

"Tell me what you remember about the man who set up your cruises where you exchanged identities in Nassau."

"That was Stanley Wilcox. He was enthusiastic but seemed preoccupied with something. I had the impression that whenever he talked with me, he was thinking of something else. He played his part

Richard Davidson

well. Nassau was in the part of the world where the James Bond saga started, and Wilcox handled things in Bond style."

"Does that mean he made a play for the women in your group?"

"He did flirt, but I didn't take him seriously. That behavior probably came with the territory of playing the tour guide."

"Emily, that's the second time you referred to Stanley Wilcox as playing a part. Did you see the real individual behind his role playing, or was he too shallow to reveal his true identity?"

"That's an interesting question, and a hard one due to the many years that have passed, but I'll take a crack at it. Stanley was always efficient at his tasks, while keeping up a light patter of conversation. He projected himself as being carefree and shallow, but he calculated the results of every move he made before he acted. I'd say that beneath his attempts at charm, he was wound up like a tight spring."

Arthur took an index card from his pocket and made several notes on it. "Did he tell you anything personal about himself?"

"I can't recall anything. It all happened long ago. He might have said that he came from Massachusetts or New Hampshire. He was trying to make us feel comfortable, and he said that while we were from England, he was a New Englander."

Arthur added to his notes as Emily watched. Then she said, "I've answered enough of your questions. Now it's time for you to tell me why you and the FBI are so interested in Stanley Wilcox.

306

After all these years, it can't be because of our unorthodox way of entering the United States with identity switching."

Arthur pondered the ethics of what he was about to say. "You've been straight with me, Emily, so I'll share something that the authorities wouldn't approve. You'll have to promise that it won't be shared with anyone else."

"I promise."

"Four people were murdered in and around that bank where Stanley's travel agency was based. One of them was Albert Rivers and another was an FBI undercover agent. Stanley Wilcox, since deceased, is the primary suspect, but his brother Gary may be involved also."

"I never met this Gary. What does he do?"

"He now runs a woodworking business in Amana, Iowa, but he was involved fraudulently in the sale of that bank that housed the travel agency you used."

"I guess we got ourselves involved with a bunch of scoundrels. In hindsight, we were so keen on pulling off our identity switching ploy that we lost our focus on other things. Thanks for telling me, Arthur."

"Thank you, Emily. Let me know if you want that NASA tour, and I'll arrange it. In the meantime, I'd better join my family at Disney World, so that I get in on some of the fun."

They shook hands, and Arthur took two extra cookies to eat during his drive to Disney World. As he rose to leave, he said, "One more thing, I

Richard Davidson

brought something to show you. Take a look and tell me whether it's a yes or a no."

CHAPTER 89 – GARY WILCOX

During one of the frequent lulls between customers, Hilda went back to the shop area in the hope that Gary would relieve her monotony. As she walked, she bound her long blond hair into a ponytail with a rubber band. Gary was a stickler for safety around his machines. He looked up and turned off his wood lathe as she entered.

"What's up, Hil?

"We've been a couple for several months now, and I have to admit I'm getting tired of our lifestyle. I sit in the front all day talking with senior citizens and students while you keep up your hobby in the back room. That's on a good day. When we don't have any visitors or customers, it's worse for me. You've hinted at having more than enough cash invested to secure the future, but all you want to do is make your wooden toys and novelties, leaving me to sit up front and make nice with the tourists. I need something more."

"I'm thinking of getting into furniture making, like the Amana Furniture and Clock Shop."

"That's fine for you, but I need something different. Didn't you say you were once in banking? Could we get into a fast-paced financial circle in a big city?"

Gary's eyes lost their focus as he stared out the window. "I wasn't a banker. That was my brother Stanley. He liked cities, but I don't. Stanley practically worshipped money, but I can take it or leave it. As long as I have enough to live on, I avoid even talking about it. If you're bored with our routine, we could take a few days off or change the shop schedule, but I like the slower pace of country living."

"I know, Gary, and we've scratched at this subject before, but I get antsy, waiting for tourists to walk in. Maybe I need a separate vacation. I have a half sister who lives in the Chicago area. Can you handle things here and let me go away for a week or so?"

"Sure, Hil, that may be just the thing for you. You could visit her every few months if she'll have you. It could be a pressure relief valve for you."

"Boredom isn't the same as pressure, but I get what you mean. I'll contact her and set something up. Thanks for seeing my side of the story."

After Hilda left, Gary mused, *I have to pay more attention to her and frost her cake to make this venture tastier for her. I'm too used to working alone, and I can't do that in this business. Life was easier when I did everything by myself. I'll have to change my style, but she's worth the extra effort. Hilda's the perfect salesperson for an Amana Colonies business. I'll have to try to add more romance.*

He restarted his lathe and focused on the prototype of the folding dining room table he had designed. His last trip to Ikea had inspired him. His goal was to create a full set of quality apartment furniture that could be folded and attractively stored to use a single room in several ways. As he worked, he reflected on the ways age had mellowed him. He no longer had to take short cuts and decisive action to get what he wanted. He didn't even care about those FBI people who had been hanging around the village for months watching him. He was a talented craftsman – that's all.

In the front room, Hilda finished her email to her half sister by writing, "I'm ready for some fun."

CHAPTER 90 – ARTHUR

From his hotel room, Arthur telephoned Mercury in Nassau. It was time to pin down a few details.

After the preliminary exchange of greetings, Arthur said, "Mercury, I consider you very sophisticated in your field. You gave me copies of the two sets of identity papers you created for Gary Wilcox, along with a copy of his edited original papers."

"That is correct Pastor Arthur."

"They all show the same place of birth. Was that a deliberate decision on your part or was it based on a request from Gary?"

"My decision. I try to keep new details as close to the original as possible because wild lies are easy to detect and because I want my customers to be able to answer questions about their identities without having to memorize a large number of new facts. Everything showed the original statistics Gary gave me."

"That applies regardless of the nature of the original data your customer gives you?"

"Absolutely, Arthur – consistency, consistency, consistency."

"I do have to tell you that your work and outlook are impressive."

"And I must applaud your perceptiveness. Please call on me again whenever your current case involves or requires documentation."

"I will do that, my friend."

After disconnecting from Mercury, Arthur turned his attention to the official records of North Conway, New Hampshire. He found them online at the site for the Conway Public Library. He thought it unusual but efficient that vital statistics for the area were handled through the library rather than a municipal department. He located the records he needed and decided to search for high school and college yearbooks. He found only reference data for two issues of the University of New Hampshire Yearbook and gave up on finding anything else that was useful at that library.

Arthur looked at his watch. It was time to leave to pick up Irma and Nancy at their Disney World hotel and head for the airport for the flight back to Chicago. This trip had been a revealing adventure in fatherhood. When he was away from Irma and Nancy, he missed both of them equally; when he was with them, he was at home no matter where they were. He enjoyed being a father, and he knew that someday Irma would remind him of the years during which he had resisted that transition. He didn't think of himself as selfish, but he knew he had been during several years of adoption discussions with Irma.

CHAPTER 91 – BOBBY ANDREWS

At Bobby's invitation, Arthur Blake drove to Parkville for lunch at House of Ming. As he entered the restaurant, he saw Bobby waving from their favorite back-corner booth.

Arthur approached the booth, threw his jacket onto the far end of the bench, and slid sideways onto his seat. "You invited me, so I assume you're treating. You arrived early, which is rare for you. You're also not smiling, which is equally rare. Is something wrong?"

"I lost my boarder. Jay is going to coach basketball for the State Police and is moving up to Rockford and moving in with Sarah Jackson."

"That shouldn't surprise you. You're a great guy, but for someone like Jay, a girlfriend is the better option every time."

"The thing is that I always wanted a son. Don't say anything to Renee. I also had ideas of convincing Jayson to work his way into a full-time position in the Parkville Police Department, so that he would be working with me. That boy has talent, and I like him."

"So the problem is that you lost out to the State Police. Their image appeals to a young guy. Don't take it too hard. There's always the possibility you'll be able to hire him back later for a higher level job."

"With our size department and our budget, the only way I could hire him back for a better job would be if he took mine."

Impasse

"By the time you're ready to do that, you may have been elected Mayor of Parkville."

"Are you serious, Arthur? Do I look like a politician?"

"You have the strong image that voters want in the age of potential street crime and terrorism. It could be a real possibility. If I hadn't moved out of town, I'd vote for you."

"Well, if I ever consider running, I'll make you move back into Parkville. I'd need every vote I could get."

"Don't look now, but your attitude just got a bit more positive. Think about it. You'd do a good job running this village. Outside of being blue, why else did you ask me to come here?"

"You know that we joined Parkville United Methodist Church when you were still pastor there because we enjoyed your messages and gained some real insights into our spiritual beliefs."

"I do appreciate that."

"After several changes, they now have a pastor who keeps preaching about secular and political problems. She hardly uses the Bible at all, and when she does, she says she doesn't believe very much of what's written in it."

"She sounds a bit self-centered instead of God-centered."

"Anyway, we think it's time for us to find another church. I wanted to run it by you before taking that step. I don't want you to think you somehow failed us or that our beliefs are getting weaker."

"What you're doing is completely natural, Bobby. You need the church to speak to your beliefs and support you. If you've found a church with a pastor who will nourish you spiritually, go for it. The United Methodist Church moves pastors around every five to ten years, so if the new church loses its luster, come back and give Parkville UMC another chance later. By that time they'll probably be led by someone else."

"Thanks, Arthur. That makes me feel much better. It's time to order our food. Order something special and expensive after that great pep talk."

CHAPTER 92 – HILDA

As she drove toward Chicago, Hilda wondered what her mother would think of her current job and outlook if she were still alive. She'd probably say, "I told you so." Mom had thought her education in electronics was a waste of time and money. She'd say, "You like kids too much to push for a professional career. Go find yourself a good man and build a loving family." Was Mom able to look down from heaven and see her bored daughter taking a break and running away from that cozy couple situation? Anyway, she didn't have kids to worry about, not that she was a worrier. She didn't agonize. She overcame obstacles through planning and luck. Hilda knew what she wanted and was quite willing to go around any obstacle she couldn't surmount.

Gary was a conniver and manipulator. She was sure her attraction for him had been her Germanic name and appearance, both assets for a tourist trade business in Amana. To be sure, he had been a good friend and lover, but she knew that she always had to look for the motivation behind each of his actions. He was a challenge, but she could cope.

The traffic slowed and flowed into a stream of red tail lights. Then everyone stopped. *There must be a bad accident up ahead.*

She turned off her engine to avoid wasting fuel. She could see a good half mile down the highway before it turned toward the right. Every vehicle between her and that turn was standing still. It was an omen.

CHAPTER 93 – RUTH AND BOB

Bob Marcus set down his desk phone and pondered the significance of the call he had just received from his boss, Ruth Daltry. She wanted to see him in the conference room right away. This could be a breakthrough in the case, or she could want to tell him in private that he was fired or transferred somewhere else. As a rule, he had been a team member rather than a leader. He knew he lost that image when he stood up to Ruth and told her it was too early to arrest Gary Wilcox. He had been right, of course, but blocking Ruth's desires had not been wise for several former agents whom she had fired or exiled to rural locations and minor duties. It was likely that he would face a confrontation in that conference room. Oh well, as that old song went, "Que Sera, Sera." He would take a full mug of strong black coffee with him.

When he walked into the conference room, he saw Ruth sitting with a larger mug of black coffee in front of her. She motioned for him to close the door behind him.

He took the initiative. "What's up, Ruth?"

"Come on in and get settled. We have to talk."

"What's the subject?"

"Gary Wilcox and how to get him once and for all."

"Are you unhappy that I told you we didn't have a strong enough case to arrest him?"

"Sure, I'm unhappy, but you were right. Now, we have to put our heads together and figure how to build a stronger case."

Bob Marcus relaxed a bit. Unless Ruth was planning a surprise at the end of their meeting, he wasn't going to be fired or exiled after all. "The problem is that we can connect Gary with the North Corner Savings Bank, but we can't directly connect him with the murders. He'll just say that Stanley, his deceased brother committed the murders, and we can't question Stanley."

Ruth drank some coffee and set down her mug with the handle pointed at Bob as though it was an arrow aimed at him. "Sometimes I hate that reasonable doubt defense. Whenever two or more people could have committed a crime, the lawyers roll out the ancient argument that the jury has to be sure beyond a reasonable doubt that the defendant is guilty. All it takes is one juror to remain uncertain and the case is dead."

"That's why it's better to watch his movements while we work on the case. If we're lucky, he might even panic and do something to reveal his guilt."

Ruth drained the rest of her coffee. "You interviewed Wilcox. Did he appear to be the panicking type?"

"Not much chance of that. He's playing it cool all the way."

"I wish we had DNA evidence, but the lab people couldn't find any that tied him to one of the long-dead bodies. I need something new to build our case."

"How unconventional are you willing to get?"

"What are you thinking, Bob?"

"We could try to spook him by putting out a story that a former cellmate of Albert Rivers is out to get him."

"Sounds like a possibility, but we'd need a reasonable way for that person to have discovered that Gary Wilcox is our prime suspect and also Gary's current location. We'd also need details about the cellmate. Wouldn't it be simpler to spread the word that Albert Rivers' son is after him?"

"Not bad, Ruth. How would you expect Wilcox to react?"

"He might pack up and leave Amana, or he might arm himself."

"Neither one of those steps would indicate a confession."

"They would at least show that the name Albert Rivers has some significance for him. Bob, did you mention Rivers' name to Wilcox when you interviewed him."

"I was very careful to mention the four bodies, but not to name them. If he knows their names, he would be admitting involvement. He'd at least be acknowledging that he was involved in dealings with Rivers at North Corner Savings Bank."

"It would be natural for him to get ready to fight or flee no matter who was hunting him. It's still not enough to prove his guilt. We'll need something else to rattle him. Think about it and see what else you can suggest. I'll do the same. I need your help on this one, Bob. I don't want him to get away with having killed Ted Higgins and the others."

Richard Davidson

As Bob left he thought, *Ruth has never been one
to share her thinking and truly partner with others.
She really must have loved Ted Higgins.*

CHAPTER 94 – HILDA SCHMIDT

As Hilda drove, she thought about her earlier marriage to Henry Schmidt. An immigrant from the former East Germany, he had been born Heinrik but anglicized his name to Henry once he reached the United States. Their marriage hadn't lasted long because Henry was a bastard who held the nineteenth century view that a wife was property and could be commanded to do anything. She had waited until three months after their divorce to arrange for the hit-and-run accident. Thank God they hadn't had children together.

She was long free of Henry, but the period of her marriage had hardened her outlook on many things. She would never marry again. The escape hatch built-into a live-in coupling suited her accumulated anxieties. The simple act of taking off and driving toward Chicago had already improved her outlook. Traffic had been light most of the way, but it grew heavier as she approached the far western suburbs of Chicago. She took one of the Aurora exits and selected a Red Lobster restaurant for her dinner.

Hilda parked her Jeep in a well-lit area by the entrance and entered without looking directly at the security camera she had located while looking for a vacant space. Then she treated herself to a steak and lobster dinner, accompanied by one of her favorite wines. She felt renewed as she leaned back in the booth waiting for dessert and coffee. As the waiter brought them, she selected Gary's phone number at the shop from her contact list.

His voice was a little gruff as he answered. "I don't understand how you knew when to leave. Business had been so slow that you were bored and I was thinking about future projects. As soon as you left, we got mobbed. There were seven busloads of tourists in town today, and I had to cover them single-handed. I'm bushed. I don't suppose you want to turn around and come back?"

"Not a chance, Gary. This is my first break in a long time. I just finished a steak and lobster dinner, and I truly enjoyed it. You're going to have to handle the shop by yourself for a while. By the time I get back you'll no doubt realize how valuable I am. Go home and get a good night's rest." As the waiter approached with her check, she smiled, raised her voice slightly, and closed her phone conversation with a statement of love. She noticed his smile as he walked away. The waiter would definitely remember her. Just to be sure, she left an extra-large tip.

Hilda returned to the road and drove an uneventful ninety minutes to her half sister's house. As she sat in the driveway, she took her cell phone from her purse and called Gary's shop again. He had gone home for the night, and the call went to the answering machine. When the messaging beep sounded, she left a message that she had arrived at her destination and that in a few days she would let him know when she would be coming back.

Impasse

She received no answer to the doorbell. Her half sister was away. Hilda punched the entry code into the digital lock pad and opened the door carefully, scanning the front rooms for any changes since her last visit. A note on the table welcomed her and said she would have to be on her own until noon the next day. Hilda took her luggage to the guest bedroom, prepared to go to sleep, and set her alarm clock for 2:30 a.m. Then she settled down to enjoy a well-earned rest.

When the alarm sounded, Hilda turned it off and reset it to seven o'clock for morning wakeup. Then she took a newly purchased second cell phone from her purse, opened an app on it, and tapped a button image on the screen. After doing so, she uninstalled the application. She smiled as she drifted back to sleep.

CHAPTER 95 – GARY WILCOX

The day had been so busy that Gary didn't bother to prepare a normal meal. He ate cold beans out of a can, washing them down with a beer. Then he sat down in his reclining chair to watch television, with two more beers to keep him company. Halfway through the last beer he fell asleep, dropping his open bottle on the floor. Most of the remaining beer stayed in the horizontal bottle, but some spilled onto his antique rug.

Gary's sound sleep was interrupted at 3:05 a.m. by firemen breaking down his front door. One of them pulled him out of his chair and led him, staggering, out of the house. The hoses were directing high-pressure streams of water everywhere, but especially on the remains of the wing where his bedroom had been. There was nothing but charred beams in that part of the house now. Now fully awake, Gary realized that he was alive only because he had slept on the family room chair instead of in his bed. He gave a silent prayer of thanks.

One fireman who also served as a paramedic for the small village checked Gary's pulse and listened to his heart with a stethoscope. Then he gave Gary humidified oxygen at higher than normal pressure and told him that they would take him to the nearest hospital for observation because smoke inhalation problems may not fully appear for twenty-four to thirty-six hours. Gary nodded his compliance as he sat on the fire engine running board. He also told the fireman that no one else was in the house. Fortunately, Hilda was out of town.

While Gary was in the hospital for observation, FBI agents in Amana busied themselves by reporting to their supervisors about the fire and Gary Wilcox's apparent good health. They requested instructions as to whether there should be any changes to their surveillance routines.

Two days later, after being discharged from the hospital, Gary visited the fire chief. They each took notes during their discussion.

Chief Henkles looked at the preliminary report in his file folder. "Mr. Wilcox, I have to say that you're a very lucky individual. If you had slept in your bed instead of that reclining chair, we wouldn't be having this discussion. I'd be attending your funeral. There was very little left of the bedroom portion of the house when we arrived."

"Does that mean that the fire started there?"

"It's quite likely, but we haven't finished our investigation."

"How did the fire start?"

"I just told you that we're still analyzing the remains of your house, but if I had to guess, I'd say that it was either due to an electrical malfunction or your electric space heater."

"I don't remember turning that heater on."

"From the beer bottles we found on the floor and your falling asleep while watching television, I'd guess that you don't remember much that happened that night."

"I suppose you're right. You don't suspect arson, do you?"

Chief Henkles stared at Gary, wondering why he asked that question. "I don't see any reason to think so. The fire started inside your house, and we had to break down the locked door to get you out. Once again, we'll examine all the possibilities, but we haven't finished our investigation."

Gary saw that the chief was getting irritated by his asking for answers before they finished their work. "Sorry, Chief, I guess I'm impatient because of the shock of losing my home. You will let me know how your review of the fire turns out, won't you?"

"Absolutely, Gary. For now, I suggest you take a few days off and rest up before you have to deal with the insurance people."

"That won't be a problem. My house wasn't insured. I took a chance because I thought it could never burn down. I bought it for cash to save all the finance charges and interest. If I rebuild, I'll have to use my own money. Next time I'll think more seriously about insurance."

"Sounds like the old saying about locking the barn after the horse has been stolen."

"I'm afraid it does. Thanks for your time and efforts, Chief."

CHAPTER 96 – AFTERMATH

Gary installed a folding rollaway cot in his workroom at the shop to avoid expenses for a hotel room or apartment. He knew he'd have to do a much better job of cleaning up sawdust each afternoon in order to have decent air to breath at night. He would wear a dust respirator while sleeping if necessary, but he hoped he would be able to breathe adequately without that awkward device on his face.

He called Hilda's cell phone. He would try to convince her to return early. She didn't answer, so he left a voice mail message.

"Hi, Hilda, it's me. We had a near tragedy here. The house burned down. I'm fine. I was sleeping in the family room, and most of the damage was to the bedroom and surrounding rooms. I've set up temporary quarters in the shop, so call me there or on my cell phone. I miss you and need you to come back and help me get fire-related things squared away while I work on keeping the business going. Call me back as soon as you can."

Gary decided to do his own search of the house remains. The fire chief had said they were still investigating the fire cause, but Gary knew they had a lot of other projects to handle and would take their time about his low priority mystery. He put on boots to protect his feet from protruding nails and other sharp objects, took his brightest flashlight, and headed for the house after posting a *back in two hours* sign on the front door of the shop.

To put it mildly, the house was a mess. What the fire didn't damage, the streams of high-pressure water did. Gary checked the kitchen area and decided that some of his utensils and small appliances might be saved and repaired where necessary, but he wouldn't eat any of the food. The family room furniture had been so soaked as to be useless. If he had a basement it would have been flooded, but his lawn mower and tools were safe in a separate shed. Except for the two bedrooms, rebuilding wouldn't be too difficult, especially in a small village setting, where nit-picky building codes were only mentioned in passing.

The guest bedroom ceiling had collapsed and the walls were charred. The closet was now a passage to the outdoors, and the bunk beds were a pile of splinters surrounding a still-soaked pair of mattresses.

The master bedroom where he and Hilda slept had suffered the greatest damage. The fire must have burned the curtains, racing upward to engulf the ceiling, which no longer existed. While the spare bedroom ceiling had collapsed, the roof above it remained, but was randomly charred. The main bedroom roof was completely gone. Once that room had become open to the sky, the burning walls had collapsed. All that remained in the room were a scorched headboard attached to a steel bed frame and the electric heater that had sparked the fire. The curtain must have been too close to it.

Impasse

Gary walked over to the heater and studied its switch, trying to force himself to remember turning it on. He made allowances for having been tired and partially drunk, but he couldn't remember that action. The sheet metal housing of the heater had melted, along with its electrical cord. All that remained where the cord had plugged into the wall was a blob of blackened plastic. Gary studied it intently.

He would have to buy some new clothes. He had only what he wore during the fire plus a couple of outfits he kept in the shop to wear while working on a dirty project. Hilda's bureau and closet wardrobe had been consumed, but she had taken several outfits with her to the Chicago area. Gary realized that he didn't know where she was staying. He would sign up for an online tracking service and use its software to track her cell phone if she didn't respond to the voice mail message he had left for her.

CHAPTER 97 – CONTACT

Hilda Schmidt knew she would have to get back on the road soon. Gary had left three voice mail messages. The first indicated that he cared for her but needed her help. The other two expressed anger that she hadn't responded and implied something else very disturbing. He might come after her. Life wasn't simple. He should have died in that fire.

Hilda soon would disappear forever. She had sold her Jeep to a used car dealer and bought a three-year-old Ford from a different dealer, so that the two transactions would not be linked. She had a new prepaid cell phone and number that she would use for one month and then discard in favor of another phone and number. She had destroyed her old phone and the special phone earlier in the day.

As she returned to her half sister's house after shopping for a style changing wardrobe, she wondered whether old friends would recognize her with her hair dyed red and cut short. She actually liked the pixie cut better than her old style, and she had tired of being a blonde. The sun dropped below the horizon as Hilda keyed in the combination for the front door lock and eased the door open.

She felt a sudden push on her back, causing her to move forward so quickly that she lost her grip on the door handle. The door swung inward rapidly, striking the wall alongside the doorway so hard that the doorknob punched a hole in it. Hilda almost fell, but kept her balance by lunging forward and grabbing the stairway railing post. She turned around to find Gary Wilcox glaring at her. His left hand grabbed her arm and held it tightly.

"Hello, Hilda; it looks as though your plan to roast me alive didn't work out."

"What do you mean? I wasn't even in the same state with you when that fire happened. I'm glad you're alive and well."

"I'll bet you are. I inspected what was left and found a portion of the remote control socket you had the electric heater plugged into. You powered up the heater from your cell phone so that it would burn the dangling curtains."

"You're crazy. I did no such thing." She tried to wriggle free from his grip but was unsuccessful.

"And you must have worried about my coming after you because you changed your appearance. I bet you wouldn't have been here if I arrived two days later."

"How did you find me? I never gave you this address."

"Cell phones can be used to remotely control smart devices like electrical sockets, but they also can be tracked by their GPS signals. Technology cuts both ways, Hilda. Tell me why you wanted to kill me, and I might let you go. That's the only thing I haven't figured out. I've been good to you, and I thought you cared for me."

Hilda knew her only hope was to talk Gary away from violence. "You have been good to me. For a while I almost believed that I could forgive you."

"Forgive me for what. I never did anything to you."

"You did the worst thing anyone could have done to me. You killed my father."

"I never killed anyone."

"Don't try that story on me. I know about that old bank."

Wilcox stiffened. "You shouldn't have said that. Now I'm going to have to kill you." He pulled a switchblade knife from his pocket and flicked it open. He held the blade very close to Hilda's throat. Then he heard a sound behind him and turned with his knife to face its source.

"Drop the knife, Wilcox. I'm with the FBI, and I'll put a bullet in your head before you can cut anyone."

He needed time to think. "Who are you?"

"The name's Linda Higgins, and you're in my house. Let go of my sister."

"I suppose I killed your father too? I didn't even know anyone back then named Higgins or Schmidt."

"You knew our dad as Marco Locante. He was an undercover FBI agent whose real name was Ted Higgins."

"I didn't know him, but he must have been the guy working with Albert Rivers."

Linda's finger tightened slightly on the trigger. "So you killed him without even knowing him. I told you to put the knife down. I'm justified in shooting you right now if you don't drop it."

"Locante was collateral damage. I had to eliminate Albert Rivers. He was the only one who could identify me and ruin the operation."

"What about Mary Lowry and Kenneth Shea? Were they collateral damage too?"

Gary thought about throwing the knife at Linda but realized his best chance was to hold Hilda hostage. He'd keep talking. "They were loose ends to neaten up the mess. Rivers was the primary target."

"Why? I don't believe your story about fear of him identifying you."

"Alright, he had to go because he and his friends were going to take over everything."

"How could he have done that?"

"I'm not telling you anything else."

"Drop the knife and surrender. You'll get a lawyer to aid your defense."

"And if I don't?"

"My phone has been connected to FBI headquarters by Bluetooth. Your confession has been recorded and by now our SWAT team is in the neighborhood or outside. If you don't put down the knife you will be shot either by me or by a sharpshooter."

Linda's earpiece emitted, "In position. Target acquired."

Gary couldn't make out the words, but he understood their implication. *What the Hell! I've had more than twenty years of easy living. How many others in my shoes could say that? There's no way I'm going to spend the rest of my life in prison.* He threw the knife at Linda, striking her in her left shoulder.

Wilcox's head exploded due to the impacts of Linda's bullet plus three more that shattered the window on their way to the target. Hilda screamed and dove for the floor to avoid the splatter. Gary's torso landed across her legs, pinning her down. Hilda screamed again and couldn't stop shaking.

CHAPTER 98 – REVIEW MEETING

They sat in Ruth Daltry's conference room. Linda Higgins had her shoulder bandaged and her arm in a sling. A subdued Ruth asked, "Will it bother you to continue living in your house after all the trauma and bloodshed?"

"No, Hilda is going to move in with me. In the past we've been distant half sisters and argued more than talked when we did get together. When I first told Hilda that Gary was our prime suspect, I didn't think she'd do anything like take the risks she did, becoming his girlfriend. She has Dad's love of undercover work. I've learned to respect her like I never did before. Now we'll just forget about that 'half' when we refer to ourselves. It will take a while to clean and repair the mess, but we've even thought of leaving one blood spot on the wall as a symbol that we avenged our father's murder."

Bob Marcus caught Ruth's eye with a gesture. "We're going to have to decide whether Hilda will have to be prosecuted for her remote-controlled arson of Gary Wilcox's house."

Ruth shook her head. "That won't be necessary, Bob. Arson is a local crime, although its interstate triggering raises some questions. The local fire department hasn't completed their investigation, and they may leave it unfinished after they learn that Gary is dead. You and I earlier discussed ways we could spook Gary into doing something or committing a new crime that might give us leverage for proving his old murders. It appears that Hilda accomplished exactly what we wanted, and thanks to Linda's opening that phone link to headquarters before she entered the house, we have his recorded confession. We wouldn't be able to look the other way if Hilda had succeeded in killing Gary, but he wasn't hurt, and the fire led him to come here and attack Hilda. It all worked out. We're rid of Gary Wilcox once and for all."

Arthur Blake had listened quietly up to this point. It was time for him to speak up. "Ruth, that statement isn't quite true."

"What do you mean?"

"You fell into the killer's trap when you agonized about the reasonable doubt defense as to which brother had committed the murders. You haven't eliminated Gary because he didn't exist. I've been off searching family records and birth papers. There never was a Gary. Stanley Wilcox was the only child in that family. Stanley faked his own death in that nursing home and became Gary. Then he flimflammed us again when he got Mercury in Nassau to make him new credentials as Stanley. He impersonated himself."

"What led you to suspect that?"

"I first wondered why there were never any records of the two brothers being together. Then I obtained copies of the documents Gary gave Mercury to use in creating new identifications. They included two different photos, one marked as Gary and one marked as Stanley. Mercury told me that Gary had yelled at him when he accidentally switched the photos. The two pictures looked somewhat different, but I asked Irma to analyze them with facial recognition software. The results proved that the two imaged individuals were the same person. In case Gary had mismarked the pictures, I showed the newspaper photo of Gary posing as Stephen George Ackerman to Emily Everett, and she identified him as the Stanley Wilcox who ran their travel agency."

"Memories can be wrong. What other evidence do you have?"

"Mercury stays as close to the truth as possible in creating new identities. Based on the data that Gary had given him, the counterfeit documents showed the correct place of birth for Stanley Wilcox. I investigated the local birth records and the family and found they had only one son. His name was Stanley."

Bob Marcus whistled long and low. "He had us fooled. We were ready to jump through all kinds of hoops to get around that reasonable doubt defense, and it didn't even apply."

Ruth stood and gathered her papers. "Well, whether there was one Wilcox or two, this case appears to be closed. Thank you all for your substantial assistance in many ways."

Irma stood and waved at Ruth. "One minute, Ruth. I've been sitting here quietly, like the proverbial fly on the wall, taking in all of your comments. I have a problem with saying this case is wrapped up."

Ruth sat down again. "Where do you see a problem?"

"You played the recording of Wilcox's confession during that final confrontation. During that recording, he said something that requires further investigation."

"I guess I missed that part, Irma. What did he say?"

"Wilcox said that he had to kill Albert Rivers because Rivers and his friends were about to take over everything. I think we have to discover who those 'friends' were and whether the 'everything' he mentioned covers more than money laundering and bringing people into the country in an unconventional manner."

Linda Higgins said, "I wondered about that at the time, but I forgot it after the shooting."

Bob Marcus picked up his papers. "I think we've gone as far as we should. We've solved the murders in that bank more than twenty years ago. We've avenged the death of Agent Ted Higgins, and we've saved the taxpayers the cost of a trial for Gary or Stanley Wilcox. I feel pretty good about the whole thing."

Arthur rose. "You're absolutely right, Bob. We have the right to feel good about what we've accomplished. Even so, I'm with Irma in more than the usual way. Let me suggest that we may have trusted witness interviews more than was justified. Wilcox referred to Rivers and his friends. What if Albert Rivers didn't defraud the twelve people from England? It's possible that they paid him that million dollars each to smuggle them into this country for an as-yet unknown purpose. What if they have been pursuing a hidden goal for more than twenty years? Shouldn't we take a closer look at what they've been doing?"

Ruth stood once more, but left her papers on the table. "You're right. I never felt quite comfortable with that lemonade and cookies sweetness of Emily Everett and her cohorts. It's all too choreographed. Let's give them another look before we mark this case closed."

CHAPTER 99 – LAWRA

The news of the baby's arrival excited Sarah Jackson more than Jayson Redshaw. She told him they should visit his mother and Terrell Martin as soon as possible. He had mixed emotions.

"My mother truly believes that our family is now restored to its original unworried condition because she had a baby girl and named her after her murdered son Lawson. A baby named Lawra may be cute, but she changes nothing."

"Of course, she doesn't replace Lawson. That's not the point. The key thing that this baby does for your mother and the rest of us is that she changes our outlook. Everyone can start to look toward the future instead of dwelling on past miseries."

"Hold it! You said, 'your mother and the rest of us' as though you were part of my family."

"So, how do you feel about that?"

"I've been learning to live in the present and not paying much attention to the future."

"Like I said, Jay, the baby will turn our thoughts from the past and present, and lead us toward building a future."

"Sarah, you are my present. Would you like to be part of my future too?"

"Man, that's the weakest proposal I ever heard, but the answer is yes."

"That's not exactly what I meant to say, but your response is amazing."

"You have ten seconds to decide whether you proposed or not."

"I don't need that long. I meant it. Get over here and confirm it. Then we'll go visit Ma and baby Lawra. I haven't even met this Terrell Martin dude."

When Jay and Sarah arrived at his mother's apartment in Skokie, his mother greeted them excitedly.

"Come on in, and let me take a look at you, Jay. I think you've grown some more. Either that or I've shrunk from getting older or childbirth. It's a gift to have another child this late in life. Sarah, welcome to our home."

Jay held Sarah's hand. "Ma, we're here to see you and your new addition to the family, but I have one too. Sarah and I are engaged."

"Congratulations, you two. If I'd known about the engagement in advance, I would have bought something for you to help celebrate it. You should have told me when you and I talked after Lawra was born."

"That would have been hard, Ma. We got engaged this morning. You're the first one to hear our news."

"I feel honored. I'll open a bottle of wine to celebrate it. Now that the baby's here, I can finally have a drink. Let's go look in on Lawra. She's sleeping."

They quietly opened the door of the room that was serving as Lawra's nursery. Jay saw the desk and file cabinet in the corner and realized that the room had been Terrell's den or office. Without having met Terrell, Jay thought better of him for having been willing to yield his private space to his new baby. *He's a family man, not one of those guys who are fathers in name only.* The baby was tiny, cute, and peaceful in her sleep. Without asking permission, Jay reached into her crib and touched her on the back. He felt her little heart pumping and her whole self quivering with energy. That contact let him grasp the fact that she was not simply a new toy for his mother. She was his half sister, despite the difference in their ages, and she was preparing to tackle the world. Somehow, that realization made him feel comfortable. Today, he had gone from being independent to having a kid sister and a fiancée to think about. Maybe family deserved higher priority in his life.

CHAPTER 100 – NEWS REPORTS

The online news reports and TV networks were all buzzing about reports from several parts of Florida and Georgia that people had seen lights in the sky that they took to be UFOs. One group of three of these bright lights streaking across the sky from northeast to southwest had been recorded by the dashboard camera in a Florida Highway Patrol car. That image had gone viral, and appeared on many news sites and YouTube. What had people excited was that the bright objects could be seen to change direction and move in formation with each other.

As usual, people advocating the truth of UFOs brought out their past photographs and testimonies. They dusted off continuing accusations of government cover-ups. Rallies by sign-toting advocates erupted in major cities.

As a counter-balance, other groups argued that the lights were reflections in windshields, classified military test aircraft, space junk re-entering the atmosphere, and meteors.

All-in-all, it gave people a lot to talk about and to post on social media platforms on an otherwise slow news day.

After viewing the morning television news, Arthur Blake commented to Irma that Emily Fiona Everett and her friends in Florida would be enjoying the UFO frenzy immensely.

Later that day, Special Agent Ruth Daltry of the FBI announced that she had obtained search warrants for the houses of all twelve of the British UFO advocates transplanted to Florida. She ordered agents to search all their houses simultaneously, so that none of them would be able to warn the others. The searches went off with only one minor glitch and large quantities of documents, computer software, and computers were seized, immediately classified, and sent to experts for analysis.

The one minor glitch in serving the search warrants was that the FBI agents found no one to receive the warrants. All twelve of the people in the transplanted UK group had disappeared, along with their families. Ruth gave the order for each team to determine when its targeted individual had last been seen and to develop leads for tracking him or her. In case the disappearances indicated something sinister, Ruth had Homeland Security issue a potential terrorism alert.

CHAPTER 101 – NANCY BLAKE

Nancy brought her mug of oatmeal and her doughnut out to the porch where Arthur and Irma were talking about their current investigation. Rex followed Nancy, hoping to get the last bite of her pastry.

Irma held up a finger to Arthur to pause their conversation. "Nancy, what kind of breakfast is that? You're having healthy and unhealthy at the same time."

"Don't worry, Mom, I'm going on a bike hike with a group from school this afternoon. I'll burn off the calories. Besides, I'm supposed to have a balanced diet, so I'm balancing the oatmeal against the doughnut."

Arthur laughed. "Nancy, she's not really being critical. Irma enjoys giving you the opportunity to call her Mom."

"That's fine, Dad. I'll give you equal treatment and give you your call-out too. What were you guys discussing when I came out?"

"We told you about those people from England who wanted to someday fly to Mars. Irma told me that Ruth Daltry called and said those folks have all disappeared. The FBI went to search their homes to see if they possibly were doing something sinister, and all their homes were empty. They didn't take any of their belongings with them – just went poof and vanished. They own companies and have major investments too."

Nancy looked up from petting Rex. "That's what I expected to happen someday."

Irma studied Nancy and concluded that her daughter was serious. "Tell us why you expected it."

"You told me that those folks all became UFO believers after sightings of strange lights in the night near a US Air Force base in Suffolk, England in 1980."

Arthur said, "That's true."

"You also said that these people wanted to encourage the development of technology for flights from Earth to other planets."

"Agreed."

"What has happened in space technology between 1980 and now?"

Arthur said, "NASA and other countries have studied the effects of long-term living in space, using rotating teams of people on the International Space Station."

"What else?"

"NASA has sent robot vehicles to Mars for up-close study of that planet and has sent spacecraft to study other planets and their moons for their suitability for manned landings."

"Correct. What else?"

"Private companies have developed the capability of launching satellites and hope in the future to offer passengers travel to the edge of space, to the moon, and beyond."

"Those are great summaries, Dad. If you put them all together, you might say that during the period between 1980 and now, we have developed the skills and the tools to someday travel to other

348

planets. What if those twelve very wealthy space travel enthusiasts somehow contributed to our space technology development while no one was watching them? They owned companies and Emily Everett said they were working on devices that might be useful when space flights happened. Albert Rivers thought his friends were going to make him a lot of money as their agent. They could easily have influenced the private firms that are now getting into the field."

"That's a possibility, but where are you going with this discussion?"

"Your group of twelve space enthusiasts first attracted attention after UFO sightings in Suffolk, England in 1980. They disappeared after UFO sightings this week in Florida."

Irma smiled and jumped into the conversation. "You're speculating that those twelve are from somewhere else and that they came to Earth to teach us about space travel. You're suggesting that they came here and returned home on a UFO."

"Yup."

Arthur hugged Nancy. "My mother would say that you have a vivid imagination. I think you have the ability to jump from miscellaneous facts to logical assumptions. You'll make a great investigator someday. I see you joining into the family business."

Irma said, "Let's take her thinking further. I'll argue that they couldn't have arrived on that 1980 UFO because they were all members of prominent British families. How do you respond to that, Nancy?"

Richard Davidson

"To use their own words, they were great fans of *Invasion of the Body Snatchers*."

-END-

ABOUT THE AUTHOR

Richard Davidson is the author of the self-help guidebook: *DECISION TIME! Better Decisions for a Better Life.* He has written the five-novel Lord's Prayer Mystery Series: *Lead Us Not into Temptation, Give Us this Day our Daily Bread, Forgive Us Our Trespasses, Thy Will Be Done,* and *Deliver Us from Evil.* He has edited an anthology, *Overcoming: An Anthology by the Writers of* OCWW. His latest project, the Imp Mystery Series, contains five novels: *Implications, Impulses, Impostor, Impending,* and *Impasse.* The Imp novels continue to chronicle the exploits of characters introduced in the earlier series, along with affiliated newcomers, taking their interests in new directions. Mr. Davidson is Past President of Off-Campus Writers' Workshop, the oldest ongoing group of its kind in the U.S. and is the founder of the ReadWorthy Books Book Review Blog. He is also the founder of the Independent Mystery Publishing Society (IMPS). Mr. Davidson is a former Lay Leader in the United Methodist Church. He is an aeronautical & astronautical engineer.

Richard Davidson

WORKS BY THIS AUTHOR
NONFICTION:

DECISION TIME! Better Decisions for a Better Life,

RADMAR Publishing

ISBN 978-0-9829160-7-0 (2nd edition paperback)

ISBN 978-1-4581-8395-8 (Smashwords eBook)

ASIN B014QFZP68 (Kindle Edition eBook)

Where you are in life today is the result of all of the past decisions you have made or which have been made for you in response to the various situations and events that have impacted your life. The decisions that you will make from this point forward will determine the degree to which your future will be positive or negative. *DECISION TIME!* gives you insight into the subjective decision-making process as applied to both small and large choices you will face. It includes dynamic aspects, cultural effects, and morality as applied to decision-making for individuals, teams, corporations, and societies. *DECISION TIME!* prepares you to face continuous decisions confidently and without hesitation.

FICTION:

Lead Us Not into Temptation (The Lord's Prayer Mystery Series, Volume I),

RADMAR Publishing

ISBN 978-0-9976381-0-3 (2nd edition paperback)

ASIN B01GEK7ZZ2 (Kindle Edition eBook)

Arthur Blake, former NASA engineer turned minister, receives an emergency appointment to be pastor of the United Methodist Church in Parkville, a distant suburb of Chicago, following the bizarre sudden death of the church's unusual former pastor. Pastor Blake's attempts to unravel the mystery that shrouds his predecessor become involved with tracking the child of a possibly bigamous soldier in World War II England; art and jewelry treasures plundered by the Nazis and their sympathizers; and the eventual results of childhood sibling conflicts in combined families. Arthur's allies in his investigation include Parkville Police Chief Bobby Andrews, County Medical Examiner Irma Custis, and the married team of Penny and Joe Gonzalez who work for a clandestine government agency. During the course of *Lead Us Not into Temptation,* the reader discovers how seemingly minor historical events lead to major present-day dislocations in church, village, and family relationships.

Richard Davidson

Give Us this Day Our Daily Bread (The Lord's Prayer Mystery Series, Volume II)

RADMAR Publishing

ISBN 978-0-9829160-5-6 (2nd edition paperback)

ASIN B01H7M47M0 (Kindle Edition eBook)

Arthur Blake, Pastor of Parkville United Methodist Church, has to deal with the aftereffects of a traumatic communion incident. He works to assist the authorities in investigating the cause while doing his best to convince members of his congregation that it is safe to return to church. Working with the police and federal agencies, he discovers that the terror of the initial event is minor compared with the potential chaotic impact of future disasters being planned by the perpetrator. The investigation is interwoven with several relationship situations that affect the final outcome.

Impasse

Forgive Us Our Trespasses (The Lord's Prayer Mystery Series, Volume III)

RADMAR Publishing

ISBN 978-0-9976381-1-0 (2nd edition paperback)

ASIN B01IQ1TJXS (Kindle Edition eBook)

Arthur Blake, Pastor of Parkville United Methodist Church, tries to assist his father to resolve his trauma after learning that his best friend, recently killed in a car accident, may have been an imposter with a heinous background. The investigation reveals that the presumed accident was but one link in a chain of murders. Blake works to determine the true identity of his father's friend, while also discovering the man's past activities and affiliations. Arthur works to solve the murders in conjunction with his colleagues at ABC Consultants. He also draws on assistance from associates at a covert government agency with which he has worked before. The coordinated effort to solve the puzzle examines incidents that span the period between World War II and the present in order to defuse the personal, national, and international dangers resulting from them.

Richard Davidson

Thy Will Be Done (The Lord's Prayer Mystery Series, Volume IV)

RADMAR Publishing

ISBN 978-0-9829160-2-5 (paperback)

ASIN B009JU6EZM (Kindle Edition eBook)

The sudden death of a young woman attending Parkville United Methodist Church infuriates her brother and leads to congregational outrage over his outburst and subsequent murder. The investigation of that slaying by Pastor Arthur Blake and his associates leads to revelations of a previously undetected criminal organization operating in the area. Unraveling the mystery and scope of this group entangles Arthur and his associated investigators in a web of conspiracies extending from Illinois to both U.S. coasts and through Mexico to Guatemala.

Impasse

Deliver Us from Evil (The Lord's Prayer Mystery Series, Volume V)

RADMAR Publishing

ISBN 978-0-9829160-3-2 (paperback)

ASIN B00EBDUXFY (Kindle Edition eBook)

Arthur and Irma's wedding day has finally arrived, but an unexpected interruption leads to their need to investigate a possible murder committed by someone close to them. With the aid of friends and federal agents Penny and Joe Gonzalez, they follow a series of clues, crisscrossing the United States to learn more about the murder, related subsequent events, and the significance of a rare object brought home by a veteran of the Iraq War. A second murder close to Pastor Arthur Blake's church involves them in a new investigation, assisting Parkville Police Chief Bobby Andrews. Are these murders and the tracking of that strange object connected? Will marriage deteriorate or improve the relationship between Arthur and Irma? Character flaws in many relationships color the outcome.

Richard Davidson

Overcoming: An Anthology by the Writers of OCWW

Edited and with an Introduction by Richard Davidson

RADMAR Publishing

ISBN 978-9829160-4-9 (paperback)

ASIN B00E80NN4I (Kindle Edition eBook)

This anthology covers many aspects of overcoming life's problems, obstacles, and challenging developments. The contributing writers have used fiction, non-fiction, memoir, poetry, historical chronicle, and drama to highlight our continuing need to overcome our problems, rather than dwell on them. The reader will learn from many talented writers the skills needed to respond constructively, energetically, and sometimes humorously to whatever obstacle bars one's path. Apply their lessons to your own needs and to those of others you cherish.

Impasse

Implications: An Arthur Blake Mystery Novel (Imp Mysteries, Volume 1)

RADMAR Publishing

ISBN 978-0-9829160-6-3 (paperback)

ASIN B00LY9IBWK (Kindle Edition eBook)

Bishop Howard Chandler has assigned Pastor Arthur Blake to investigate the burning of a church in the small city of Amboy, Illinois. He learns from that church's pastor that she had to overcome past improprieties by former members. During the investigation of the fire's cause, Arthur and the other state fire investigators uncover disturbing aspects of the ninety-year-old church's design and history. Arthur calls on his federal associates for assistance, as the investigation of a local church fire expands to seeking solutions to related crimes occurring from the present to recent years and back to the Prohibition Era. Progress in the investigation intertwines with new developments in Arthur's family life.

Richard Davidson

Impulses: An Arthur Blake Mystery Novel (Imp Mysteries, Volume 2)

RADMAR Publishing

ISBN 978-0-9829160-8-7 (paperback)

ASIN B012LFQXYI (Kindle Edition eBook)

Several disturbing dreams cause Arthur Blake to wonder whether he is trying to do too much for the many people who seek his services. These qualms are complicated by Bishop Howard Chandler's suggestion that Arthur temporarily set aside his official duties and take an extended sabbatical leave. His resulting internal debates about career moves are set aside when the pastor who replaced him at the Parkville church dies in an apparent suicide possibly linked to several deaths at the Parkville Rehabilitation Home. The bishop assigns Arthur to determine the circumstances behind the new pastor's death, while Arthur and Irma, his wife and constant investigative partner, also study a mysterious shipment at his father's antiques shop. The sudden disappearance of a young associate provides another mystery and leads to questions of life after death and reincarnation. Events that initially appear simple become increasingly complex as the true natures of many people come into question.

Impostor: A Genealogical Mystery (Imp Mysteries, Volume 3)

RADMAR Publishing

ISBN 978-0-9829160-9-4 (paperback)

ASIN B01FZQZEK4 (Kindle Edition eBook)

When Debbie Danforth discovers a flaw in the genealogy of her live-in boyfriend, Jeremy Hadley, he and his family try to discredit her findings, but eventually admit they must be true. Jeremy and Debbie run a private detective business, the Sandley Agency and commit their skills and resources to learning about the impostor Debbie has discovered in the Hadley ancestry. They are assisted in this effort by Penny and Joe Gonzalez, principals in a covert federal agency, with whom Jeremy has previously worked as a consultant. Their joint investigation uncovers both unique details concerning the mysterious Hadley impostor and little-known facts about events leading up to World War II in both Britain and the United States. Was the person who masqueraded as a Hadley a villain or a hero? Did other Hadleys know he was a fraudulent member of their family? Did his actions assist or impede the British and the Americans as they faced the growing menace in prewar Europe?

Richard Davidson

Impending: A Genealogical Mystery (Imp Mysteries, Volume 4)

RADMAR Publishing

ISBN 978-0-9976381-2-7 (paperback)

ASIN B072KPHN7K (Kindle Edition eBook)

Young married private detectives, Debbie and Jeremy Hadley, discover that Debbie's family, the Danforths, have a family secret. Grandma Marie Danforth summons them because she fears that alienated family members and underworld characters will attempt to wrest control of the secret from her. The history of the secret begins at the American Civil War Battle of Gettysburg and develops through a century and a half of Danforth family twists and intrigues. Although written as one story, *Impending* actually is effectively two novels in one: the saga of how the secret developed from its inception to the present day, and the mystery of how to counter multiple attempts to hijack it. *Impending* is history and mystery all-in-one. Debbie and Jeremy team with police from two cities to unravel the mystery and reach its surprising conclusion.

Impasse

Impasse: An Arthur & Irma Blake Mystery

RADMAR Publishing

ISBN 978-0-9976381-3-4 (paperback)

The discovery of human bones while excavating a property to build a new church requires all work to stop. Arthur and Irma Blake investigate and find an earlier structure on that lot was involved in illegal activities, requiring FBI leadership of the inquiry. Further research reveals a group of foreign citizens who replaced Americans illegally and an elaborate money laundering scheme. What are the foreigners trying to do? Who killed the people unearthed during construction and others discovered later? How will the killer be brought to justice more than twenty years after the crimes?

Richard Davidson

Learn more about the writings, humor, and random thoughts of Richard Davidson at: radmarinc.com davidsonbookshelf.com and at the Independent Mystery Publishing Society (IMPS) https://www.mysteryimps.com and https://www.mysteryimps.net

Richard Davidson's author page on Amazon is located at https://www.amazon.com/author/richarddavidson
Follow and *Like* Richard Davidson, Author on Facebook at https://www.facebook.com/richarddavidsonauthor?ref=hl
Follow him on Twitter @mysteryimp